COMEBACK
LOVE

COMEBACK LOVE

A NOVEL

Peter Golden

WASHINGTON SQUARE PRESS
New York ◆ London ◆ Toronto ◆ Sydney ◆ New Delhi

WASHINGTON SQUARE PRESS
A Division of Simon & Schuster, Inc.
1230 Avenue of the Americas
New York, NY 10020

Originally published by Staff Picks Press

First Washington Square Press trade paperback edition April 2012

WASHINGTON SQUARE PRESS and colophon are registered
trademarks of Simon & Schuster, Inc.

For information about special discounts for bulk purchases, please
contact Simon & Schuster Special Sales at 1-866-506-1949 or
business@simonandschuster.com.

The Simon & Schuster Speakers Bureau can bring authors to your
live event. For more information or to book an event contact the
Simon & Schuster Speakers Bureau at 1-866-248-3049 or visit our
website at www.simonspeakers.com.

Manufactured in the United States of America

10 9 8 7 6 5 4 3 2 1

Library of Congress Cataloging-in-Publication Data

Golden, Peter.
    Comeback love: a novel / Peter Golden.—1st Washington
Square Press trade paperback ed.
        p. cm.
    I. Title.
    PS3607.O4525C66 2012
    813'.6—dc23

                                                    2011039945

ISBN 978-1-4516-5632-9
ISBN 978-1-4516-5634-3 (ebook)

For my son, Ben,
And my wife, Annis,
With love and gratitude beyond measure

For winter's rains and ruins are over,
And all the season of snows and sins;
The days dividing lover and lover,
The light that loses, the night that wins;
And time remembered is grief forgotten,
And frosts are slain and flowers begotten . . .

—ALGERNON CHARLES SWINBURNE

Part I

Present

Chapter 1

TWO DAYS AFTER Christmas, the snow was still falling.

I should have been at my older sister's outside Boston, visiting with Elaine and her husband, but the snow had started on Christmas Eve, closing the airports, and by morning the world was white and silent.

I decided to drive to Elaine's from DC and make a couple of stops on the way. Traffic was light and the plows were out on I-95, but with the storm it was slow going, so I didn't get to the Mt. Lebanon Cemetery in New Jersey until early afternoon.

The snow had piled up between the long rows of carved granite, and after tucking the cuffs of my corduroys into my boots, I high-stepped through the drifts to the Meyers family plot. My father had bought these dozen graves in 1951. Around then, my mother was bugging him to buy a house in Jersey, like his brother, but my father had refused to leave Brooklyn, saying he had plenty of time to go to Jersey—when he was dead.

Now he was there, with mom, my aunt, and uncle. There was even space for me. Someday. And probably sooner rather than later, since the men in my family weren't notable for their longevity.

I cleared the snow from the footstones with a windshield brush, then stood in the pale gray light, talking to my parents, Aunt Lil, and Uncle Jerr until tears were freezing in my eyes.

Then I drove to Manhattan and checked into the Grand Hyatt.

Much of my life has been passed alone in dilapidated hotels and guesthouses in the peskier backwaters of Europe, Asia, and the Middle East—not necessarily places you'd go unless, like me, you had been a civilian consultant to a handful of intelligence agencies.

Yet even in the most genteel cities, when the accommodations were five-star, the rooms filled me with loneliness.

Television helps. So does vodka. And after turning on the news and pouring a Stoli from the minibar, I sat on the bed and reread the page I'd printed from the DoctorFinder on the American Medical Association website:

Glenna Rising, MD

Location:	**Office Phone:**
289 W. 51st St	212-555-0422
New York, NY 10019	

Residency Training:	**Primary Specialty:**
NY AND PRESBY HOSP	PEDIATRICS

Medical School:
COLUMBIA UNIV COLL OF
PHYSICIANS AND SURGEONS
NEW YORK, NY 10032

I doubt the cold warriors who initially funded the Internet suspected it would become a popular method for tracking down ex-girlfriends. I hadn't seen Glenna in over thirty years, and given my career collecting and analyzing intel on foreign armies and paramilitary groups, I could have used my skills to uncover far more about her. But I didn't want to ruin my vision of Glenna: beautiful, available, and willing to concede that she, too, was subject to this strange power that had kept us connected across so many years.

Reaching into my daypack, I took out a photograph of her. Long ago, I had sealed it between laminated sheets: the edges were curled with age, but the image had remained as detailed as an etching. Glenna is standing in the golden autumn light outside a hotel in Bennington, Vermont, with leaves falling all around her. Her long hair is the color of maple syrup with sun shining through it. A breeze blows it off the shoulders of her sweater, swirling it around her face, but you can still see the cameo perfection of her features. She is smiling, and yet doesn't seem happy, appears suspicious instead, and to this day I don't know if it was happiness she didn't trust or me.

Perhaps it was both.

Someone once said a photograph is a far cry from a memory. I'm not so sure this is true because I remember looking through the viewfinder of the Minolta on that breezy, sunlit Saturday, smelling the woodsmoke rising from the white-brick chimney of the hotel, and thinking that no matter what became of us, I would love Glenna—and be haunted by her—forever.

I put away the photo, then picked up my iPhone and went through the saved voice mails until I heard the last one from Alex: "Hey, Dad. Thanks for dinner and the advice about Julie.

Things're up and down, but I'm trying. I'll be in touch. Love you." Alex started laughing. "And, Dad. Stay out of Dorkville!"

I loved hearing my son laugh—in part, because his mother and I had split up when he was in fifth grade, and I'd taken away an enduring guilt-curdled image of him on his bed sobbing into his pillow. When Alex was fourteen, my ex remarried and left DC for Potomac, Maryland, and Alex decided to live with me in Georgetown. From the day he moved into my town house, Alex had been trying to fix me up—with a few of his teachers, some divorced soccer moms, and once with a woman who struck up a conversation with him in the cereal aisle at Safeway. Eleven years later and living in his own apartment in Baltimore, he was still playing matchmaker, but I wouldn't cooperate, which, according to Alex, made me a distinguished resident of Dorkville.

The dinner Alex mentioned was three weeks ago at Bourbon Steak. We were splitting a porterhouse when Alex told me that for months he'd been fighting with Julie, the young woman he'd been seeing for two years, an auburn-haired beauty who worked at the State Department and spoke half a dozen languages. Alex said the fights were over nothing and came out of nowhere. I suggested he listen more and argue less; perhaps he'd discover what was really bothering Julie. He said, "Dad, I'm scared. When I imagine losing Julie, I can't imagine ever getting over her." Alex had some red in his hair, courtesy of his mother, but the greenish-brown eyes, cleft chin, broad shoulders, and thick chest came from me, and as I looked at him across the table, I felt as if I were watching a dismal rerun of my own life. I comforted my son with a lie. I told him these things worked themselves out, but whatever happened, time took care of every wound. He smiled at me, a sign, I thought, that he believed me. But outside after dinner, before Alex got into his car, he hugged me, holding on longer than usual, and remembering that now, drinking by myself in a hotel room, I was convinced that I'd failed him as a father.

I finished my vodka and glanced at the television, where the newscaster was announcing that two soldiers had died fighting in northern Iraq, killed in an ambush outside the city of Mosul. Sadness and disgust rose up in me, and I shut off the TV and went to take a shower.

Standing under the hot spray, I considered calling Glenna, but odds were her receptionist or answering service would pick up, and I'd have to leave a message, which might not be returned.

Of course, Glenna might not be at her office when I showed up. She could be on vacation with a husband or lover or seeing patients in the hospital.

I dismissed these possibilities for the best and worst of reasons: I didn't want them to be true, because even though I knew that my reunion plan was ridiculous, I also knew that if I didn't feel as though my life were splitting at the seams, then I would never have stopped in New York to see her.

Chapter 2

IT WAS DARK when I exited the Hyatt and walked past Grand Central Station. The snow had let up, but the plows were working overtime, and the streetlights sparkled on the ice-crusted peaks that ran along the curb like arctic mountains.

Crossing Madison Avenue, I glanced downtown and saw the office building where my father and Uncle Jerry used to work in public relations for Danzig Pharmaceutical. An ache of loss went through me like the icy snap of the wind, but thinking about my dad and his brother, usually locked in a ferocious debate over something—which way the rivers flow, for instance—always made me smile.

My father, Alex, was seven years older than Uncle Jerr. Their parents died young, and Uncle Jerr was in Eastern District High School and living with my mother while Dad was off fighting with the Fourth Infantry Division in the Hürtgen Forest, where he won the Silver Star. My father kept his medal in his dresser, and I remember coming into his room when I was a kid and seeing him, big and broad-shouldered, standing in his boxer shorts and staring at the ribbon and medal cupped in his hand, his handsome face as hard as stone and his sepia, gold-flecked eyes filled with a grief and rage I didn't understand. He showed me the Silver Star a few times, and Uncle Jerr told me that he'd won it for taking out three Nazi pillboxes by himself, but my father seldom spoke about his war.

As I headed north on Fifth Avenue, the city felt deserted in these lost, snowbound days between Christmas and New Year's Eve. Turning up the shearling collar of my coat to keep the cold off my neck, I was curious why I couldn't stop thinking about my father and uncle, and then it struck me that they had been responsible for my meeting Glenna.

It was the summer of 1968. I was working in the public-relations department at Danzig because I had recently earned some of the lowest grades in the history of Brooklyn College and failed to graduate after four years, which led my father to insist that I get a real job. Since he was head of PR, and either traveling or in a meeting, Uncle Jerr showed me the ropes. Banging out press releases and proofreading direct-mail pieces was a cinch, and it was a gas working for Uncle Jerr, who took PR a little less seriously than the fate of the Mets, Jets, Knicks, and Rangers. He wasn't exactly a degenerate gambler, since he avoided money trouble, but in the mornings when I went to get my assignments from him, my uncle had several sports sections opened up on his desk, and we would spend an hour going over the day's starting pitchers before he called his bookie.

Sometimes, my father would drop in to see me. Once, he stopped by while I was reading Bernard Fall's *Street Without Joy*. Fall had been killed in Vietnam on patrol with the Marines, and evidently, from the concern on my father's face, he was familiar with Fall's obituary.

My father asked, "How's the book?"

"Interesting."

He eyed me suspiciously. "There's things more interesting than war," he said, lighting a Lucky Strike. "I thought you'd like coming to work here. It's no great shakes. But we'd be together. And you gotta work at being something."

A tremor of guilt rolled through me. I hated disappointing him. "I've been thinking about being a writer. Like those stories I wrote for the lit mags."

"Gordon, that writing was fine for high school and college. But how you gonna support yourself?"

I shrugged. Truth was, I didn't have a clue of what to write about. Nor did I have any knowledge of how one becomes a writer, and I was convinced that I had no experience worth recording, which partially explained my attraction to Vietnam. Even if the war was shaping up into a grotesque mistake, I still wanted to see it for myself, though I was enough of a middle-class kid to be ashamed of feeling thrilled by the idea of going.

My father crushed out his cigarette in the ashtray on my desk. "We'll talk about the writing," he said.

We didn't talk about it again until August. Aunt Lil and Uncle Jerr had been to another peace rally in the city, and afterward they drove to Brooklyn. We were at the redwood table in the backyard, and my father was barbecuing steaks and knocking back Chivas on the rocks when he said, "Gordon, this writing plan is bullshit. You got better things to do."

I took a slug of Michelob. "Like public relations?"

Uncle Jerr said, "Alex, you gotta give the boy room to grow."

"What is he?" my father said. "A plant?"

Uncle Jerr said, "Gordie, so you want to be a writer?"

"Butt out," my father said. "Quit tryin' to raise my son. You don't have any kids, so you got no idea what you're talkin' about."

With their thick bodies, intense, dark-eyed stares, and the Yardley pomade in their wavy, graying black hair, my father and uncle looked so much alike it was as if one person were arguing in a mirror. I drank my beer and listened. Once those two got going, there was no percentage in my getting involved.

My uncle said to me, "You wanna write, you can try journalism; I got contacts with some papers."

My father snapped, "He'll do it on his own."

Uncle Jerr ignored him. "I'll help you, Gordie. But you gotta buckle down in school and hold on to that student deferment."

"I told you to butt out," my father said.

"I'm tryin' to keep your son out of a goddamn war."

"Go back to your peace march, Jerr. Don't tell me about war."

Aunt Lil walked out the back door of the house with a wooden bowl of salad. Under her bleached, brassy bouffant, her face was as round and sweet as a cider doughnut. Her miniskirt didn't flatter her stubbiness, though it did testify to her abundant courage.

"Darling," she said to me, "you stay in college till you're a hundred and seven. That Two-S can save your life."

My mother, small and slender in an ivory summer dress dotted with sunflowers, came out right behind my aunt with a platter of corn on the cob. "What's this deferment talk?"

"Relax, Renée," my father said.

He must have mentioned my reading Bernard Fall to her because my mother glared down at me, her light blue eyes suddenly as cold and colorless as frost.

"Gordon," she said, placing the platter on the table, "I sat home worried sick while my husband went to war. I don't want to do it for my son."

All these years later, it was still painful for me to recall the fear and resentment in my mother's eyes, and as I cut across Rockefeller Center, passing the glass angels blowing trumpets and the Christmas tree shining like a pillar of flame, I was grateful for the wind whistling through the dark spaces between the skyscrapers, the wintry blast proving that I was no longer at a summer cookout in Brooklyn.

Glenna's office was only a few blocks away, but as I stopped on the terrace above the enormous gilded statue of a reclining Prometheus and watched the skaters in brightly colored knit caps gliding through the lights of the ice rink below, I had a disquieting moment of sanity and asked myself two questions: What was I doing here? And what could I possibly accomplish by seeing Glenna?

I didn't like the answer to either question.

No doubt, it had been easier meeting her that first time. At work, a couple of days after the barbecue, my uncle said, "You got everybody nervous with your lousy grades and your reading material. Get yourself out to the *Long Island Press* in Garden City tomorrow and see the managing editor."

His name was Mack Grunch, and he had the pallor and squinty eyes of a man who'd spent years underground running a tarantula farm.

"Nice to meet ya, Gordon Meyers," Grunch said, handing me a slip of paper with a name and number. "Your Uncle Jerry tells me you got ability but no experience. Listen, here's the play. There's this organization of med students over at Columbia doing abortion lobbying. A few guys and lots of modern broads. Go talk to one of the bra burners, type me four pages, and you'll make the double sawbuck. And don't sweat it. Reporting ain't like playin' ball in the bigs. If you had to be that good, would there be so many papers?"

Armed with Grunch's philosophy of excellence, I called the number he'd given me, and my interview turned out to be with Glenna.

The skaters were leaving the ice. Across the way, I looked at Prometheus, the Titan who stole fire from Zeus and passed it along to humanity. For his trouble, Prometheus was shackled to a rock, where an eagle arrived to eat his liver, which would grow back every night so the eagle could eat it again.

Ever since reading that myth, I'd wondered why his statue was in Rockefeller Center.

Maybe it was a warning to the tourists.

And now, I wondered, if it was a warning to me.

Chapter 3

Acording to the directory on the wall in the lobby, Glenna Rising, MD, occupied Suite 1515. I rode the elevator up, and my heart was pounding as I walked down the corridor to her office. When I reached the frosted-glass door with her name stenciled on it, I had to step back to let a UPS deliveryman out.

Having imagined seeing Glenna again for so long, I viewed myself as ready for anything—anything, that is, except entering the waiting room and actually seeing her with a UPS box in her hands, standing amid the tube-framed chairs and low, laminate-topped tables that made me think all doctors shopped at the same discount-furniture outlet.

"Can I help—" Glenna said, and then she went silent, gazing at me.

I was stunned, not quite believing it was her. From the looks of it, she had been getting ready to leave. She was wearing a wraparound, camel-hair coat and sheepskin boots. Her hair was shorter than I recalled, cut even along her shoulders, the soft, luminous brown highlighted by strands of silver. The age lines in her face were visible under the harsh gleam of the fluorescent ceiling panels, but she was still beautiful, the features softer now and just as lovely.

Although I had rehearsed several clever remarks, the best I could do to break the ice was "We've got the same boots."

Glenna didn't reply. I had expected a melancholy rush of nostalgia. Instead, I felt the torment of unfinished business, regret without end.

But then, thankfully, Glenna laughed, her own special music, irony always playing around the edges of joy.

She put the box on the receptionist's desk, then came over and lifted up my Irish-tweed cap. I didn't spot a wedding ring on her finger, and while I was processing that information, Glenna touched my short gray hair.

"We're old, Gordon."

"We're getting there."

I can't say who made the first move, but hugging her was perfectly natural, as if we had seen each other that morning, before Glenna left for the hospital and I returned to my writing, as though over thirty years hadn't vanished. When her arms came up around me and the side of my face touched hers, memories flashed through my head like a movie being rewound so fast the scenes are reduced to a blur of colors. The smell of her hair, though, that was real, like crisp apples in the fall. My throat constricted; I almost started to cry; and yet, I also had the comforting illusion that my whole adult life was starting again, and everything that had happened had not happened at all. The disturbing sense that I had taken a wrong turn and lived the wrong life was gone.

She stepped back, looking up at me, and I remembered how I used to love the amused spark in her big green eyes—a deep, startling green, closer to jade than emerald.

"What's the occasion?" she asked, grinning. "You lose your mind or something?"

"Something."

"Well, that clears it up."

I had prepared a lengthy answer for her, but what I said was "I wanted to see you."

"C'mon, Gordon."

I shrugged. "Do you have to get home?"

"No," she said, staring at me, her eyes narrowed. I recalled that look. As if she was studying a slide under a microscope.

"Gordon, you all right?"

I nodded, wondering if I still had the heart to tell her my story. "Is there somewhere we can have a drink?"

"In New York City?" Glenna replied, smiling. "Probably."

"You done for the day?"

She continued studying me. "I'm done. Let me lock up."

OUTSIDE, IT was snowing again.

"Let's walk," Glenna said, slinging her leather briefcase over her shoulder. "I skipped the treadmill today."

We went up to Broadway and headed downtown. I didn't know where to begin, and when the silence became awkward, I said, "So you finished your internship and residency."

"I started right after I saw you the last time."

"I shouldn't have taken off like—"

"It's okay, Gordon. It was my fault, too."

The snow was falling through the velvety blue evening the way it falls through a dream, slow, steady, the flakes big and bright, as if each one had been cut from a doily by a child's jubilant hand.

Glenna said, "Are you still with that consulting firm?"

"I sold my partnership last month."

"What were you doing? I remember you told me it was like journalism, except it paid better."

I gave her the abridged version. "I ran around the world, watched military exercises, talked to people, and wrote up my impressions for the government."

"Sounds dangerous." Though she tried to keep her voice neutral, I heard her disapproval, dismissing the work as another of my risky adventures.

"For the most part it was safe."

"And when it wasn't?"

"I brought company."

We trudged on, saying nothing. As we stepped around a mountain of snow at the corner of West Forty-Seventh, I said, "I want to give writing another try."

"Good for you." The confidence in Glenna's tone took me back to when she had believed that I could do anything, and her faith was the only proof I needed to believe that all I dreamed would be mine.

Glenna said, "What're you going to write about?"

"My misspent youth."

"About us?" she asked.

"I'm not sure I know the end of the story."

"Is that what you came for, Gordon? The end of the story?"

I didn't answer, but a familiar pain and numbness spread through me, an iciness that made the wind blowing over us seem like a breath of summer.

"You know I had a life," Glenna said.

"Had?"

"Have. I have a good practice. I was married for twenty-two years. My husband died eighteen months ago."

"I'm sorry," I said, and I was, even though I'd felt a flash of jealousy.

Stopping and staring up at me, Glenna said, "You never did understand, did you? About me. That there is other sadness in the world besides your own."

"I—"

"Do we have to dig up ancient history?"

"No." I couldn't bring myself to meet her gaze and aimed my eyes downtown toward the lights of Times Square, a neon kaleidoscope glowing through the snowy haze, with silhouettes, outlined against the blazing colors, moving slowly along the sidewalks.

"Gordon, why are you here?"

"For the nice weather?"

I don't know what Glenna saw in my face; snowflakes were landing on my cheeks and melting; maybe she thought they were tears, or maybe they were. She reached up and wiped the water away with a gloved hand.

Softly Glenna said, "What do you want?"

"A drink. I want a drink."

She started walking again. I followed her up a block and into Lally's Tavern, a dimly lit joint with barn-wood paneling and a big stone fireplace. A few people were drinking on the stools at the horseshoe bar, but the rough-hewn-plank tables in the dining area were empty.

"Manhattan rustic," Glenna said, and began slipping out of her coat. I helped her off with it, letting my hands linger on her shoulders. She glanced back at me, the tightness in her features a sign that my touch had come as an uncomfortable surprise. I removed my hands, feeling myself blush.

Glenna turned. She had on a white turtleneck under a charcoal-gray herringbone jacket.

"This is confusing," she said. "I feel—I think I might still be mad at you. And I'm angry at myself for—"

"For?"

"For still being mad," she said, and tried to smile, but didn't quite make it. "Hold on to my coat while I find the ladies' room."

I watched her wend between the tables, her hips swaying in smartly tailored dove-gray slacks, and suddenly I had the dizzying sensation of bouncing from the past to the present and back again. I stood there, unable to move, frozen by memory's guile, its sad and evil magic.

Finally, I went and sat at a table by the fireplace.

Part II

———————

Past

Chapter 4

THE FIRST TIME I met Glenna Rising, she was thirty-nine minutes late. I waited for her inside the main entrance of Columbia Presbyterian Hospital, while doctors and nurses passed, patients in wheelchairs rolled by, and visitors strode in with baskets of fruit swaddled in cellophane.

At last, I saw a young woman in a white lab jacket with a stethoscope curled in a pocket and a section of rubber tubing looped through a buttonhole. She was smiling and walking toward me, every curve of her body as smooth as water. The sight of her was disconcerting, the helplessness I felt when confronted with her heartbreak of a face and all that maple-silk hair spilling past her shoulders.

"Oh, fuck a duck," she said sweetly, after we'd exchanged names. "Am I late? I've got to remember to bring my watch."

I almost asked her how she had been able to take a patient's pulse, but my own was galloping off, and it was about to get worse. She led me to a dead-end corridor and pulled up her white skirt.

"Pantyhose are a hassle," she said, her voice clipped and breathless, as though suppressing some private joke. "They fall down to your ankles and you waddle around like Old Mother Hubbard. I don't need them to be interviewed, do I?"

It was a rhetorical question. After a cursory glance to make sure no one was in the hall, she stepped from her white sandals and peeled the offending nylon down her shapely legs.

"That's better," she said, cramming the pantyhose in a pocket of her lab jacket.

In the cafeteria line, Glenna described her organization: New York Medical Students for the Repeal of Abortion Laws. NYMSRAL consisted of med students, interns, and residents whose primary function was to provide legislators with data that could be used to sway votes in Albany. The organization had started out by doing a study for Assemblyman Bert Cohane, a Manhattan Democrat, who had pioneered the reform effort, which indicated that abortions could be performed without overnight hospitalization. At the moment, NYMSRAL was combing emergency rooms for victims of back-alley jobs and documenting the cases of cervical tears, perforated uteruses, chronic pelvic pain, severe hemorrhaging, and runaway infections—typically peritonitis or septic shock.

Through it all, I kept replaying her peeling off her pantyhose and only managed to keep my head straight by focusing on the plates of chow mein on the steam counter. Then after paying for my coffee and Glenna's tea, I sat across from her at a Formica-topped table and got lost looking at her. She was discussing the moral debate surrounding abortion and the scientific response to it, and I could neither stop staring nor follow what she was saying.

Glenna said, "I don't know much about being a reporter, but aren't you supposed to be writing this down?"

"This is background," I said, uncapping my Bic pen and opening my spiral notebook.

I had just started taking notes when guys in white lab

jackets—other medical students and doctors with bald spots and bifocals—began stopping at our table to say hello. They asked about her summer ("I was around," she replied vaguely), or where she was living ("In the Bronx," she said, equally vague). I was annoyed; I did have an interview to do; and furthermore, I didn't want her paying attention to anybody but me.

I was on my second page of notes when another guy, built like a cross-country runner, tapped Glenna on the shoulder. His face, with its perfectly planed nose and jutting jaw, had a studied indifference, and his fine, straw-colored hair was receding at his temples and tumbling in his eyes. Under his lab jacket, he wore a candy-striped, button-down shirt and a red tie with black stripes. His cuffed khakis were baggy, and his Top-Siders were so beat he must have had them since Mummy and Father sentenced him to Choate or wherever rich WASPs dumped their kids so they could dissipate the family fortune in peace.

This guy was particularly annoying because his hand was lingering on her shoulder. He was also the only one that Glenna introduced me to: his name was Palmer Chilton, but I was already thinking of him as Biff the Brooks Brothers Mouse.

"When will you be home for dinner?" Biff asked, and my heart sank. "I'm barbecuing lamb chops."

Glenna looked at me. "Are we almost done?"

Not ready to ask her out, I said, "We can stop. But I need to do another interview."

Her eyes narrowed in a way that hinted she may have been onto my game. She told Biff that she'd be home by seven, and he departed without mentioning how nice it had been to meet me. I'd figured him for better manners.

"I've gotta split," Glenna said, standing up. "I think I'm late again."

"Who's Palmer?"

"Palmer's president of NYMSRAL. He's an ob-gyn resident here."

Hoping to sound casually inquisitive, I asked, "You and Palmer been living together awhile?"

"A couple years. Is this more background?"

"Just curious."

"Curiosity's good for a journalist," she said. "Being handsome must also help."

"Don't know. This is my first story."

"I suppose you'll find out." She started to walk away. After a few steps, she turned. "Palmer and me: same house, different beds."

I tried to play it cool, but my relief must have shown on my face, because that was the first time I saw her grin, as sly and delighted as a child who knows all your secrets.

Then she was gone.

Chapter 5

I MET WITH GLENNA a week later at the College of Physicians and Surgeons. She referred to it as "P and S" and suggested that we talk in an empty classroom when I told her that our interview would go smoother without interruptions. Glenna was eighteen minutes late, and her pantyhose must have fit because she did not remove them.

During the interview, I discovered that Glenna was a third-year student, done with her classes and med boards, and beginning her clinical rotations.

"I'm doing psychiatry now," she said. "It's nine to five, hardly any overnight on call, and weekends are usually free. Medicine is next, at the end of October, and that's a drag."

The huskiness of her voice didn't help my concentration, but unlike our interview in the cafeteria, I managed to ask plenty of questions and to scrawl enough notes on NYMSRAL to fill the N volume of the *Encyclopaedia Britannica*.

I said, "You never told me why you got involved in abortion reform."

"After Palmer started treating women who'd been to the illegal butcher shops, he joined NYMSRAL and asked me to help."

"So it was Palmer asking?"

"Great tie," she said.

"Thanks."

It was a Peter Max, with a colorful pattern of planets and stars, and a prime feature of my reporter's ensemble: safari jacket with my hair combed over the collar, blue work shirt, denim bell-bottoms, and new low-cut construction boots from Smitty's Army-Navy.

"There's more to it," Glenna said, and undid the rubber tube that was laced through a buttonhole of her lab jacket. "Do you have to quote everything I say?"

"No. It can be off-the-record." I thought Glenna was going to tell me that she'd had an abortion, and I wondered about the guy who got her pregnant. What he was like. How I compared.

Glenna said, "You have hazel eyes."

"That's what it says on my driver's license."

Glenna laughed, a muted, fleeting sound. "I've never told anyone this before. My parents knew. It was years ago."

I watched Glenna pull the tubing out of the buttonhole.

"Her name was Vicky Wyland. We met at sleepaway camp in the Poconos when we were fifteen. She was small and shy with short blond hair. The girls in our bunk thought she was weird; I thought she was cool. When everyone was reading romance comics or movie magazines, Vicky was reading a history of the Incas. When we were making lanyards, Vicky was painting watercolors of winged canoes flying over the lake. I liked talking with her, and she liked that I wasn't shy and danced with boys."

Glenna wrapped the rubber tube around her index finger. "Vicky used to disappear after dinner, and I finally found her in the woods behind the mess hall. She was playing a guitar and singing 'The Water Is Wide.' The purity of her voice was hypnotic. Vicky stopped when she saw me and said, 'I borrowed the guitar from the office. I'm not very good.' I said, 'No, you're great.' She didn't believe me, but I began going to the woods with her to listen."

Glenna unwound the tubing from her finger and noticed me watching her. Smiling as though I'd caught her doing something shameful and stuffing the tube in her pocket, she said, "It's a tourniquet. For drawing bloods."

I was tempted to hold out my arm as a joke, but I didn't want to distract her.

"In August, I convinced Vicky to enter the talent show. Most of the performances were worse than the weird-animal acts on *Ed Sullivan*. Then Vicky sang 'Moon River' as if it was part folk song, part prayer. I was thrilled she was up onstage, but her singing scared me. She sang 'Moon River' as if she knew more about longing than anyone on earth. You know that longing, Gordon, that terrible, bottomless longing?"

I nearly replied, *Yes, every second I look at you.* Instead, I nodded, and Glenna said, "Vicky got a standing ovation, and for the rest of the summer she was a star. She sang all over camp and always drew a crowd, and she even started dancing with boys. On the last day, we were about to board our buses for home, and Vicky began sobbing. I'd had my arms around her, and when I let go, she said, 'Thank you, Glenna,' and ran for her bus. Before getting on, she turned and shouted, 'Thank you for everything!'"

Glenna leaned back in her chair. "In September, Vicky wrote me she had a boyfriend who looked like Steve McQueen. He was a freshman at Dartmouth, and I thought that was weird. What kind of college freshman dates a fifteen-year-old? But Vicky wrote that he was wonderful, and in two hours they were driving to Amherst to see Joan Baez at UMass."

Tears glistened on Glenna's cheeks. A lump was rising in my throat.

"I wrote Vicky that she should be careful, but six weeks later, I still hadn't heard back, so I called. Her mother answered. She sounded drugged, and as soon as she heard my voice, she said, 'Oh, Glenna, we've lost our Victoria. You girls have to watch out. You—'

"Vicky's mother dropped the phone. I kept saying, 'Hello,' but no one answered, and I hung up. I was sure Vicky had died in a car accident on her UMass trip. I told my parents and then cried myself to sleep. A few days later, I got a letter. Some other kids at our camp were from New Hampshire, where Vicky lived, and one of them had sent me a clipping about her from the *Manchester Union Leader*. She'd been pregnant and gone to some slaughterhouse in a motel behind a truck stop. The state police arrested the guy doing the abortions. The article said Vicky had died from a massive hemorrhage. I'm guessing the asshole perforated her uterus."

I reached over and touched Glenna's hand with my fingers. She ran her hand over mine, then dabbed at her cheeks with the sleeve of her lab jacket.

"I felt so fucking guilty," she said.

"Why? Because if Vicky had still been too shy for a boyfriend, she wouldn't have gotten pregnant?"

Glenna studied me with a half smile of either admiration or disdain: I couldn't say. But her silence made me uncomfortable, so I was relieved when she said, "Something like that."

"It's how I'd feel. Fact is, all you did was help her."

Glenna nodded and, leaning back, closed her eyes. I had an image of her sitting alone on a beach—a still life painted with the palette of summer, the sun streaks in her hair and her tanned face setting off the delicately sculpted symmetry of her features. It was an idyllic image, soulful, and yet unspeakably sad in its loneliness.

Glenna looked at me. "I was thinking, this interview isn't fair. I don't know anything about you."

"What do you want to know?"

"Everything," she replied with such seriousness that it made me nervous, since it was hard to believe Glenna would be interested in me.

"You have that much time?"

"No." She grinned. "But you didn't ask me that. You asked me what I wanted to know."

"Are you high?"

Glenna burst out laughing as if she were gone on a dime of weed. "Not during working hours."

It was heartening to hear her laugh, and the sound seemed to float, like music, on the balmy September air coming through the open windows.

I said, "I'm starting my fifth year at Brooklyn College. I have to stay enrolled for my Two-S or I'm draft bait. I have zero interest in graduate school. What I want to do is write fiction. And what I don't want to do is bore you."

"All med students talk about is the hospital, and that's boring. C'mon, Gordon. If you weren't interested in anything, you wouldn't be writing this story."

I took a breath. "I want to get my life down on paper and make it behave—or at least understand more of it. I think I can do that in short stories or a novel. And that would be interesting. Like traveling but you don't have to go anywhere except inside your head."

I had never spoken about this stuff because it sounded weird even to me, like the noise that flitted through your brain when you were peaking on a tab of sunshine. Yet, as I spoke, Glenna leaned closer, her eyes locked on mine. No one had ever listened to me so intently. There was something passionate about the keenness of her concentration as I went on, and it would be years before I understood that I'd just had the most intimate experience of my young life.

"Writing," I said, "is the one thing that makes sense to me."

"Anyone who can write—that's a gift. You should do it." Glenna glanced up at the clock over the door. "Gordon, I don't want to, but I have to leave."

Both of us stood, and Glenna said, "I appreciate you listening to me go on. No one's ever—I'm glad I told you about Vicky."

"Me, too." I should've asked her out on the spot. Ordinarily, I wasn't so lame, but I was afraid she'd say no, and not only because she was good-looking enough to frighten just about any guy. It was that talking about the future with her had made me feel as though I'd actually have one, and if she said no, then what would I have?

"Is that it?" Glenna asked. "We're done?"

"I'll have to check your quotes with you when I'm finished." She hesitated. Then she said, "Give me a call."

EAGER TO see Glenna again, and with the deadline for the article two days away, I decided chemical assistance was required and went to see my best friend, Todd Elhoff. He was perched on his regular stool at the far end of the counter in the Sugar

Bowl, a noisy, smoky hangout across from the Brooklyn College campus.

We had grown up next door to each other on Fifty-Ninth Street, right off Ralph Avenue. Unlike me, Todd had graduated from Brooklyn on schedule. Long term he planned to go to Hollywood and get into the movie business. Short term he worked at Incense & Peppermints, a head shop in the East Village, where he swapped his hours for the studio apartment above the store. He made his real bread by dealing ups, downs, mescaline, and acid to more of Brooklyn College than would have pleased the dean of students.

"What's happenin', Meyers?" Todd said, as I sat on the stool next to him. "Man, it was in the *Voice* today. Jimi's coming to the Fillmore. You in?"

"I'm in." Todd was a fanatic on the subject of Hendrix, which accounted for his wild Jewish Afro, fringed, white-leather vest, and frilly, tie-dyed shirt with puffy gambler's sleeves.

He gave me a Marlboro, stuck one in his mouth, and lit us both up. "How's your *Long Island Press* thing going?"

"Have to pull an all-nighter."

Todd said, "Two black beauties to go," and reached down to the floor, dunking his hand into one of the complimentary airline flight bags he always carried—this one from Pan Am.

"Hey, Meyers," he said, pressing the pills into my open palm. "Now that you're a reporter, you can forget about joining the army."

Todd was the only person I'd told about wanting to check out the war. He said I must be mentally handicapped. Todd didn't have to sweat the draft. Last summer, we were playing ball at Manhattan Beach when he landed wrong after grabbing a rebound and tore the ligaments in his left knee, which

got him an operation, eight weeks on crutches, and a 4-F clas-
sification from our draft board.

I put away the speed and said, "Met someone who'd be
worth staying home for."

"That mean you and me won't be doubling up on Gina and
Marie Ianolli anymore?"

"She's amazing. Not just for a roller-coaster ride. Let me
know about the Hendrix tickets."

As I got off the stool, Todd said, "Meyers, guys get fucked
permanently in Vietnam. You better wait for the movie."

EARLY THAT evening, I popped a black beauty and started writing.

"You're up," my mother said, stopping by my room at midnight to investigate why I was hunt-and-pecking on my sister's
old portable Smith-Corona. "I'm proud of you. I told Dad if
you found something you liked, you'd be able to concentrate.
Should I fix you a sandwich?"

Buzzing along on the speed, the thought of food made me
gag. I declined and went on working, downing another black
beauty at 2:00 a.m. and finishing the article as the sun rose.
Glenna had told me she woke up about seven, and after pac-
ing my room for an hour, I called her. She said that later in the
afternoon she had to go to the library at Columbia University
to read through some psych journals, and we agreed to meet
nearby at the West End Bar.

Glenna was a mere nine minutes late. I was at a table in
back, surrounded by a rowdy bunch of jocks swilling beer,
intellectuals eating hamburgers, and revolutionaries munch-
ing potato chips and debating what SDS had accomplished at
the Democratic Convention in Chicago. ("Scared the country
enough to vote for Nixon!" one of them shouted. "That's what

we'll get! Nixon!") I waved to Glenna when I saw her come in wearing a rose-and-violet batik peasant dress. She paused to say something to the radical conclave, then sat across from me.

"Is NYMSRAL part of SDS?" I asked, when the waitress had gone off with our order.

"They're Palmer's pals. And Robin's—my other house-mate. Palmer's a gourmet cook, and he invites them over for dinner. They rant and rave about poverty, racism, and the war with Palmer's beef Wellington stuck to their faces."

Glenna rummaged through her burlap shoulder bag and extracted a paperback of *Portrait of a Lady*.

"I have this friend, Rick Siner," she said, handing me the book. "He wanted to be a writer, but went to med school instead. I asked him, and he says Henry James is the great modern novelist. So I bought this for you."

I was touched and astounded by the gift. My response was to demonstrate my masterly humor and the brassiness of my balls by saying, "I've read James, *The Golden Bowl*. And the thing is, the word *fuck* wasn't in it one time."

Like all bad jokes, it had seemed funnier when I thought of it. Spoken, it had sounded crude. Glenna didn't laugh; she seemed confused, hurt, and I castigated myself for being a jerk. Finally, after the waitress delivered Glenna's gin and tonic and my Jack Daniel's, Glenna said, "You like that word?"

"What word?"

"*Fuck*."

"It's one of my favorites."

"Then why don't you ask me out? Or do we have to do another interview?"

I swallowed my bourbon wrong and started coughing.

"Very romantic," she said.

Chapter 6

"Wнат'd you do?" I asked my father. "Knock off Grabstein's Deli?"

I was in the den lacing up my work boots, and Dad was sitting upright in his Barcalounger, transforming a TV tray into a smorgasbord, spreading out plates of seeded rye and pastrami, cans of soda, a jar of mustard, and a container of coleslaw.

"Jerr's comin' over to watch the Mets and Pirates with us," he said.

"Got a date," I said, expecting him to say what he'd been saying before every one of my dates since high school: *Be nice to the girls. Remember, you got a sister.* Instead, he came back with "A date? With the Mets on and Uncle Jerr coming over? Must be some girl. She a stripper?"

In my excitement about Glenna, I'd overlooked his potential objection to my breaking our Sunday baseball-season ritual. "She's a med student," I replied, letting some pride seep into my voice. "She's at Columbia."

"What'd ya know. If my son can't be a doctor, he can marry one. I used to figure that'd be for your sister. Not for you." He shot me his caustic sideways glare in case I was unaware that his wisecrack was intended to piss me off.

"Elaine marry a doctor? She's bumming around Europe with a guy who has braids down to his ass. When you met him, you told her he looked like he belonged in a Turkish prison."

"That kid—what's his name, Gary?—he'll shape up. His father's a big tax attorney."

"That's logical, Dad." In her last letter to me, Elaine wrote that she was about to dump Gary. He had gotten a gig as a drummer at the Rock 'n' Roll Circus, a club in Paris, and he was shooting smack three times a day.

"Stick around," my father said. "Tell me about this article Mom says you did for the *Long Island Press*."

"It'll be in Sunday," I said, and dashed out of the den as my father said, "What's the hurry? I got your Dr. Brown's black cherry here."

GLENNA HAD predicted it was an hour ride from Brooklyn to the house she rented. Since she didn't strike me as being on eastern standard time, I was skeptical, but her prediction and her directions were accurate, which gave me a rabbit punch of paranoia to go along with my appreciable first-date jitters; she undoubtedly passed out directions to guys by the hundreds.

I would've gone nuts with that line of thinking, except that exiting the bucolic stretch of the Henry Hudson Parkway and driving into the cityscape of Riverdale was jarring, with all those opposite images collapsing on each other. Along Kappock Street, the apartment towers formed a concrete skyline worthy of a Russian prison complex; it was cold and gray and dead despite the reddish-gold patina of sunlight. Then the concrete horizon suddenly surrendered to a silver-blue stretch of the Harlem River with the span of the Henry Hudson Bridge above. Glenna lived on Edsall Avenue, and circling down the narrow, leafy winding lane that dipped toward the railroad tracks along Spuyten Duyvil Creek, I felt as though I'd been transported to an earlier century.

The houses were terraced into a hillside overlooking the water, and after parking on a wooded slope along the creek, I opened a rusty iron gate and climbed a steep set of cracked stone steps to Glenna's house, an old, white colonial with a big bay of four-paned windows on the third story and a yard shaded by gnarled oaks. I rapped on the door with the brass knocker and had the feeling that once she let me in, I wouldn't want to leave.

Inside, I heard someone stamping down a staircase, and then the door was opened by a chick in a waffled thermal-underwear shirt and bleached-denim overalls.

"I'm Robin. Glenna's housemate. You met her already so you know you'll have to wait. Hope you brought a book."

I followed Robin across the warped pine floor into a living room with windows on either side of a fieldstone fireplace. The room was furnished with a shabby brocaded couch with carved walnut arms, a wing chair covered in the same shabby oyster-white cloth as the couch, two chipped walnut rockers—one of which I sat in—and a chipped walnut coffee table. A plaque proclaiming George Washington had slept over wouldn't have been out of place were it not for the posters on the white plaster walls: the Stars and Stripes with a peace symbol stamped on it; Malcolm X leveling his forefinger during a speech; and a garish poster above the fireplace, with a black light gleaming on it, that depicted twelve sexual positions, each corresponding with a zodiac sign and dates.

Hopeful that this was Glenna's contribution to the decor, I checked my sign, Libra. No sweat—basic doggie style.

"When's Glenna's birthday?" I asked Robin. She was standing at a card table by the fireplace, running pages off a mimeograph machine.

"February nineteenth. Don't worry. You have time to send her flowers."

Glenna was a Pisces. Uh-oh. A position that would stump the Flying Wallendas.

"What're you doing?" I asked.

"SDS is helping the Black Panthers publicize their free-breakfast program."

Showcasing my wit, I said, "Which group do you belong to?"

Grimacing to let me know she thought I was about as droll as a malignant tumor, Robin replied, "Glenna said you were strange."

From upstairs, Glenna called, "Gordon, I'll be right down."

Winking at me, Robin said sarcastically, "The anticipation must be killing you."

I appreciated the implied conspiracy of her wink, as if we were allies, and she was rooting for me not to be intimidated by Glenna's beauty. And her sarcasm was understandable; it couldn't be much fun for her living with a stunner like Glenna; and I assumed that her envy overflowed on a regular basis. This isn't to say Robin was unattractive. She had an exotic face with flawless olive skin and raisin-dark eyes, but it seemed as though she had decided to protest that she wasn't as blessed as Glenna by making herself as unappealing as possible. She was a few pounds past zaftig, and her overalls didn't help. Robin wore them a couple of sizes too big, so she appeared to be floating around inside a bleached-denim potato sack, and her long, thick raven hair, which would have been lovely had she bothered to tend it, was piled up carelessly on her head and clipped down with a plastic swarm of bumblebee barrettes.

Still, even with Robin as an ally, I felt lost in a fog when Glenna waltzed in with her hair falling past her shoulders like a silken cape. Getting up out of the rocker, I heard myself say hello and tried, with mixed success, not to gape at her sheer, white bell-sleeved blouse, with no bra underneath it, and the black velour bell-bottoms hugging her hips.

"Late again," Glenna said with a smile. "God, I never know what time it is."

"So sometimes you're early?" I asked, startled by how suddenly I disliked her for always making me wait and never apologizing for it.

"No," Glenna answered, losing the smile. "I'm not."

Robin said, "She's practicing for stacking up patients in her waiting room."

I shared Robin's amusement; Glenna did not. She said to Robin, "Aren't you going into the city for a poetry reading at the Y?"

"There're no real guys there," Robin replied. "Only poets."

"Try the Teamsters," Glenna said, paying off Robin for her waiting-room remark.

Robin's social reflexes were acute enough to feign amusement, but then she took a quart carton of Breyers mint chocolate chip from the mantel of the fireplace, pulled out the spoon sticking in the top, and dug into the ice cream with the grim methodicalness of a gravedigger shoveling into frozen ground.

Watching her, I had one of those ephemeral insights that you dismiss as irrelevant: Robin should be my date. But dating unkempt, sad-eyed girls in baggy overalls wasn't my thing, so I said see ya to Robin and helped Glenna on with her champagne-colored shawl.

DRIVING INTO the city, we traded personal trivia. Because Glenna was well along in her schooling, I was surprised that she was my age. Turned out she was an only child who'd been a brain in school, skipping the eighth grade at Fieldston, a tony, progressive private academy close to her family's house in Riverdale, and graduating from the University of Vermont in three years. She'd gone to UVM to be near the skiing at Stowe and to needle her pushy parents, who had hounded her to apply to Wellesley, Bryn Mawr, Smith, and Radcliffe. Her father, Dr. Herman Rising, was an anesthesiologist, and for med school she chose Dad's alma mater.

"I'd grown up by then," Glenna explained. Her mother, Kay, was born some species of Protestant in Maine; Herman was a Bronx Jew; and both now worshipped at the Riverdale-Yonkers Society for Ethical Culture.

"Not that you can categorize what Ethical Culturists do as worshipping," Glenna said. "It's more like AA meetings for atheists."

She fiddled with the radio. When a classical station came on, she turned it off. "I hate Bach."

"Why?"

"Reminds me of my last date."

"You went out with Bach?"

She rolled her eyes. "I went out with a radiologist who was a closet harpsichordist. He had a compulsive desire to hear string quartets at Philharmonic Hall."

"You're safe from string quartets with me."

"Figured that," she replied, resting her hand on my leg for an exquisite instant.

Then I believe she said that she loved the Beatles, and the song "Here, There and Everywhere" was her favorite, and I'm sure that she said some other things, but I can't recall, because by the time I'd parked on Bleecker, and we were walking to Little Italy, Glenna had stuffed my heart in the lusciously curved back pocket of her bell-bottoms.

DURING THE Feast of San Gennaro, the patron saint of Naples, Mulberry Street is transformed into the midway of an urban carnival, and the thousands of lights strung above the revelers glitter like constellations in the evening sky. The canopied booths of roulette wheels, ring tosses, and card games are mobbed, and when people aren't trying to win goldfish or parakeets, they're bellying up to the food stands, which was where Glenna and I stood in line with the spiced steam of frying sausages washing over us.

Glenna was squinting in concentration, as though opting for a calzone or slice of Sicilian pizza were a decision of some magnitude.

"What're you having?" she asked.

"Pizza."

"I'll have pizza, too."

As I shouldered into the throng to order, Glenna nodded over at the next booth, saying, "What do they have there?"

I backed out of line, and we approached a counter serving puffs of fried dough powdered with sugar.

"Zeppoli," I said. "They're great."

"Maybe I should have a zeppoli."

I got into line, and Glenna said, "Zeppoli're for dessert, aren't they?"

"Only if you've already eaten dinner."

"Oh, right. What do they stuff the calzone with?"

I told her cheese and sausage, but before I could vouch for their quality, the brawny guy working the counter said to me, "Youse two gonna eat or what?"

I bought some zeppoli, gave the paper plate to Glenna, then went to the other stand and got two slices of pizza, a calzone, and sodas.

"Take your pick," I said when we were seated at one of the sidewalk tables with the Cinzano umbrellas.

"If I'm by myself or with friends, I can order. Go out on a date, I get sort of stuck." She smiled sheepishly. "Part of my charm."

"Which part?"

She laughed. It was a warm night, and after draping her crocheted shawl over her chair, Glenna sampled everything, which was fine with me, since I was so struck by the sheerness of her bell-sleeved shirt, with the whitish-pink fullness of her breasts and the tawny shadows of her nipples showing through, I lost interest in the food.

"You like my top?" Glenna said.

"It's distracting."

"You want a closer look, we'll have to go home." I readjusted my gaze and heard her chuckle. "Let's have a drink. My treat."

Young, miniskirted waitresses were wheeling carts among the tables, and when one of them stopped by, Glenna asked for a gin and tonic and I ordered a Chianti. The waitress poured the drinks, while Glenna stood, sliding her hands in and out of the pockets of her bell-bottoms, an impressive feat given that the velour seemed inseparable from her skin.

"Oh, God," she said, her cheeks reddening. "I changed three

times before we went out. I left my money in my other pants. I'm really sorry."

"Don't worry," I said, and paid for the drinks. After moving her chair beside mine, Glenna kissed me quickly on the lips and began to eat. She didn't touch her gin and tonic.

"Care for a different drink?"

"Thank you, no," she said, then took a small sip. "I always order gin and tonic. It saves me a decision." She gave me a beguiling smile. "What do most of your women prefer—a draft?"

I didn't reply. Let her worry about my other women.

The remainder of the evening was devoted to walking the fragrant streets of Little Italy, reveling in the improbable intimacy that arises between a couple when they are alone in a crowd. We held hands, listening to the Neapolitan love songs filling the soft, slate-blue air, passing boys hawking miniature plastic saints out of cigar boxes, stopping to eat lemon ices and to watch children ride the Ferris wheel. As we approached the corner of Mulberry and East Houston, a teenage girl, dressed in a jersey that was the green, white, and red of the Italian flag, blew by us on roller skates, her ponytail flying behind her.

"One of my favorite summer jobs," Glenna said.

"You were on Italy's roller derby team?"

Glenna grinned. "Very clever, funnyman. But, no, not a roller-skating team. I was a carhop at a drive-in outside Burlington. The summer after my freshman year at UVM. Never dropped my tray once."

"That's the summer I worked at the Laurels Hotel in the Catskills."

"What'd you do?"

"Won a trophy for dancing the cha-cha."

"You were a dance instructor?" Glenna asked.

"You sound skeptical."

"Only a little."

"Okay, I was a busboy. But a group of grandmothers came up from Miami Beach. They'd paid for dance lessons, and since most of them were widows, the social director recruited busboys to be their partners. Eva Cohen and I took first place in the cha-cha. Want me to show you?"

"No music."

"Follow me," I said.

Under the streetlights, I'd spotted a plum-colored Cadillac with Batmobile tail fins parked at the curb. The top was down, and the heavyset guy behind the wheel must have been hard of hearing because he had WINS cranked up like he was broadcasting the news to Brooklyn.

"Excuse me, sir," I said.

He lowered the volume on the radio. What was left of his salt-and-pepper hair was combed back in a duck's ass, and he was wearing a Yankees warm-up jacket over an undershirt.

"Yeah?" he asked.

I said, "My friend here doesn't believe I can do the cha-cha and—"

"Gordon, I didn't say—"

"And," I said, "I need some music to show her."

He looked at Glenna, who was giggling, and stared at me as if I'd recently dropped in from Mars.

"Make it quick," he said. "I'm waitin' for my wife. She comes out and sees you two playin' Fred Astaire and Ginger Rogers, she'll be hustling me over to Roseland Ballroom."

After cranking up the volume, he jabbed a radio button, and we heard, "More music on seventy-seven WABCeeeee!" and Cousin Brucie was on the air, sending out a song for Gus and Lorraine in Astoria, an oldie from Jay and the Americans, "Come a Little Bit Closer."

"It ain't a cha-cha," the guy said, "but get goin'. The wife's comin.'"

I raised my arms; Glenna took my hands; and before we'd made our first turn, I felt as though I were dancing with a shadow—if the shadow had long brown hair and radiant green eyes and a body that gave off a perfumed warmth while moving with precise, exquisite steps.

"Hey, Fred," the guy called out. "You havin' trouble keepin' up wit Ginger?"

"No," I said, and Glenna laughed.

When the song ended, Glenna leaned into me, placing her palms on my chest, and said, "Am I better than the grandmothers?"

I smiled down at her. "Much. And prettier, too."

"Good answer. You ready to take me home?"

We thanked the guy in the Caddie, and as we headed to my car, I decided that when we got back to Spuyten Duyvil, I wouldn't try to talk Glenna into bed. Not to pique her interest or put her down, but because I thought that I was on the verge of having something real with her and hoped to avoid confusing passion for love, and the best way to do that was to keep my hands to myself.

It seemed like a logical strategy on that mild September evening, with the festive sounds of Little Italy simmering behind us, yet had things proceeded logically, I wouldn't have been moved, decades later, to write them down.

"HI, PALMER," Glenna said as I followed her into the house. "You remember Gordon?"

Biff the Brooks Brothers Mouse, in a madras, collarless

surfer shirt and white shorts, was sprawled on the living-room couch, reading a Freak Brothers comic. He brushed his lank hair from his eyes and gave me the once-over, appearing less than thrilled by what he saw.

"The reporter," he said. "What paper was it?"

His tone was unfailingly polite, which in my opinion didn't make him any less of a douche bag, because his question implied that I'd have to work for the *New York Times* before he could be expected to remember my employer.

"The *Long Island Press*," I said.

"Where'd you go?" he asked Glenna so peevishly that I wondered if their past or present was less platonic than Glenna had led me to believe.

She told Biff, and he said, "Outta sight," the sardonic lift to his eyebrows intimating that the San Gennaro festival was anything but—unless you were a camera-toting rube from Toledo.

"C'mon upstairs," Glenna said to me.

I hadn't altered my outlook on opening-night sex, but I wasn't about to decline the invitation in front of Biff, who looked me up and down as if I'd wandered into the living room by mistake and then refocused on the reefer madness of Fat Freddy, Phineas, and Freewheelin' Franklin.

Trailing Glenna up the stairs, I surveyed the velour seat of her hip-huggers as it shifted with raw, animal grace, and on the second-floor landing, Glenna abruptly turned and commented, "Tits'll do, but the ass is a winner."

Her comment breached the blockade of my self-discipline, and as I reached to press a palm on her winner, she said gleefully, "Race ya," and sprinted up the stairs, crossing the threshold ahead of me.

Her room occupied the entire third story, and after turning on the overhead fixture, a four-pronged Japanese lantern with red, green, yellow, and blue bulbs, Glenna stepped over the hillocks of laundry on the floor and demonstrated a flair for understatement by saying, "I probably should've straightened up."

Her room looked like it had been robbed—by amateurs. Clothes spilled out of the open drawers of an old cherrywood bureau, and a metal desk was cluttered with medical tomes, spiral notebooks, half-filled mugs of tea, a tall, greenish-gold bottle of Jean Naté after-bath lotion, two smaller exotic-shaped bottles of Shalimar perfume, and a lamp missing its shade. A rubber tree stood in one corner; in another, there was a potted palm and Glenna used both as racks for her bathrobe and towels. At the foot of the unmade bed—a double mattress and box spring—was a midget-legged bamboo table that held a stereo with albums crammed underneath.

Glenna put on *Rubber Soul*, and then we sat on the striped Mexican blanket covering the bay window's recessed seat. This high up you had a view out across the Hudson River, and beyond the water I could see the lights above the Palisades on the Jersey shore.

John was singing "Norwegian Wood" when Glenna said, "Room's a mess, but the view's cool."

"I can't complain. I live with my folks."

Hanging from ceramic planters above the window were spider plants and asparagus ferns, shedding their hairy leaves. Glenna brushed a few from my shoulder, then ran her fingers down my arm until she was holding my hand.

"You can stay here," she said, studying me, her green eyes warm as summer seaside light.

"Maybe this works out better if we don't rush it."

"Maybe it does," she said, and smiled. "But I think you want to remain a mystery."

"An enigma wrapped in a mystery."

Glenna laughed. "You're an enigma wrapped in a blintze. But I'll wait. I'm a good sport. And I'll try anything once." She laughed again when she saw me pondering her last remark. Then she said, "Only kidding. You'll kiss me, won't you?"

I kissed her, and she shimmied over to sit on my lap. Leaving was becoming an increasingly arduous concept to put into action, but then she broke off the kiss.

"Good night," she said, and smiled at me, a complicated smile. A smile that made me think she might not be such a good sport after all.

Chapter 7

My NYMSRAL PIECE was published as the abortion controversy heated up. Governor Rockefeller pledged to sign a reform bill if the legislature forwarded one to him, and the traditional liberalism of Long Island and New York City—bastions of civil-rights support and war protest—was on a collision course with the Catholic Church and its devout flock in the boroughs and upstate.

Mack Grunch called me at home and said, "Congratulations, Gordon Meyers. We got alotta mail on that one. The fruitcakes are outta the woodwork and they're buying papers. Go hunt me up some stories that'll drive people nuts."

I guessed that night court in Brooklyn would be a good hunting ground, and Glenna, who had gotten a kick out of reading her quotes in the paper, thought court sounded like a blast when I invited her to join me. Sitting on the curved-back benches, we mainly saw a bored judge slapping the wrists of hookers. The one possibility that I thought would amuse readers was Enid Henstrom, a spectrally thin, chain-smoking divorcée from Red Hook, who had once again gone into the Macy's on Flatbush Avenue and paid for a shopping spree with a check that bounced out of Brooklyn. The judge asked

Enid to explain the rubber check, and when, visibly outraged, she replied, "What can I do? Macy's won't give me a credit card," the courtroom broke up.

After the judge arranged for her to repay Macy's, I asked Enid for an interview. She said, "Pay my bill, we'll talk," and since I couldn't do that, Glenna and I left. I dropped her off in Spuyten Duyvil, sticking to my decision not to hop into the sack with her by refusing to go inside. I was home in bed when my phone rang.

"Don't you want to fuck me?" Glenna said.

"Can't say till my mom gets off the extension."

I heard an intake of breath on her end and laughed.

"You're not serious?" she asked.

"My folks are out."

"Gordon, do you . . ."

"Do I?"

"Think there's something wrong with me?"

"Besides your awful taste in guys, you're perfect."

I thought Glenna would laugh; she didn't. "You're not that awful."

"What a nice thing to say."

Now Glenna laughed. "I mean—nothing I can't help you with."

"Then we should get going."

"Tomorrow night at seven?"

"I was thinking we could get started on the phone."

"That's a lovely thought, Gordon, but I'm the hands-on type. See you tomorrow."

WE SAT cross-legged on her bed, her room lit by the rainbow glimmer of a Japanese lantern. Glenna tamped out the joint we'd been smoking in a pearly violet abalone shell, then stretched out on her stomach, curling into herself, head turning on the pillow, looking up at me.

"Great weed," I said, floating, contemplating the designs on her Indian-print quilt.

"Robin's homegrown," Glenna said. "She hangs the plants from the curtain rods in her bedroom."

Revolver was playing, and even though the stereo was only on the low table at the foot of the bed, the music sounded far away and I watched my hand push up the back of Glenna's yellow polo shirt. She wasn't wearing a bra, and a white line left by a bikini top ran across her like a narrow strip of buttercream frosting. My hand roamed along the soft slope of her back, then under the faded denim of her cutoffs, caressing round, taut flesh before moving up again, her skin a rosy copper color in the lantern light. I knew that I should get on with it, but I didn't want this moment to end, didn't want to turn it into a different moment, maybe better, but not this exact moment, with its boundless promise, its serenity, its grace.

I glanced out the bay window, where the evening sky was purple with a satiny sheen, the dark wisps of clouds like wrinkles in the satin.

I said, "I feel like I've known you my whole life."

Glenna, more impressed by science than mystery, replied, "You haven't."

"But I wanted to."

Now she had another expression entirely, serious, hesitant, vulnerable. "Here I am," she whispered.

Kneeling over her, I moved the long hair from her neck and began to kiss the strands at the nape, lightly at first, then nibbling at her. Glenna smelled like lemon flowers and vanilla, and she must have turned over because we were kissing, floating together, happy, weightless. It seemed to take forever for our clothes to come off, but I'm sure they did because her breasts were heavy in my palms, and my hands left ghostly prints on her sun-bronzed stomach and thighs. Her breathy murmuring thrilled me, a wondrously intimate sound, and I lost myself in the cadence of her breath, and soon the room was scented with the bouquet of our bodies, and our breathing was a persistent song, becoming part of the music on the stereo as the album played again and again.

FOR THE next seven weeks we were off on our own version of the decathlon, astonished by the events we created and the finish lines we crossed. Did we love each other? I was sure of it then, less sure later on. But I'm jumping ahead of myself here. Laying out the end of the story when our story hasn't really begun. That's because there's no story without conflict, and during those first fevered weeks Glenna and I got along like lovebirds off a funny little valentine. Best of all, she seemed to believe in our infinite future together, the proof being that one night, with the wind sighing in through her bedroom windows and drying the sheen of perspiration on our bodies, she presented me with a new, buttery calfskin case with the key to her house hooked inside.

I held the case in my hand, staring at it.

"Is that okay?" Glenna asked.

I nodded.

"Then what's wrong?"

"I feel—embarrassed. Embarrassed that I can't give you one."

"Someday," she said, and I don't think I ever felt more gratitude toward anyone.

I started staying at her place for days at a clip and leaving my belongings there. The bottom two drawers of her bureau were empty—no surprise there since most of her stuff was on her metal desk or thrown around the room or hanging from a rubber tree and a potted palm. I stored my clothes in the bureau, and my razor, toothbrush, and the black-and-white-covered composition books I used for journals in a dented, putty-beige, two-drawer filing cabinet. But the mess flipped me out, and I regularly straightened up while Glenna sat on the bed, watching.

"This is far out, Gordo," she said, grinning. "Lots of guys wanted to get in my bedroom. None of them ever offered to clean it up before."

"Think of it as foreplay."

"Foreplay for me or for you?"

She asked that question as I picked up what I thought was an empty box of Screaming Yellow Zonkers off the floor, and a ribbed, plastic vibrator fell out.

"Medical instrument?" I asked, flicking the on-off switch, seeing the tip glow and feeling the plastic hum in my hand.

"Things were a little slow before I met you."

"Glad to hear it."

One real bonus to moving in was that Biff was put out by my presence. Whenever he was around, he was seized by an urge to plop down in the rocker across from where Glenna and I were sitting on the couch watching the tube. Then he would recount his latest conversation with a state legislator who, impressed by NYMSRAL's evidence of the casualties caused by illegal abortions, had switched sides and now favored reforming the law.

"That's great, Palmer," Glenna would say, while I went to jack up the volume on the TV.

Chapter 8

THE DINNER WITH my folks came about because one evening, when I went to Brooklyn after staying in Spuyten Duyvil for a few days, my mother asked me what I'd been doing, and my father cracked, "Boy's past puberty, Renée, what do you think he's doing?"

His tone offended me. I was too proud of having a gorgeous, brainy girlfriend to dismiss her with a leer. Glenna was the first woman I'd been with who made me realize that sex was an expression of something other than a wish for a little exercise after a movie. And for me, young, directionless, and officially residing with my parents, my feelings for Glenna were a signpost to adulthood, to freedom.

I'd believed writing an article for the *Long Island Press* would help. But after my father read the NYMSRAL piece, he commented, "Interesting. What'd they pay you for it?" And when I answered twenty bucks, he frowned and said, "That'll buy a fifth of Chivas, except you'll have to borrow a glass to drink it."

I thought, Fuck you, while Mom beamed with dependable maternal pride over my byline. Yet whenever I blew by the house to grab some clothes, she bugged me about my whereabouts. I didn't want her disapproving of Glenna because she was letting me sleep with her. My mother had liked some of my other girlfriends, but who knew what she thought about my sex life. I had never lived with a girlfriend before, and thus she hadn't been forced to consider it.

I suggested to my folks that they take us to dinner. My father was hepped up to try Zalman's, a restaurant on the Lower East Side that had just received a four-star review in the *Times*.

That night, in bed with Glenna, I mentioned the dinner, and she was all for it. I asked her if we had to get there early so she could mull over the menu.

She started laughing. "Why? You think it'll make a better impression on your parents if I appear to know how to order in a restaurant?"

"That was my thinking."

"Nice of you to ask. But that only happens when I'm on an official date with a guy."

ZALMAN'S WAS in a dim, tin-ceilinged basement, and by six fifteen it was already packed and noisy with a line out onto Delancey Street.

"Girl's a knockout," my father said, after Glenna excused herself to go to the ladies' room. "Lighten her hair, you got Veronica Lake."

My mother said, "I read in a magazine that Veronica Lake is a drunk."

Dad made a smart move here. Instead of commenting further on his favorite erstwhile movie star, he put an onion roll in his mouth.

My mother's estimation of Glenna was harder to discern, and I hoped the unpleasant pucker of her lips was due to the sour tomato she was eating. Judging from the photo albums in the den, she had also been a knockout in her prime and still was if you were knocked out by a middle-aged, blue-eyed brunette who had kept her shape. At the moment, though, that wasn't doing the trick for my father. He was more interested in Glenna coming out of the ladies' room.

As she squeezed past the close-set tables in her tight, salmon-pink shirtdress, my father couldn't take his eyes off her, and my mother spritzed some soda water into his glass from the seltzer bottle and said, "Take a drink, Alex. And cool down."

My father, gentleman that he was, rose to hold the chair for Glenna. I beat him to it, and he said to her, "I gotta tell you how nice it's been meeting the girl who got my son to comb his hair."

"My pleasure," she replied, and after treating him to a smile that I thought would bust the brass buttons off his double-breasted, navy-blue blazer, she gave me a quick kiss.

My mother's puckered expression remained in place, even though she was done with her tomato, but my father didn't seem to care. From the moment my parents had entered the restaurant, he had been weird. Zalman's didn't have a liquor license, and he had brought a couple of bottles of wine, one of which he finished by himself while he glanced around as if looking for someone.

My father calmed down when the waiter delivered our dinner. The food gave us something to talk about. You can have quite a discussion about rib steak topped with mushrooms, chicken fricassee, stuffed cabbage in sweet-and-sour tomato sauce, whipped eggplant, and potatoes mashed with chicken fat.

When we ran out of food, my father quizzed Glenna about the effectiveness of a new tricyclic antidepressant, Trelozin, that doctors were prescribing during her psych rotation. Danzig had been involved in developing the drug, and it sold so fast Danzig's stock price had jumped 20 percent.

"We're such a happy country," my mother commented, and then my father picked up where he had left off.

Long ago, I had observed that when my friends were over, my mother invariably asked them about school or their plans, and she acted genuinely interested in their responses. Nobody asked her anything. If my father was around, they asked him. Not her. Maybe it was that kids are taught not to ask embarrassing questions. I mean—what would a mother say? I cook and clean. I worry about everyone.

Glenna, to her credit, addressed her answers to both my parents. Mom, however, wasn't talking. She could have mentioned that after high school she had worked for Dr. Himmelmann, a psychiatrist who had trained with Freud. Being a secretary must have seemed inconsequential to her compared to Glenna's schooling, and perhaps it was, but Glenna was becoming uneasy with my mother's silence, her answers getting shorter and faster. The waiter brought pints of milk and a jar of Fox's U-bet chocolate syrup for dessert, and as my father mixed himself an egg cream, I rerouted the talk by saying, "Ma, what's happening with you and the Russians at Temple Hillel?"

Glenna relaxed, and my mother spoke primarily to her. "I'm helping eleven new immigrant women get acquainted with New York City. Yesterday, we were in Korvettes when Olga Urofsky, who, I'm telling you, must have had the greasiest hennaed hair in the whole Soviet Union, inspects a dress and says to me, 'We have like this in Odessa.' All of the women agreed with her, and they must have nicked a patriotic nerve, because I got so . . . so indignant, and I took them to Saks, where I almost pushed Olga into a rack of Puccis and said, 'Mrs. Urofsky, do they have like this in Odessa?'"

"Right on, Mrs. Meyers," Glenna said, smiling. I was smiling, too.

My father lit a Lucky Strike and said, "Renée, you're a regular propagandist. You did good. You turned Russians into JAPs."

My mother didn't react, and I felt like slapping my father across his face. He started glancing around again and finally saw what he'd been looking for—the hostess, an older woman with a black turban and dress, and spooky eyes that made her seem better suited for reading palms than directing traffic in a restaurant. She had been at the door when Glenna and I arrived, but off in the kitchen when my folks came in.

The hostess walked toward us, beaming. My mother stared at my father. It was an intimate stare, and seeing it embarrassed me. Glenna also saw it, and she concentrated on mixing an egg cream. With a heavy European accent, the hostess said, "Alexander, this is you, yes?"

My father dragged on his cigarette and stood, giving her a fast hug. "Tamara, how are you? You remember Renée?"

The hostess shut off her beam. "You married her, yes?"

"Yes," my mother said.

My father introduced Glenna and me to the hostess. She was the proprietress of Zalman's. The restaurant, she said, had been owned by her uncle, who, like her, had never married. It had closed after his death, and she had, as of late, reopened it.

"Food's terrific," Dad said.

Tamara replied with a racy, theatrical laugh, saying, "It's terrific, yes. What did you expect?" Then she rested her hand on my father's shoulder and reminisced about a 1939 trip they had made to Washington, DC. I remembered my mother telling me about it when I was a teenager. My father, along with his Zionist pals, had gone to protest FDR's refusal to grant entry visas to Jewish refugees from Hitler. Tamara was in that group, and my mother had characterized her as a Romanian hussy inclined to quote Theodor Herzl while rubbing my father's leg. Now, listening to Dad and Tamara nostalgically rehash the past—not bringing up that my father was arrested for coldcocking a Nazi supporter and that my mother, his steady girl, had to wire him his bail—I decided that Dad had been screwing Tamara in 1939, and Mom knew it.

"Magnificent times, Alexander," Tamara cooed. "And my restaurant, it is magnificent also, no? See what becomes of you if they put your name in the *New York Times*."

"They put your name in?" my mother asked.

Tamara stiffened at the question, offended. "Yes, yes, they did. Why would they not use my name?"

From the look of outrage on my mother's face, I assumed that we had reached the same conclusion: my father had known that Tamara owned Zalman's from the review, which was why he wanted to eat here, and he had been looking for her during dinner.

"Alexander," said Tamara, "I must get back. It has been lovely, yes?"

Dad bussed her cheek and stepped back to gaze at her. While he was gazing, he went to puff on his Lucky Strike and stuck the lit end in his mouth. Tough as Bogart, he withdrew the cigarette without giving any indication that he had burned his lips. I noticed it—so did Tamara, Glenna, and my mother. And if my father figured he was going to get off without being humiliated in front of his ex-flame, he was in outer space.

"That was clumsy, darling," said my mother, picking up the seltzer bottle. "Burning your mouth like that. Here, let me help."

My father started to protest, but before he could speak, my mother sprayed seltzer in his face. He sat there, too proud to wipe himself off, and my mother said, "Tamara, get us some napkins, will you?"

AS THE wind hurried the litter along in the gutters, Glenna and I waited for the attendant to retrieve the GTO from the lot on Chrystie Street.

Glenna took my hand. "Dad's a little hard on the family, hmm?"

"Tonight was an improvement. He usually concentrates on me. But he liked you. So did my mom."

"Not really."

"She kissed you good-bye, hugged you. She liked you, Glenna."

"No, your dad liked me. Men are easy. My dad also likes me."

"What about your mom?"

Unflappable as usual, Glenna said, "She doesn't like me."

"You know, you hardly mention your parents." All Glenna had said about her folks since San Gennaro was that I shouldn't answer the phone in the morning in case they were calling because they might ask her what some strange guy was doing there so early, and she didn't want to lie. Glenna never even raised the idea of my meeting them, and I assumed she thought that they would disapprove of me—my five years at Brooklyn College, my half-ass career, and that I was living with their daughter.

Glenna said, "You're changing the subject," which I was, because now I wasn't sure what my mother thought of her.

And it annoyed me that I wanted to know her opinion. I was too old for that, wasn't I?

Apparently not, because on Monday, after my Modern Lit class, I dropped by the house in Brooklyn.

My mother was in the kitchen, sticking a meat loaf in the oven. She poured me a cup of coffee from the pot on the stove, and I said, "Glenna doesn't think you like her."

"Was it the seltzer? Your father says I shouldn't have made a fuss."

"The seltzer was dynamite, Ma. Glenna thought sending Tamara for the napkins was even better."

My mother chuckled. "She's clever, your Glenna."

"Why don't you like her?"

"What's not to like? A girl going to be a doctor, she's smart as a whip. And so pretty. I told Aunt Lil on the phone this morning how smart and pretty."

"Ma?"

Opening the refrigerator, she said, "Glenna reminds me of your sister."

"What'd you mean?"

"Elaine's very smart and very pretty."

"Dumb and ugly's better?"

"Easier," she said, bringing the creamer to the table and sitting down. "Today it's easier. Like with Elaine. At Boston University she wants to be an anthropologist. She graduates and then gets a master's in social work. She says she loves Boston, and the next week, she says a job in New York appeals to her, and maybe there's one in Los Angeles she'll take. So what does she do? She goes running around Europe. It was the same with her boyfriends. This fella's swell on Tuesday, and by Wednesday he's not, but there's another swell fella she met on a train, and the fella she met in the park, he's also swell. Girls like your sister, like Glenna, they have too many choices. They can't make up their minds." My mother put some cream in her coffee cup. "I don't dislike Glenna, but I love you, and she's a girl like your sister, and they . . ."

"They what, Ma?"

"They hurt men."

Since my mom wasn't in the habit of dispensing wisdom to hear herself talk, I should have considered what she had to say. But I couldn't imagine Glenna hurting me, and being in bed with her night and day did little to stimulate the darker regions of my imagination.

Besides, 1968 wasn't a very good year for listening to your mother.

Chapter 9

So, WHEN DOES our story begin? After Glenna finished her psychiatry rotation and started playing doctor for real on the wards. If psych was a vacation, medicine and surgery were sentences to the rock pile, and Glenna had those two rotations back-to-back, beginning with medicine.

She was assigned to the team directed by Dr. Arthur Feldstein, coauthor of *Internal Medicine*, the specialty's twenty-seven-hundred-page bible. Glenna described Feldstein as a diagnostic wizard with intelligent eyebrows, whatever that meant, and halitosis, a malodorous consequence of his postnasal drip. Monday through Saturday, Feldstein led his team on rounds, which jumped off at 7:00 a.m., and God help you if you were late. Feldstein was an acerbic taskmaster and greeted the tardy with nose-to-nose harangues, and with that breath of his it was like being trapped downwind from an elephant with a chronic bowel disorder. With Feldstein at the head of the column, the resident, interns, and students slogged from room to room, examining their twenty-odd patients, and presenting their cases and suppositions to Feldstein, who entertained himself by clearing his throat and picking lint off his tie. When his team was done, Feldstein generally responded,

"It's lamentable that sloth and ignorance cannot be readily treated," and concluded by doling out the relevant pearls of wisdom and commanding his team to get to it.

Getting to it meant entering the status of your patients in their charts and dealing with any flux in their status; inking in request forms for X-rays or electrocardiograms; checking lab results of urine, stool, and sputum; drawing bloods, inserting intravenous tubes and catheters; and performing the two-hour admittance procedure on new patients. And because third-year students were at the bottom of the team totem pole, and because gravity mandates that shit roll downhill, they got buried in it.

Here was the ostensible source of our problems. In late October, Glenna vanished from my life. Every morning, except for Sundays, Glenna left the house at six. Twice a week, she did on call, so I wouldn't see her for a minimum of a day and a half. Otherwise, if things went well with her patients, she returned around seven at night. If things didn't go well, as they frequently did not, there was no saying when she'd show up.

Since I was busy making it to an occasional class at Brooklyn College, writing short stories and profiles for the *Long Island Press*, the change didn't register right away. And in the beginning, Glenna was turned on about playing doctor, and I liked hearing about it.

"Gordo, guess what?"

"You—"

"I diagnosed an anemic."

"Do tell?"

"I tugged on his lower eyelid and it was rimmed with white instead of the normal red. Want me to check you?"

"Absolutely."

She pulled on my eyelid.

"Am I all right?"

"You'll live," she said.

"Then can we eat dinner now?"

Sometimes, I'd be sleeping when Glenna came in, and she'd crawl into bed and tickle me awake.

"Dr. Fecal Breath told me I'm the only member of his team who can be relied on to read an X-ray."

"What did it say?"

"A resident thought he saw lung cancer, but I could see it was pneumonia. 'Eyes like an eagle, Miss Rising,' Fecal Breath said. 'Keep it up, you'll have quite a future.'"

"Did he mention if your future will include sleep?"

Glenna laughed. "He said nothing about sleep."

I wasn't surprised that she had impressed Feldstein: Robin had told me that Glenna was in the top 5 percent of their class. But Glenna had confessed to me that she felt like an airhead, which I suspected was not an uncommon complication for good-looking women with brains. Glenna was afraid that she wouldn't make it through med school, would screw up and kill a patient, or flunk out and disappoint herself and her parents. Her doubt fueled her doggedness at the hospital. So after the novelty of doing her doctor thing wore off, she often came back to Spuyten Duyvil exhausted and appeared annoyed to find me sitting in bed and writing on the legal pad in my lap.

"Don't you go out?" she asked.

"During the day. Like normal people."

"Wouldn't hurt you to get some exercise."

"I am, Glenna. I'm splitting infinitives."

"And stop smoking cigarettes. It stinks."

"I'll get some more incense."

"Here's a suggestion," she said. "You like to read. Read the side of the pack."

"Soon as I buy another one, I will."

"Fucking nurses," she said.

"What?"

"The floor nurses are resentful bitches. Never send your specimens to the lab or tell you when your patient's been moved. They hate med students. And they hate female med students the most. Like we should be making beds, not learning to give them orders."

Complaining, however, wasn't Glenna's bag. She was too controlled for it. Her style was promising to be back from Presbyterian by seven and not making it till quarter of ten and not bothering to call. I'd be sitting in the bay-window seat gazing out at the lights across the Hudson when I heard a train pull into the station down the hill by Spuyten Duyvil Creek. Two minutes after the train had chugged on to Yonkers came Glenna's rapid footfalls, the gate swinging in and scraping the mossy stone walk, the front door opening and closing, and Glenna climbing the three flights of stairs.

She kissed me briefly, the brevity of her kiss compounding my anger. I was happy that she was home, but resented my happiness because it depended on her return.

"You could have called," I said, and that I sounded, even to myself, like an overwrought housewife didn't help matters.

"I had an admission to do. This woman, Katherine. She has a carcinoma of the liver and had been in for a colostomy. She must weigh seventy pounds. Her husband left her years ago, and her daughter lives in Oregon. Katherine held my hand, her hands were like claws, and she cried, said I made her think of her daughter. I had to stay. She's dying and she's alone."

I'm alone, I thought, and felt shitty for being so selfish.

Peeking out from behind her hair, she kissed me. "Try to understand."

"I understand," I said, choking on my anger. "And I don't like it. You're never late for Dr. Feldstein."

"It's work. It's important."

"What am I?"

"You used to be fun," she said.

Frankly, fighting with Glenna was more satisfying than missing her; at least when we fought I had her attention. So we had our share of fights, and they began to center around Palmer Caldwell Chilton III.

"Glenna," I said one night as we lay in the dark, "when did you and Biff form your mutual-admiration society?"

"Don't call him Biff. And why are you interested in Palmer?"

"Because he's interested in you."

"Is not," she said.

I wasn't sure what made me angrier: Biff the Brooks Brothers Mouse constantly eyeballing Glenna or Glenna's refusal to admit that he had the hots for her.

She said, "And don't you dare ask me if I ever slept with him. That's disgusting. Our parents are friends from the Ethical Culture Society. Our fathers play golf together in Palm Beach. Our mothers go shopping together on Worth Avenue."

"How does any of that disqualify you from sleeping with him?"

"I've known Palmer since I was in first grade and he was in fourth. Do you think I'd share a house with a guy I was sexually attracted to?"

"I won't take that personally."

Glenna laughed. "C'mon, Gordo."

I doubted that she was screwing Biff. Something about him was almost asexual, and he never brought women or men to the house to sleep over. Yet, he lingered in the kitchen after dinner to talk with Glenna, standing beside her at the sink with their hands submerged in the soapy dishwater. He handed off his old oxford-cloth shirts to her, and she wore them around the house with the white sweatpants he'd given her from the Sun Isle Polo and Country Club, where every December he competed in the club's amateur polo tournament.

"Nice sweats," I said. "Could Biff get me a pair?"

"Gordon, don't be so possessive."

"I'm not possessive. I really want a cool pair of white sweatpants."

"Stop it. You have no right to tell me who I can be friends with."

"What are my rights?"

"You can stay or you can leave," she said.

"The essence of democracy. Choice."

Whether we argued about Biff or her grind at the hospital, I had the feeling that our real conflict was about something else entirely, but Glenna wasn't ready to tell me about it—at least not while I was awake.

Instead, in the evenings she would grow distant, and even though we were in bed reading, we might as well have been on opposite sides of the planet. When she grew tired, she would click off her light without a word and turn away from me, and I would move toward my edge of the mattress and curl up alone.

Later on, in the middle of the night, Glenna would wake and spoon herself around me. Through the curtain of my own slumber I would feel her trembling and hear a faint sob.

She would press her hand against my shoulder until I turned toward her, and she could come into my arms, and I would dimly perceive that she was entwining her body with mine, huddling into me as if seeking shelter, whispering, "I don't want to lose you."

I was stunned that Glenna was scared of losing me, for I had thought it was the other way around, and though I was too clouded with sleep to answer, I held her tighter, drawing her close enough so that in my mind we became a single sculpture of flesh and bone, impossible to separate.

Yet, in the morning, after the clock radio went off, and Glenna put on her terry-cloth robe and went downstairs to shower and then came back up to dress for the hospital, and I lay in bed watching her brush her hair, she would look over at me, her eyes holding mine, but never mention the fear that had disturbed her sleep or the affection that had helped her sleep again.

I wondered if she thought it had all been a dream, not her life at all, or mine for that matter, only a silent storm that would pass if she let it, if she answered it with a silence of her own.

ON A Monday, when I had to be at the *Long Island Press* in Garden City to pitch a new profile to Mack Grunch, I offered to drop off Glenna at the hospital, figuring I could ask her about her restlessness.

The fall was warm and sunny that year, as though reluctant to surrender to winter, and I put the top down. Driving into the city, I told Glenna about the subject of my profile, Izzy Aronowitz, a seventy-three-year-old ex–carnival barker, with a white ponytail and rakish goatee, who owned the head shop where Todd worked and who was revered around the East Village for his extensive collection of groupies, both young and old. As I spoke, Glenna sifted through my eight-tracks, unable to decide which one to play. She gave up and stared out the windshield, focusing on that place I imagined she saw in her sleep, her own badlands, all dust and sorrow.

"You've been having trouble sleeping," I said.

Glenna said, "You're the first thing I thought about when I opened my eyes this morning."

Her statement wasn't exactly a coherent response to my observation, but Glenna was clearly trying to tell me something, even if she wasn't sure what it was.

"What do you usually think about?" I asked.

"My patients, or what I have to do on rounds."

"Very romantic," I said, kidding around.

That was not how Glenna took it. "I thought about you first thing. What else do you want?"

"You know that song, 'I Want a Girl, Just Like the Girl, That Married Dear Old Dad'?"

"The world's out of stock," she said with a sad smile. "Permanently."

"What's going on, Glenna?"

"When I'm—"

I waited.

"When I'm at the hospital and I have a second when I'm actually not busy, I think about you—about coming back to the house and seeing you—and it takes me another five minutes to concentrate again."

I glanced at the fuel gauge. The needle was on E.

Glenna said, "I feel like there's not enough room in my life for me. Like I want more space and can't get it."

"Can't get it? Why?"

"Because then I'll lose you."

"I'm right here," I said. "You won't lose me."

Tears were leaking from her eyes. She took a Kleenex from her burlap bag and wiped them away. I swung into an Esso station, handed the attendant $4, and as he gassed up the GTO, I went in to get change and buy a pack of Marlboros in the cigarette machine, stuffing the box in the knapsack with my notebooks so I could avoid a cancer lecture.

Back in the car, Glenna was looking around for me, her eyes narrowed with concern, like she thought I'd abandoned her in a gas station. Partially hidden behind an island of pumps, I was, as always, awestruck by the creamy naturalness of her skin and the sublime planes and angles of her face, but that was secondary to the fact that Glenna seemed frightened that I wouldn't come back. At last, she spotted me, then smiled with an uninhibited joy she hadn't shown me before, and for the briefest of moments I was certain that she loved me. Later, I'd be haunted by the possibility that I'd fallen in love with Glenna alone, fallen in love with the reflection of my own appetite to be loved, which was as voracious as Robin's for Breyers ice cream. But not at that moment. The wind was blowing Glenna's hair off her shoulders, and we gazed at each other, not daring to move, for movement could break the connection. I heard the cars and trucks going by and realized that Glenna had put the Mamas and Papas in the eight-track. Above the whoosh and rumble of the traffic, I heard them singing "California Dreamin'," and their poignant harmony stayed with me so that for years afterward, whenever I heard that song, I remembered Glenna smiling at me from a candy-apple-red convertible with the brilliant autumn sunlight in her eyes.

After I got behind the wheel, Glenna said, "You want everything from me, don't you?"

There was no hint of accusation in her tone. She was simply asking a question.

"What's 'everything'?" I said.

"Don't have a clue. But after rounds on Saturday, we're going to Vermont. You want to help me look for it there?"

"Aren't you on call?"

"Found someone to switch with me," she said, and kissed me softly on the lips. "So you want to help me look?"

"Absolutely."

Chapter 10

BENNINGTON WAS A classic Vermont college town, its quaintness marred only by the occasional pizzeria or factory outlet. Along the narrow side streets, past the grassy commons, stone churches, the stacked rock walls, and the saltbox houses built before the Revolutionary War, old men in plaid lumber jackets raked leaves into fires, and because the top was down on the GTO, the smoke washed over us in a sweet mist.

We checked into the Paradise Inn, which sat up on a hill in the center of town, and after Glenna and I took some pictures of each other with my Minolta, we ate lunch at the Brasserie, a rambling clapboard building attached to the Bennington Potters. A young freak with long, stringy sandy hair and tinted Ben Franklin specs provided the entertainment by waiting on us at one of the tables in the courtyard.

"What's the soup du jour?" I asked.

Peering at me as though I'd asked him to elucidate the meaning of existence, he replied, "Like I don't know, man. It's different every day."

I skipped the soup, and we had some white wine from a local vineyard and ate salad and cheddar-cheese-and-tomato omelets and a freshly baked baguette with sweet butter and strawberry jam from a farm a mile outside Bennington. We were too full for dessert and sleepy from the wine and the meal, so we drank espresso and then wandered over to the potters' gift shop, where Glenna bought four place settings of aquamarine stoneware.

"Glenna, you think fine dining at home is eating take-out Chinese. What's with the fancy dishes?"

"Palmer," she said, paying the cashier, a flinty old woman with a white bun on her head that was so tight it had to be a method of Puritan torture. "He loves these dishes."

I was suddenly angry, but there was no use fighting about Biff in Vermont; we could do that in New York.

"Let's go explore," I said.

We drove north on Route 7, and twenty minutes later we left the car on the side of the road and climbed to the top of a rise above a lake. A farmhouse and a barn with a silver-domed silo were beyond the dark blue water, with a redbrick church beyond the farm, its steeple pure white against the flaming maples, and beyond it all were the mountains and leafy tree-tops standing out against the clear sky in clouds of russet, orange, and gold.

We spread a blanket and pillows on the grass behind a wall of pines, took off our shoes, and lay next to each other reading.

After a while, Glenna said, "That for school?"

"No. It's a collection of stories by James Joyce. In this one, he uses the falling snow as a metaphor for the loss of love and the hope for redemption. I'll never be able to write like him, but his use of snow is a function of craft, and I might be able to learn that. It's such a trip trying to—" I stopped when I saw Glenna smiling at me. "What?"

"Writing's a lot more interesting than this." She held up the *New England Journal of Medicine.* "It's an article about tissue rejection and heart transplants."

"It's remarkable they did it. Seventy years ago, that surgeon, Paget—"

"Paget's disease? That's a bone disease."

"Same guy," I said, putting my book down and sitting up. "Sir James Paget. He predicted that science would never be able to fix a heart."

"I don't get you. All you do is read and write. You're so smart, but you blow off school and you get up every day like you're on some personal intellectual adventure. How do you do that?"

"It's my life. Who else is supposed to do it?"

"I admire it. I couldn't do it."

"You don't have to. You want to be a doctor."

She shrugged. "Well, I didn't want to be a nurse."

"What's wrong with nurses?"

"Nothing when they're not hassling me. I was almost a nurse. My mother's plan was for me to find an Ivy League husband. After I told her that wasn't going to happen and chose UVM, my father tells me he read in the catalog that Vermont offers a BS in nursing. Fine, I'll try that. So I start taking bio, physics, organic chem. The girls in those classes were going to be nurses; the guys were applying to med school. We had to take the same courses for God's sake. I switched to premed."

Glenna fell silent, gazing up at me. Then she said, "I love when you look at me like that."

"Like what?"

"Like you're listening."

I said, "That's what I'm doing."

"No. Really listening. Guys don't know what a turn-on that is—listening."

"But you listen, too."

"Women always listen."

Glenna had on a pair of beige jeans that fit her like a second skin, and the fingers of my right hand were drawing circles on her thighs.

"You really like that?" she asked. "The listening?"

"I like listening to you."

Glenna was studying me as if trying to peek behind my eyes. "I can't tell what you're thinking."

"You're not supposed to. It's private."

"But being inside me. You like that."

"Best of all."

"Not the fucking, Gordo."

"No, not the fucking. Being inside you."

"It's different," she said.

"Philosophically speaking."

Glenna laughed. "I'm serious."

"Me, too," I said, my fingers going, the circles widening.

"Not the sex part. *The fact* of being inside me. That's what you like."

I nodded, unsnapping her jeans, my hand sliding down.

Glenna closed her eyes. "When you're first inside me, you don't move."

"I like being inside you."

"No, that's not it."

"You like my not moving at first," I said. "You push back and stop."

"Because then it feels like *I'm* inside *you*."

She raised up and shed her jeans and panties, and my fingers touched tight, damp curls.

Glenna opened her eyes. "Gordo. Can we, here?"

"Yes."

"Yes only if you tell me why."

"Why what?" I asked.

"Why you don't move right away."

"It'll end if I start moving."

"Not for a while."

"No, but sometime," I said, unbuttoning my dungarees and lowering myself on her as her hands came around behind me, pushing down my underwear.

"Now you can," she said.

"Now I can?"

"Just be inside me."

"I am."

"I know," she said. "That's not what I mean."

"You mean what?"

"I mean everything. I mean all the way inside me."

"That's 'everything'?" I asked.

"Everything, yes."

"There?"

"Everything there," she said. "That's what you want."

"Everything I want."

"Everything all the way inside me."

Glenna pushed up against me, hard, and I pushed back, and we pressed together and clung to each other so tightly that it was an effort to breathe. I remained still until it was no longer possible, then I began to move, and Glenna slid her knees up around my hips, murmuring, "All the way, alltheway-insideme," and I seemed to whirl away somewhere else, and

Glenna was calling my name, summoning me to a place I was fast approaching, and neither of us lasted too long, not on this dazzling afternoon, in the drowsy, pine-scented air, with a golden light shining through the trees, and a breeze whispering over us, and I heard myself call back to her, and there was a long, sweet pause—perfect stillness—and when it was over, Glenna and I were wrapped up together, gasping, holding on, each of us inside the other.

Chapter 11

MY BASIC STRATEGY for dealing with Biff was to ignore him, but that was impossible once Glenna and I came back from Vermont, because he started putting me down with subtle and not-so-subtle insults.

One evening, Biff, Robin, Glenna, and I were at the trestle table in the kitchen, eating Biff's latest culinary masterpiece, a brussels sprout soufflé, off the aquamarine Bennington stoneware. A black-and-white, portable TV was on the counter, and clips of the presidential candidates were rolling on *The Huntley-Brinkley Report*: Hubert Humphrey promising that he would bring peace to Vietnam; Richard Nixon promising that he would bring an honorable peace to Vietnam; and George Wallace promising that if a peace demonstrator sat down in front of his car, he'd run him over.

Sporting his customary expression of studied indifference, Biff said to me, "You're voting for Wallace, aren't you?"

"What makes you say that?" I asked, though I knew he was messing with me. Wallace, the former governor of Alabama, was a fervent racist and about as low as rattlesnake balls.

Biff said, "You're always reading those war writers—Mailer, Jones, Shaw. I thought you'd be a fan of Wallace's running mate."

"General Curtis LeMay? Why?"

Biff snickered. "Because LeMay wants to bomb North Vietnam back to the Stone Age."

"Funny," I said, and concentrated on my soufflé. Nineteen sixty-eight was going to be my first chance to vote for president, but with Bobby Kennedy dead the election seemed a lot less interesting, since RFK had, if nothing else, represented the hope of expanded possibilities.

Biff said, "If you're not supporting Wallace, maybe you could help us with the Humphrey campaign." Biff, as the head of NYMSRAL, had the organization drumming up support for the vice president. Glenna was stuffing envelopes and working the phones at the cramped office on 116th and Morningside, and so was Robin, even though she regarded mainstream politics as a bourgeois plot to bilk the masses and sporadically slipped up on the phone by quoting Marx.

"It's not my thing," I said, promising myself that if Biff made one more crack, I would slap him.

He didn't get the chance. Robin fired up a joint, toked on it, gave it to Glenna, and blurted out, "The attending in charge of my ophthalmology team says he's gonna kick me out of school."

"Dr. Stroop?" Glenna asked, taking a hit off the J and passing it to me. "Why?"

"Because he's a racist pig."

"Robin," Palmer said. "You're not black."

"I'm a woman and that's about as bad," Robin said, going over to the freezer and taking out a carton of mint chocolate chip. "Today, Stroop tells me if I don't wear a bra on rounds, I'm gone. I told him Stroop was the name of the Nazi in charge of wiping out Jews in the Warsaw ghetto, and was that his daddy?"

Laughing, I coughed on the smoke and said, "Did Stroop appreciate your command of history?"

"Nah," Robin said, sitting down and going to work on the Breyers. "But I flashed my SDS membership card and said I wasn't doing anything I didn't want to."

Handing the joint to Glenna, I asked, "SDS has membership cards?"

Haughtily Palmer said, "Of course they do."

I said, "Can you use it to get into movies free?"

Before Palmer could fire off a comeback, Robin said, "Meyers, call Stroop and say you're a reporter investigating discrimination against women. Your editor will let you do it if he's not some Establishment lackey. It's a dynamite story. Stroop takes me into an exam room. He gets fatherly and says it's not simply improper to go without a bra, it's unhealthy. Then I say to him, 'Check it out, my thirty-six D's pass the pencil test.'"

"The pencil test?" I asked, and Glenna started giggling and put the joint in the pincers of a mosquito clamp, a miniature forceps that Robin had swiped from the hospital to use as a roach clip.

Robin said, "Stroop never heard of the pencil test either. And this is what I did."

She unbuttoned her madras shirt, and there they were, a set of centerfold-quality 36 D's. Robin stood up straight, placed a pencil under her breasts, and it fell to the floor.

"If the pencil doesn't stay put," she said, "you have the uplift to ditch your bra."

Taking the mosquito from Glenna, Palmer said, "Robin, put those away."

"Palm, you sound exactly like Stroop," Robin said, grinning and rebuttoning her blouse. "Meyers, you have to off that pig in the newspaper. Otherwise, I'll have to get Phillie's lawyer on the case. My mother'll freak out, and spending money for shit people can't admire isn't where my father's head's at. Will you call Stroop tomorrow?"

I said, "Not gonna happen, Robin. But I'll give you the money to buy a bra."

"Does the *Long Island Press* pay you enough for bras?" Palmer said.

I locked eyes with him, and Glenna defused the situation by saying, "Palmer put the coffee on. I bought a pumpkin pie for dessert."

I made a tactical miscalculation by not laying out Biff then and there, because the putdowns continued. Sometimes, he would make snide remarks; other times, he would conduct a medical colloquy with Glenna, speaking of bilirubin or blastomycosis like a shaman reciting kabbalistic abracadabra. But whatever the conversation, Biff never failed to pause and explain the technical terms to me with the exaggerated simplicity of a teacher instructing a drooling idiot on the intricacies of tying his shoes.

Afterward, alone with Glenna, I'd say, "What's Biff's problem?"

"Palmer can get weird, but he's only fooling around, and he likes talking about work. You're—"

"Too touchy?"

"Exquisitely sensitive," she said.

Maybe I was. The literary pornographer and sage Henry Miller once observed that a writer must grow accustomed to living with humiliation. With the two short stories I'd submitted mailed back in my self-addressed, stamped envelopes with preprinted rejection slips, and my query letters to do articles for the national magazines rarely answered at all, I recognized the wisdom of Henry's observation. Humiliation, though, must have been easier for him to get used to than it was for me, because he was cavorting with Parisian whores, while I was hanging out with med students and an ob-gyn resident. My father had been right about one thing: he raised me to be a doctor, not to marry one.

I voted for Humphrey and told Biff about it, but he pecked at me until the Saturday before Christmas. Glenna was flying to Palm Beach in the morning to join her folks at the Breakers hotel, and Biff was flying there on Tuesday to stay at his family's forty-seven-room cottage and to play in a polo tournament. Glenna would be in Florida until the day of New Year's Eve.

"You'll be okay, won't you?" she said late that afternoon as we lounged in bed.

"I'll miss you."

"I'll miss you, too. When I'm down there, all I do is follow my mother around and watch her charge goodies at Cartier and Chanel."

"Those are educational excursions," I said.

"How's that?"

"She's showing you the advantages of choosing a proper husband."

"Gordo, that's not me, you know that." She kissed me. "I'll be back soon. And you have an assignment to do; you can use your Christmas presents."

Mack Grunch had told me that he laughed so hard when he read my profile of Izzy Aronowitz that he busted a couple more veins in his nose, and now he'd gone for another one of my oddball ideas, a story about Dan Kamminski, an old friend of Uncle Jerr's, whose job selling beer at Knicks games had started in 1957 and ended last week when the cops busted Kammi for booking bets on the games with fans as he passed them a cold one. The gifts, which were on the quilt amid scraps of wrapping paper, included a burgundy-leather-topped lapboard so I could write in bed, and a Webster's dictionary and thesaurus bound in the same burgundy leather. I'd bought Glenna a handmade, scarlet silk Spanish shawl with an ivory fringe from Eartha's, after reading in *New York* magazine that it was the hippest boutique in the city.

Downstairs, the doorbell rang. Robin, who was going to spend her Christmas break at an extended-Blumberg-family reunion in Atlantic City, had ordered pizza for the three of us. Glenna and I went down and ate with her in the living room.

We were finishing our pizza when the front door opened, and Biff stamped in, the crepe soles of his L.L. Bean boots squeaking wetly on the pine floor. It was below zero outside, so Biff's garb could only be categorized as preppie macho: a muddy-patterned tweed sports jacket, a white, button-down shirt, khaki chinos, and, in his solitary concession to the arctic weather, a Black Watch plaid scarf coiled around his neck like a Scottish python, an image that I relished contemplating.

Robin said, "Will somebody take me to the movies? I want to see *Funny Girl*. It's playing at the Riverdale Cinema."

"Can't," Biff said, turning on the television to Channel 13—the public TV station—and plopping down in the wing chair. "There's a program on about polo. We've got to catch it." He looked at me. "Doesn't hurt to learn."

The BBC production opened with helmeted gentlemen galloping up and down a field on ponies and smacking a wooden ball with mallets, while the narrator, with an upper-class British lisp, recounted the history of polo from its origins in Persia to its spread to India, where, in the nineteenth century, the game became popular with British army officers who took it home to dear old England.

"Along with ninety new strains of VD," I added.

Robin didn't react; she was reading the movie listings in the local paper; but Glenna whacked me playfully in the ribs with her elbow. Biff glared in my direction.

When the program paused partway through so the Channel 13 fund-raisers could make their pitch, Biff said to me, "Play much polo, do you?"

"Used to," I said. "After school behind Meyer Levin Junior High. But I kinda thought it'd be more interesting if the players hit each other with the mallets."

Robin and Glenna laughed, which twisted Biff's nose out of joint.

He responded by launching into an ultratechnical soliloquy about a patient of his in her last trimester who had developed uremia. Predictably Biff segued into addressing me like an imbecile.

"Urea," he said, "is a nitrogen compound. You've heard of chemical compounds, haven't you? Urea is the chief product of protein breakdown. We excrete it in our urine."

He went on like I cared about urea or uremia as long as I could drain my vein when I needed to, which is what I told Dr. Brooks Brothers Mouse.

"This isn't difficult to understand," he said, and resumed talking.

I walked over to the wing chair, wrapped the woolly ends of Biff's scarf around my hands, then tightened it crosswise around his neck. This brought his soliloquy to a close. He tried to sustain a bemused gaze but failed. I had the advantage because I knew he wouldn't swing at me, my confidence rooted in the fact that men, in some marshy inlet of our brains, remain twelve years old forever, and the playground pecking order prevails, and each of us knows who can whip whom and behaves accordingly. That's why I was positive Biff wouldn't fight. I wasn't that tough. I just knew that I was tougher than him. And he knew it, too.

Scissoring the scarf tighter around Biff's neck, I said, "You speak to me like that again, I will kick your ass."

His mouth opened and nothing came out.

Robin said, "Hey, Palm, let's go see *Funny Girl*."

I said, "That's a swell idea, isn't it, Palm?"

Biff nodded, and I let go of the scarf and stepped back. He stood up, showing me his hard-guy stare. It would have been more effective if he hadn't tossed his head to the side to remove a limp forelock from his eyes. He stayed well back from me—a smart move, since I was thinking about sucker punching him.

He said, "Let's split, Robin," and left the living room and went out the front door.

Robin said, "Way to go, Meyers. Now all you gotta do is threaten a guy into being my boyfriend."

"Next week," I said.

When Robin was gone, Glenna said, "That wasn't very nice."

"But it was fun."

"Would you really have hit him?" she asked with a breathless hint of wonder, as though she might have relished the action while being repulsed by it.

I nodded.

"I don't believe you."

"Then you don't know much about men."

"Oh?" Glenna said, and kissed me.

"You're not mad?"

She shook her head. "Palmer sort of deserved it."

"Good. Then can we turn off the polo show?"

"Never thought you'd ask."

Chapter 12

"I T'S COOL," I said to Glenna. "Your dad'll be watching the game."

On a frigid January afternoon, we were driving to the Risings' house in Riverdale for Sunday dinner. The game was Super Bowl III, and the New York Jets were eighteen-point underdogs to the Baltimore Colts. The huge point spread, and that the upstart American Football League had never beaten the National Football League in a Super Bowl, hadn't phased the Jets' quarterback, Joe Namath, who guaranteed sportswriters that his team would win.

Uncle Jerr wasn't as confident as Namath about an outright victory, but, "Jesus Christ," he'd said to me over the phone after the betting line was printed in the papers, "Joe wouldn't let New York down, he's gonna cover that spread." Uncle Jerr bet four grand on the Jets with his bookie, and although I didn't mention it to Glenna, I'd risked one-fifth of my life savings by springing for a grand of my uncle's action. I doubted she would've been impressed with my investment strategy.

"My dad won't be watching the game," Glenna said. "My mother says football's disgracefully violent."

"Which is why it's fun to watch. And I'll be watching with your dad, not your mom."

When Glenna had returned from Palm Beach and informed me that her parents had invited us over, I was still myopic enough to believe that her reluctance to introduce me had been a symptom of her uncertainty toward me. Thus, I was glad to be presented for parental blessings and wanted to make a decent showing. I'd let Glenna trim my hair and gone to Brooklyn to grab my rust-brown corduroy suit and black cashmere turtleneck. Glenna had been uptight as we got ready to go, putting her coral-and-white Fair Isle sweater on backward. Her nervousness made me feel calmer about our visit, but my calmness disappeared in the GTO when I realized that the fate of my money would be decided in the dark, that I wouldn't have the satisfying delusion of influencing the game's outcome by watching it on TV.

I swung onto West 247th, a wooded road of expensive homes. Her parents' house was a futuristic, flat-roofed hexagon of redwood with triangular glass wings on either side. While the exterior owed its inspiration to *Sputnik*, the interior was as gloomy as a medieval hall. The cavernous living room had a slate floor with Persian rugs here and there in lonely islands of color. A massive, freestanding steel fireplace commanded the center of the room like a Space Age idol, and the only light besides the failing orange flicker of the logs was the feeble light gathering at the hexagonal windows that were scattered like stars across the redwood walls.

"Glenna," a woman called, "I'm in the kitchen," and a swinging door opened, and the woman came out, saying, "I expected you ten minutes ago."

"Sorry, Mother," Glenna said, tensing up beside me.

I'd anticipated seeing some of Glenna's beauty in her mother. And it was there, except that it had been frighteningly transfigured by chic apparel and a rigorous diet. Mrs. Rising was twice her daughter's age and looked half her weight. Her leopard-print blouse and miniskirt hung on her gaunt frame, and her black, geometric-patterned tights and white Courrèges boots drew special attention to her swizzle-stick legs. Her hair was teased back from her face in a cloud of dark smoke, a style that seemed calculated to exhibit her splendid tan and assert that here was a woman who vacationed regularly in the sun. Unfortunately that same sun had given her complexion the texture of an alligator purse, and the effect of her outlandish modishness and conspicuous middle age on me was the sensation that I was beholding a psychedelic human flower in the throes of a simultaneous bloom and wither.

Glenna said, "Mother, this is Gordon."

Considering Mrs. Rising's appearance, I had expected her voice to be a scratchy whine, but it was polished to a cultured gloss. "Yes, yes, hello. You're the young man who wrote about Glenna and her abortion business."

"A pleasure to meet you," I said.

Glenna said, "I'm not in the abortion business."

Mrs. Rising replied, "You would think young women today with their opportunities could choose nobler causes than terminating pregnancies. I've always thought that issue was the bailiwick of men who don't want to accept the consequences of their actions."

Glenna said, "But the women they impregnate are saddled with the children."

Peering keenly at Glenna, Mrs. Rising said, "*Saddled*, yes. Saddled with children. Very good, dear."

I glanced at Glenna and thought she was going to start crying or cursing, and just then Dr. Rising emerged from the kitchen carrying an acrylic tray of hors d'oeuvres. Given his wife's taste, I was expecting a fiftyish hipster in a paisley Nehru jacket, but he was attired for a day of billiards at a swanky men's club: a maroon, shawl-collar cardigan, powder-blue shirt, gray flannels, and tasseled cordovan loafers.

He shook my hand, and I wanted to laugh. He was a dead ringer for Babe Ruth, the same severe part in his hair, the flat nose, and overhanging brow, the big shoulders and belly.

"The fire needs fixing, Kay," Dr. Rising said.

"Sit, Herman," said Mrs. Rising as she and her daughter sank into a leather settee. "Glenna's friend will see to the fire."

Dr. Rising obeyed, and I arranged more logs in the fire pit, along with kindling and sections of last week's Sunday *Times*, one of which was sports and featured an interview with Jets' coach, Weeb Ewbank. As flames rose from the newsprint and kindling, I checked my watch. Kickoff was in midair.

Hors d'oeuvres were a selection of cheeses, French bread, and carbonated Pellegrino water. I could have used a real drink. Nobody offered me one. The conversation was now devoted to Mrs. Rising's fear of getting hijacked to Cuba on her flight from Palm Beach to Newark. Dr. Rising had raised the topic, and Mrs. Rising was clearly uncomfortable with it, which lit up Glenna's face like a thousand-watt bulb.

"It's horrifying," said Mrs. Rising. "The morning before we left, a National Airlines jet from Key West to Miami winds up in Havana."

Trying to impress Mrs. Rising, I feigned as much interest as I could and asked her, "Do they have many hijackings from Palm Beach?"

Glenna snickered like the smartest girl in class when the dumb kid asks if two plus two equals zero. She said, "A crime wave at the Palm Beach airport is when the baggage handlers steal golf clubs."

Mrs. Rising retorted, "Don't be absurd. Palm Beach has crime like everywhere else."

Chewing a wedge of Swiss, Dr. Rising said, "Kay, I did lose my putter to the baggage handlers."

"Herman," she said, "don't talk with your mouth full." Dr. Rising swallowed his cheese, then asked Glenna what rotation she was doing. Glenna answered, "Surgery," and Dr. Rising commented, "That's tough," which was when Mrs. Rising, perhaps miffed that the discussion no longer centered on her, grimaced and said, "Glenna, help me with dinner."

BY FOUR fifty, I was the unhappiest adult male in the New York metropolitan area who was not locked in solitary confinement. If I was going to flush a grand down the toilet, didn't I deserve the privilege of seeing it sucked into the sewer? Dinner was no consolation. A meal fit for a nursing home: poached chicken, diced carrots, and baked potatoes. The conversation was as dull as the food. The Riverdale-Yonkers Society for Ethical Culture meetinghouse was being renovated; Mrs. Rising was chairing the kitchen committee; and we were treated to a synopsis of her agony over the project.

"It's been nightmarish," she said to Glenna. "I'm dreading this week. I have to decide on the flooring. Your father's been so busy with patients in the afternoons he can't help, and his headaches have been keeping him in bed mornings."

Glenna, who had shown a courteous, if somewhat aloof, interest in her mother's tale of woe, said to her father with genuine concern, "You didn't tell me you were still having headaches. Let me make an appointment for you to be seen by neurology. I passed Gardner in the hall Tuesday, and he asked for you."

"It's nothing," Dr. Rising said. "If they keep up, I'll phone Gardner myself."

Mrs. Rising said to her daughter, "If you do have a chance, I could use your help with the flooring."

"I'd like to, Mother, but I'm in my surgery rotation."

From Mrs. Rising's frown, she apparently thought her daughter was being evasive, but Glenna wasn't using surgery as an excuse. It was a monster. At the hospital for pre-op rounds by 6:00 a.m., she didn't complete her post-op rounds until after her patients had eaten dinner.

Dr. Rising broke the uncomfortable silence by saying to me, "Glenna tells us you're writing short stories. You know my wife majored in Russian literature at Wellesley."

"I'm partial to Gogol," Mrs. Rising said.

"I'm not quite in his league," I said, and listened to her discourse, with astonishing acuity, on Gogol's incandescent realism, all the while thinking that her preference for Russian authors was fitting since she had the personality of Nikita Khrushchev, and you knew that she wouldn't be above banging one of her Courrèges boots on the table if you disagreed with her.

As Mrs. Rising threw her engine into idle to serve dessert—a real treat, canned pears and graham crackers—I found myself, against my will, feeling sad for her. Underneath her frown I'd seen that her daughter's refusal had hurt her, and not for the first time. Mrs. Rising was cruel, but she was also bored, and it was impossible to know if the boredom gave rise to the cruelty. I mean, what was a middle-aged woman, who had studied Russian literature at Wellesley, doing dolled up like a go-go girl and stewing over a remodeled kitchen as if she had been directed to redecorate the Kremlin?

And you had to admire Mrs. Rising's persistence. As we drank our coffee, she tried to interest Glenna by describing the wallpaper she'd chosen for the meetinghouse kitchen—a white background brightened by sprays of tulips and daffodils. Glenna yawned, twice, and Dr. Rising looked reproachfully at his daughter, as though signaling her that they must hear out these childish preoccupations. I could only guess at how Mrs. Rising must have resented Glenna's freedom to be a doctor and *not* to be interested in wallpaper.

Dr. Rising put his coffee cup in its saucer, and his wife said to him, "Glenna and I will clean up. Why don't you take Gordon for a walk."

Mrs. Rising may not have meant anything insulting by her suggestion, but the severity of her tone made it sound as if she were referring to a dog who better be taken outside before he shit in the house.

As my appreciation of Glenna's viewpoint soared, Dr. Rising said, "It's chilly out, Kay. We'll go to my study."

His study was in the southern wing of the house, but we walked right by it. Glancing furtively over his shoulder as if making sure we weren't tailed, Dr. Rising led me down a steep flight of stairs, keyed a double-locked iron door, and flipped on the fluorescent lights. Inside, metal utility shelving sagged under the loads of canned goods and bottled water. The wicker chairs and couches had summery pastel cushions, as though after World War III everyone would adjourn to the patio to enjoy the nuclear sunset.

"Let's have a drink," Dr. Rising said, and unlocked a six-foot metal cabinet that was bolted to a cinder-block wall. On the cabinet shelves were crystal decanters of Rémy Martin Louis XIII cognac. Dad once gave Uncle Jerr a bottle for his birthday, remembering to tell his younger brother that the stuff went for five hundred bucks a bottle. I counted twenty decanters in the cabinet. Christ, ten times what I had riding on the Jets.

With a loving twist, Dr. Rising withdrew a crystal fleur-de-lis stopper from a decanter. He may have been an Ethical Culturist who fancied pricey cognac, but he poured it into cheap grocery-store *yahrtzeit* glasses, which, before they held the Rémy Martin, had contained the candles Jews light to honor the anniversary of a family member's death.

"To the New Year," Dr. Rising said, sitting across from me. We raised our glasses and drank. Rather, I sipped and he drank—three glasses of the 80-proof nectar to be exact. "Like to come here at night and unwind," he said, which explained why he stayed in bed mornings with a headache. The guy was a lush.

"Had the shelter done in the summer of '61," Dr. Rising said.

"When the Soviets threatened us in West Berlin."

"When President Kennedy determined that what people in my tax bracket could do for our country was install luxury caves under our cellars. Cigarette?"

Dr. Rising fished a pack of Dorals and a Zippo lighter from the pockets of his cardigan. He lit us up and said, "Mrs. Rising doesn't tolerate smoking and drinking in the house. This shelter cost thirty thousand dollars. Thirty thousand dollars to have a drink and cigarette in my own home."

"Makes the Rémy Martin look cheap."

Dr. Rising actually laughed. You could credit my superb humor or the additional *yahrtzeit* glass of cognac he had knocked back. I voted for the cognac. After pulling out an empty Campbell soup can from under his chair, he set it on a wicker end table and said, "That's my ashtray."

As we smoked, Dr. Rising was gazing behind me, so I swiveled around. On the shelf was a framed photograph of a teenage boy in a cap and gown who bore a striking resemblance to a young Dr. Rising, and therefore to Babe Ruth in his rookie season.

"My son, Richard," the doctor said with pride. "His high-school graduation."

I was astounded that Glenna had lied to me about being an only child, and I was trying to come up with potential explanations for the lie when Dr. Rising said, "Richard was a prodigy, a true genius in science and math. Ten years older than Glenna. Does medical research in Colorado. Glenna distinguished herself in school, but Richard's work was of another order."

I was distracted from the mystery of Glenna and her brother by the sight of a boxy portable radio on the shelf next to Richard's photo. If you could tune in the news in the aftermath of a missile strike, it should be a cinch to raise a football game under peaceful skies. I asked Dr. Rising if we could listen to the Super Bowl.

"Never played that radio before," he said. "Paid for the installation of a special antenna on the roof. And I never forget to change the batteries every six months. But I've forgotten to play it. Let's give it a go."

I reached back and clicked on the radio.

"Marvelous," Dr. Rising said as I spun the dial through the stations and tuned in the game.

The third quarter was under way, and miracle of miracles, the Jets were up thirteen-zip. Late in the period, Johnny Unitas, the greatest play caller and passer in history, who had been nursing a sore elbow all season, replaced Earl Morrall at quarterback. But even if Johnny U. could save the game for the Colts, he wasn't going to beat the eighteen-point spread. So I was a grand to the good, which is pleasant knowledge to have while listening to the Super Bowl and sipping cognac in a bomb shelter.

Dr. Rising was also having a bang-up afternoon, though I think that was because he ordinarily drank alone, and today he had more to keep him company than the Rémy Martin. He surely didn't follow football. At the outset of the fourth quarter, when Turner's field goal bumped the Jets' lead to sixteen, Dr. Rising told me that he was rooting for New York because he'd once taken Richard to watch them play the Cleveland Browns at the Polo Grounds. I was too polite to indicate that he was talking about the NFL's Giants, except then he asked me when the Giants had changed their name to the Jets, and I diplomatically explained pro football's expansion.

"A new league," he mused. "I must've missed that. When did they start it?"

"Oh, let's see," I said as nonchalantly as possible so as not to offend him, "eight, nine years ago."

He raised a *yahrtzeit* glass and said, "I'll drink to that," which he did, and kept doing, until the Jets won the game 16–7.

I had a thousand bucks, and Dr. Rising had the makings of an all-pro hangover. We left the bomb shelter, and he shambled unsteadily up the stairs. Weaving in the doorway of his study, he offered me a mint from a roll of Life Savers, popped one in his mouth, and said, "Do me a favor, will you? Tell the girls I'm under the weather and napping on the couch. And Gordon—this is the best afternoon I've had in a while, so you make certain my daughter knows she's welcome to bring you any Sunday."

"Will do," I said, and hoped that I would never have to come back here again.

Chapter 13

Glenna was staring blankly out the windshield as we rode back to Spuyten Duyvil.

"Jets won," I said.

"That's nice," she said, and then she said nothing else, which may have saved our lives because, juiced on the cognac, I needed all my concentration to avoid driving off the road.

In her room, she dropped her maxi coat with the clothes piled on the floor, and without a word, kissed me with an insatiable hunger, a furious hunger—furious, perhaps, because it was insatiable. Pushing me onto the bed and straddling me, she undid my pants and lifted her skirt, hooking her thumb in her black panties and tights and tugging them off. A fleecy patch brushed my knee, then went up over my stomach and chest to cover my face, and I got lost recalling summer days at the beach, the hot wind redolent with the tides. The curls receded, and Glenna flattened herself against my body as though she were trying to crawl inside me, and she began sliding up and down, back and forth, picking up speed, none of her sensually drawn-out moaning as she moved, but blunt, explosive shouts instead, and then rising to her knees, still rocking with that truculent cadence, a scream quaking in her throat as she pummeled my shoulders with her fists, releasing the hurt she'd brought back from Riverdale, another hurt heaped onto the years of hurt, screaming, "Fuck you, you fucking bastard!" and me straying through that turbulent darkness, lost now, disappearing into the terrifying uncertainty of where I began and Glenna ended, and no longer caring about the distinction, just surrendering myself to the ecstatic rhythm of her rage.

IN THE after-haze, we retreated underneath the covers. Glenna dozed against me while I clasped my hands behind my head, mesmerized by the moonlight shining through the bay window and crowning the rubber tree in the corner with an icy halo.

"Gordon," Glenna said, her voice small, frightened. "Was that—was that—"

"Great," I said, putting my arm around her.

Snuggling into me, she asked, "What did you and my father do?"

"Listened to the game."

"You had a drink, too. I could taste it when I kissed you."

I didn't want to upset her further—she'd had enough for one afternoon—but she was going to be a doctor, and she might be able to help her dad. I said, "Your father had more than a drink."

"How many?"

"I lost count."

"Are you saying he's a drunk?"

"I didn't say that, but it could be why he has those headaches."

"Gordo, you're becoming a med student—diagnosing everybody. My father has a drink once in a while. He's no alkie."

"No, he isn't." I kissed her on the forehead and dropped the subject.

"My dad's a great guy. Did you get a chance to talk to him?"

"Yep."

"What did you talk about?"

Glenna was giving me a chance to mention her brother. I wasn't so uptight now that she hadn't told me about him, mostly curious, and I didn't want to sound as if I were accusing her of being a liar. Gently, casually I replied, "He said your brother's a genius."

Sitting up, Glenna reached over to the varnished apple crate and turned on the lamp. "Half brother. I never told you about him because—"

Glenna was shivering, and she tugged the quilt up around her shoulders.

I said, "Because?"

"Because he screwed up my life, my mother's life, and even if my father doesn't know it, his life as well. That's why I put off introducing you to my parents. My family's a mess."

"How'd you wind up with a half brother?"

"When my father was a freshman at CCNY, he and his friends met these girls at a dance in the city. The girls were visiting from Cleveland, and they snuck the boys into their hotel. The one my father spent the night with was Felice Dudek. Six weeks later, he got a long-distance call from her. She was pregnant."

"Your dad told you all this?"

"My mother. And according to her, my dad told Felice he'd heard of an abortionist in Pennsylvania. He offered to pay for everything and go with her. But Felice was raised a serious Catholic and she wouldn't hear of it."

"Did your mom know about it when your parents got married?"

"Some of it. Not that my father had volunteered to marry Felice. My father told my mother that years later—in the middle of a fight. But Felice said no. Her parents were not especially fond of Jews, and they wouldn't let her marry one. Felice just wanted financial support. She never did marry or get a job, and my father's been supporting her and her son for thirty-five years."

I took her hand, lacing my fingers through hers.

"Twice a year," she said, "when Richard got older, my father would fly to Cleveland to see him. My parents fought like tigers before he went. They fought constantly about Richard. My mother always wrote the checks for the bills, and one night every month when we'd sit down for dinner, she'd drop the checkbook on the table and say, 'You write the one for your girlfriend and your son.' When Richard used to come East to visit, my mother would go see her sister in Maine, and I'd stay home with the maid while my father and Richard went into the city."

The image of Glenna as a child, alone in that sterile monstrosity of a house, sent a wave of sadness through me.

"My whole life," she said, "it's been Richard, Richard, Richard. Well, Richard was thrown out of three colleges. My father still sends him money, but has seen him once since 1960. My father's sick about it. He's sure Richard's a genius. Just like he's sure I'm his cute baby girl—incapable of anything important. Meantime, only something like nine percent of medical students in the whole country are women. Me, I'm seventh in my class at P and S, out of a hundred and forty-eight. And do you know what Richard the genius does?"

"A medical—"

"A medical researcher! Is that what my father said? For your information, Richard was kicked out of a clinical psych program at Northwestern for experimenting on undergrads with LSD—my father had to fly to Illinois to get him out of jail. And now Richard lives on a commune in Boulder, where he and the freaks he *communes* with all fuck each other like Nero's throwing the party, then write pseudoscientific horse-shit about their fucking and publish it in their own journal."

Switching off the lamp, she curled next to me and began to cry quietly. I held her, desperately wanting to comfort her and judging it within my power to do so.

"Glenna, I've got a question."

"I can't talk about it anymore."

"Not about Richard," I said.

"Okay."

"Who dresses your mother?"

Her laughter confirmed my grandiose belief in my power. "God," she said, "her redecorating makes me insane. And she doesn't like me. But she's always loved me."

I told Glenna that I loved her, and she said, "I love you, too, Gordo. So much."

I pressed myself against her warm, milky skin and couldn't believe my good fortune. Yet it would be some time before I understood that this was precisely the problem, the beginning of our end, that Glenna loved me.

So much.

Part III

Present: New York

Chapter 14

LALLY'S TAVERN WAS lit by hanging wrought-iron octagons that bathed the paneling in an amber glow. Through the arched hallway that separated the dining area from the bar, I saw a couple of customers on the red-leather-topped stools, but all around us the tables were still empty.

"Usually people drink cognac after they eat," I said. "You want a sandwich?"

"I'm fine," Glenna said, sipping from a snifter of Rémy Martin. "I started drinking cognac after my father died."

"Sorry, Glenna. When?"

"Seven—almost eight—years ago."

"And your mom?"

"She moved back to Maine—to Bangor. To live with her sister."

"You two getting along?"

"About the same," Glenna said. "When I go see her, she has her projects for me to help with. Her first one was for me to fix up and sell the house in Riverdale. After the house sold, I cleaned it out. There were three crystal decanters of Rémy Martin in the bomb shelter. I'd been down there before, but I'd never seen them. They were locked in a cabinet."

I saw where this was going and had a sinking feeling.

"David, my husband, told me it was excellent cognac. So I saved it. One night, I was missing my dad, and I drank some and liked it. Now I order—" Glenna put down her glass. "You knew, didn't you? My dad used to take you down there to drink, didn't he?"

Nodding, I shifted my gaze between Glenna and the fireplace. Orange-blue gas flames were flickering up through ceramic logs.

Glenna said, "I knew he drank. I could smell it on him sometimes. But he didn't do it in front of my mother and me, and I guess I didn't want to admit he had a problem. At least not till it hit me in the face. He was taken to the ER one night. My mother called me, and when I got there, the charge nurse let me read his chart, and I saw he was being treated for cirrhosis. He was still drinking when he died. I tried to get him into a program. My mother even called Richard."

"Was he any help?"

"No. Richard's done with the commune, but not with being pissed." Holding the stem of her snifter in two fingers, Glenna twirled the glass on the table and gave me an apologetic smile. "I remember you trying to tell me about my dad. And I know it couldn't have been easy for you to do, and I—I appreciate it."

"You're welcome."

Glenna drank some more cognac. "Catch me up with you."

"Well, you know my father's gone."

She nodded and started reaching across the table, as if she were about to squeeze my hand, but she seemed to think better of it, pulling back and saying, "Whenever I'm channel surfing and the Mets come on, I remember those games your dad took us to at Shea."

"Nice times," I said, and then we were silent.

Glenna said, "Your mom?"

"Mom's gone. Her, Uncle Jerr, and Aunt Lil. All within two years."

"I'm so sorry, Gordon."

"Thanks. At least my sister's fine. Elaine lives in Belmont, outside Boston, has a husband, two daughters, and three grandchildren. I was on my way there when I stopped in New York."

"I knew you two were close. I always wanted to meet her."

"You'd like her. My mother said you had a lot in common."

"How so?"

"Smart and pretty," I said, skipping the part about their both hurting men.

Outside, I heard the scrape of plows clearing the streets.

Glenna glanced down at her hands. "Married?" she said.

"Hard question for you to ask?"

"Maybe. A little."

"Good," I said.

She looked up at me with a small, tight grin, and even in the dim apricot light the meshwork of creases around her eyes and mouth stood out like cracks in a cameo. Yet her power to hold my attention had not diminished. I had an overwhelming desire to touch her, but I'd already made that mistake helping her off with her coat. I took the plastic sword with an olive speared on it from my martini and held it toward her.

Glenna leaned over and stopped, as if hesitant to share an act of intimacy with me—however innocent. Then she ate the olive, and a spurt of affection for her warmed me to my toes, and I wondered whether the warmth had come from memory or this moment.

"Divorced," I said. "For a while. My ex, Beth—she's a nice woman. Talented. A graphic artist. Works in advertising. But she had no business being married to a man who always had a plane to catch."

"Children?"

"A son. Alex."

"After your dad. That's wonderful. How old?"

"Twenty-five," I said. "When he was in high school, I cut down on my traveling because Alex wanted to live with me. That was a good—a great time. Then he went off to Berkeley."

"You mean the university or like Alex ran away from home?"

"The university."

"How'd Alex do at school?" Glenna was grinning.

"You're asking if he repeated my stellar academic career?"

"More or less."

"Are you kidding? Not with what Berkeley cost me. Alex was Phi Beta Kappa. I was so proud of him. But I wasn't surprised. He was always a terrific student and so responsible. After he came to live with me, I wasn't sure if I was taking care of him or the other way around. He was a pleasure from the day he was born."

"You're lucky."

I looked over at the gas flames in the fireplace, recalling the muggy gray morning that Alex had moved out of my town house. The moving men were carrying a couch to their truck, and Alex was standing on the sidewalk under a willow oak, holding the box with the iPod dock and speakers that I'd bought him for his new apartment in Baltimore. My son had seemed so happy then, standing in the shade, close enough for me to touch.

"Gordon?"

I moved my eyes from the fire. "Tell me about your husband."

"David. David Aldrich."

"Surprised to hear you were married," I said, regretting the words as they came out of my mouth.

She flinched. "Don't say that, Gordon."

"Forgive me. That was out of line. Tell me about David."

"Presbyterian brought David up from Philadelphia to become chief of ophthalmology. It was at the end of my internship. David was twenty years older. He'd been married before and had twin boys. He didn't want more children and . . ."

I took a slug of my martini.

"I—I wasn't sure what I wanted. I was going into pediatrics, so I'd be around kids, and the twins were with us a couple weekends a month and for vacations. I must've been a decent stepmother. One lives in Seattle now; the other in San Diego; and they both still call and come to visit."

Glenna was twirling her snifter again. "David was so easy for me to get along with. He was busy at the hospital and did committee work at the med school, and he was just glad I was young and pretty and around. Even after he was diagnosed—with bladder cancer—all he needed was for me to make sure he made it to radiation and chemo and to talk to him when I got home. He was sick for five years. The cancer had metastasized. 'Olympic organ hopping,' David called it. The last several months, he couldn't work. I offered to take in an associate or scale back my practice. He said no, hire a nurse for him. All he wanted was for me to sit with him at night and tell him everything I'd done during the day. Funny thing is—as sad as those nights were—it was the only time I felt useful."

She was still twirling the snifter, and I sensed that she wanted to tell me something else, but couldn't decide if she should or how she would feel about it if she did.

"You're making me dizzy," I said, reaching over and putting my hand on her glass. "Tell me the rest of it, Glenna. It's all right."

"I don't want to hurt you."

"You never did want to," I said.

"You know that, don't you? It's important to me you know that."

"I'm middle-aged, Glenna. I know everything." She smiled, and I said, "It's all right. Go ahead."

Despite the reassurance, she held back. Then: "I was so grateful to David."

"For?"

"For the calmness. For—for not feeling the way I did about you."

"Ouch," I said, trying to keep it light, yet stung.

"You made me feel like the ground was going to open up and swallow me. I used to get furious with you about it. I would wake up with it."

"It didn't seem that way. Not to me."

"I know, Gordon." She was quiet again. I noticed her eyes misting up and handed her a napkin. She shook her head. "After David died—right after David died, I felt like I'd cheated him. Like I didn't love him the way a wife should love a husband. But gratitude is a kind of love, isn't it?"

"Not the kind on valentines. But, yes—I think gratitude is a kind of love."

"Maybe the best kind," she said.

"Definitely the easiest."

She lowered her head. "Was it that way with you and—Beth?"

"Beth. We dated. We lived together. I married her. I'm not sure I loved her till Alex. I loved her for having Alex."

Glenna pinned me to my chair with her eyes, and I saw her dissolve backward through her fifties, forties, thirties, and twenties, and then back again to now. It was unsettling, as if my vision had lost its ability to decode past, present, and future.

I said, "Did you ever think about—" and then stopped, embarrassed about asking the question.

"Think about you? Sure. Don't you believe you were important to me?"

"Sometimes." I started twirling my martini glass by the stem.

"You still haven't told me why you're here."

"I wanted to go out on a date."

Glenna shook her head. "I'm . . . what do they call it? 'Geographically undesirable.' And you could've been in touch years ago. For God's sake, you can tell me, Gordon. I want to know."

"Nothing to tell."

From her shrug, I knew that Glenna wasn't buying it. As she drank the rest of her Rémy Martin, she stared past me, with a faraway look in her eyes. I turned and saw that she was staring out the front windows of the tavern, where snowflakes were fluttering through the streetlights as gracefully as silvered butterflies.

"What're you thinking?" I asked.

"About that winter."

"Our happy winter?" I said, unable to keep the sarcasm out of my voice.

"It was, Gordon."

I was angry now and amazed how old wounds can bleed like new.

"Gordon?"

I finished my martini. The vodka didn't help my anger.

"You look ready to leave," Glenna said.

"You wanna go?"

She sighed. "It was a lovely winter."

"Absolutely lovely."

"Stop it," she said.

"Absolutely lovely. Till you planned your party."

"I wasn't trying to make you feel bad."

"You didn't have to try. You had a gift for it."

She stood up. "I won't do this."

"Do what?"

"This," she said, taking her coat off the chair at the next table. "This evening of—of you getting even."

On the verge of losing her again, a feeling of dread came over me, and I pictured myself walking back to the Hyatt alone, drowning in the nighttime blue.

"Sit down," I said.

"Excuse me?"

"Please. Sit down."

She stood there, her eyes traveling over my face.

"Are you hungry?" I asked. "I'm hungry. Let's split a club sandwich."

"You're done?"

"I'm done."

She draped her coat back over the chair. "I'd also like another cognac."

I went to the bar. The bartender, a guy about my age with steel-gray hair slicked up like an Elvis impersonator, appeared transfixed by the images on the flat-screen TV up on the wall. Down at the end of the horseshoe, two twentysomethings in jackets and ties sat on stools, talking and drinking beers. The one in the blue pinstripe suit reminded me of Alex, with his chestnut hair and how he sat straight up on the stool, his hands moving as he spoke, as though he were conducting an orchestra.

"Helluva thing," the bartender said, nodding at the flat screen.

Fox News was running footage of a marine convoy in eastern Afghanistan that had been hit by an IED. A marine was dragging the driver from the cab of the lead truck. The driver's arms and legs were limp, and his helmet had fallen off, so I could see how young he was, and from the way his head was rolling around on his neck, it was even money that he was dead.

"Yeah," I said, my stomach contracting into a fiery knot.

I gave him my order and pulled my iPhone out of my pocket; no messages, though I already knew that because I had the phone on vibrate.

As the bartender scooped ice into the cocktail shaker, he said, "Our waitress got snowed in on Long Island. I'll run the sandwich over to you."

"I'll wait," I said, glancing away from the TV and over to our table.

Glenna was gazing out the window again, watching the falling snow.

Part IV

Past

Chapter 15

THAT WINTER, GLENNA and I lived in glorious harmony. Sympathetic vibration, she called it, tuning forks humming at equivalent frequencies. Her metaphor was a tad scientific for my taste, but I couldn't dispute its precision. Glenna was different from what she had been in the fall, and consequently, I was different, too. I can't clarify exactly what motivated the change, but once Glenna lowered her guard enough to tell me about her half brother, our daily activities away from each other became no more than a pause in an unbroken conversation.

On most evenings when Glenna wasn't on call at Presbyterian, we sat side by side in bed, Glenna reading *The Merck Manual* while I hunched over the lapboard she'd given me writing stories. Sometimes, when Glenna finished up her surgical rounds early, I met her at the hospital, and we caught the subway to Chinatown and ate sesame noodles or went to the movies or explored the Village.

As my relationship with Glenna progressed, my interest in Vietnam waned, but the luster of the war was further dulled for me as it became apparent that I could be a writer without getting shot at. The profile I'd done on Dan Kamminski, the beer-selling bookie at Madison Square Garden, had caused a small stir. The local New York TV stations had featured Kammi on the news, citing my *Long Island Press* piece, and Mack Grunch jumped my fee from twenty bucks an article to thirty and heaped assignments on me.

Ultimately, though, I viewed journalism as an apprenticeship for fiction, and I began turning out one short story every two weeks. Glenna read each of them, frequently over my shoulder as I sat at her desk typing the final draft on my Smith-Corona.

"Gordo, did your father really take your mother to see the Patterson-Johansson fight at the Polo Grounds for their anniversary?"

"He also took me and my sister."

"That's funny."

"My mother didn't think so."

"No, I mean the story. It's very funny. I know somebody's going to publish it."

Because this was our glorious winter, I let myself believe that Glenna was right, and on this particular evening, after I rolled the last page out of the typewriter, we went into the city for Irish coffee at the West End Bar, then strolled along the river, the snowflakes glazing the hills and hollows of Riverside Park. The night was like many other nights that winter. The streetlamps always seemed to be on, and the smoky-blue darkness was always descending as softly as the snow, through which Glenna and I lightly stepped, with a delicious symmetry to our wills and our wishes that would not survive the spring.

IN MARCH, Glenna and Robin traveled to Albany with a busload of NYMSRAL members to lend support to Biff, who was testifying before the Joint Legislative Committee on Public Health. NYMSRAL had issued a voluminous report on the health risks of illegal abortions, and when Assemblyman Cohane, the sponsor of the reform bill, read it, he invited Biff to testify. According to Glenna, Biff was at his didactic best when he summarized the report, bowling over the committee with a ghastly litany about the cases of endometriosis that occurred when untrained hands punctured a uterus, an excruciating mishap whose outcome was often sterility for the patient. He cited the gruesome statistic that in New York City, 74 deaths per 100,000 resulted from illegal abortions, while in nations that legalized the procedure, the rate plummeted to 3 per 100,000.

Biff was so enthralled by his performance that he decided to throw a party. Robin and Glenna were also psyched about it, and when the three of them got done with the guest list, they had invited every member of NYMSRAL, Biff's fellow residents, and the 1970 graduating class of the med school.

"Did I make the list?" I asked Glenna as we got into the shower together.

"Lucky you. You're my date."

"That Friday night I might be hanging out with my friend Todd."

"Invite him," she said, moving directly under the nozzle to wet her hair.

"Wouldn't be his thing," I said, standing outside the hot spray, shivering.

"You don't want to come?"

"I do but—"

"But?"

"But I'm freezing here. Let me under the water."

She made room for me and said, "You're ashamed to be around my friends."

"Why the hell should I be ashamed?" I replied, knowing the exact source of my shame: Glenna and her friends were en route to their medical degrees and a fortune, while I was profiling geeks at $30 apiece. It wasn't a real job, which my father pointed out to me whenever I stopped by the house. And my writing fiction had been a complete bust. My stories came back from the literary journals and magazines almost as fast as I sent them out, and I'd felt too humiliated by the rejections to mention them to Glenna.

Picking up the bar of soap, she said, "I don't know why you should be ashamed. Because you're not the most famous writer in America? I'm proud of you."

Of course, the problem was how I felt about me, and I would have explained that to her, except at the moment she was rubbing the soap on me in a manner that I suspect the chemists at Procter & Gamble had not intended.

"I'll come," I said.

"I'm counting on it," Glenna said, then I shut my eyes and let the water wash away my shame.

Chapter 16

I HAD PROMISED MYSELF—AND Glenna—to drop by my classes to hang on to my 2-S. But driving to Brooklyn for poli sci and contemplating Professor Gould's lecture on Rousseau forced me to smoke a J, and the munchies came on like an epileptic fit. After detouring to the Sugar Bowl for a burger and a chocolate malt, I was far too happy to hear a professor explain how an onerous society had corrupted my inborn goodness.

So off I went to pursue my favorite school activity—time traveling via old newspapers in the library stacks. And it was there, leafing through plastic-sheathed pages, that I discovered Madame Restell, a freethinking seamstress who escaped the savage poverty of the nineteenth century by becoming New York City's preeminent abortionist.

Back then, birth control was considered an affront to God's will, and abortion was outlawed. Still, great numbers of married and unmarried women sought to manage their own fate, and Madame Restell, along with her husband, opened for business in Greenwich Village. Their challenge was to inform the populace of Madame's practice while dodging jail, and their solution was so clever that it reportedly made one robber baron weep with envy.

Advertisements were placed in newspapers proclaiming that Madame Restell specialized in concocting pills that cured the fairer sex of every disorder from a deranged stomach to a despondent spirit. The ads claimed the pills should never be used when ——. Delicacy precluded the ads from filling in the blank, but everyone got the idea, and customers flocked to Madame Restell. When the pills, a compound of harmless powders, didn't induce a miscarriage, Madame was ready with a pricier, foolproof alternative, using pliers and wire to pierce the amniotic sac.

Over four decades, Madame Restell was indicted, imprisoned, and vilified as "the Wickedest Woman in New York." She salved her wounds with the traditional American balm—money. She and her husband built a spectacular four-story brownstone on Fifth Avenue, stocking it with servants and the latest European furnishings.

By 1878, though, on the eve of a trial in which her conviction was assured, Madame climbed into her bathtub and slit her throat.

"A fit ending to an odious career," was the judgment of the *New York Times*.

I stayed in the stacks, thinking. With the vote on the abortion-reform bill scheduled in Albany and abortion a hot topic nationally, why not do a piece on Madame Restell for the *Long Island Press*? Then, when I mailed my writing samples with the query letters proposing articles to *Esquire* and *Harper's*, I could show the editors something beyond my profiles of geeks. I called Mack Grunch from a pay phone in the library and did an abbreviated song and dance for him on Madame Restell.

"Amazing," he said.

"Amazing, hunh?" I replied, figuring he was going for it.

"Amazing you call a newspaper with crap that happened a hundred years ago. We do today, kid. And the future if we can figure it. Your Uncle Jerry's a guy knows the future. Talked me into betting the Jets against the Colts. You know the future, kid?"

"I'm not winning a Pulitzer?"

"There ya go." He took a ferocious bite of what sounded like a stale bagel or plate-glass window. "But even if you're no genius, you gotta live. Here's what we'll try. Sarah Dunlop, who edits the Sunday magazine, has been buggin' me to recommend her writers. I'll pitch her you and Madame Restell, and you get in touch with her in an hour."

Sarah Dunlop was as nice as pie when I phoned, saying that she had enjoyed my profiles. She assigned me the article and promised a $250 fee, the most I'd ever earned for a piece. As if that didn't elevate her in my estimation to the greatest editor in the Western World, Sarah said that if I did a good job, she'd consider the story for the May 4 cover of the magazine.

WHEN I got back to the house, I didn't have a chance to tell Glenna about Madame Restell because preparations for the party were in full swing. Robin had set up a brass hookah with eight stems in the alcove off the living room, and she was slicing an ounce of black opiated hash into squares small enough to fit into the bowl. Glenna was screwing black-light bulbs into lamps, and Palmer was roasting Cornish game hens, which he set on the kitchen counter to cool, their butts raised as though waiting for a gang of roosters to stop by for an orgy. My job was to pick up the soda and beer at Waldbaum's. After I returned from the supermarket and unloaded the GTO, I showered and changed into my corduroy suit and cashmere turtleneck.

Glenna was breathtaking in a long, clingy crimson-velvet dress, and I stood near the front door with her. She introduced me to guests as they came in, saying, "This is my boyfriend, Gordon," which, along with my new assignment, made me less nervous about being around the med students and doctors.

Soon, people were pouring in, and with the stereo blasting and the air clouded by a reefer-and-hash smog and Day-Glo balloons bobbing above the crowd, I felt as if I were backstage at the Fillmore. The black lights gave the faces a twilight-zone tan, and in the hot, noisy press of bodies I got separated from Glenna and wandered back to the alcove, where a merry circle was seated around the water pipe.

"Having fun?" I said to Robin, sitting on the cushion next to her. Her dark eyes and flowing raven hair brought to mind an Indian princess, but she had swapped her standard bleached-denim overalls for a billowy, tiger-striped jumpsuit, which made her look like a young, man-eating Buddha.

"You're bored," she replied, dipping a spoon into a quart of Breyers butter pecan. "Guys are only interested in me if they're bored."

"No mint chocolate chip?"

She chuckled. "Mint chocolate chip's too fattening."

Someone on my left passed me a stem, and I did a few tokes of the hash.

"You're being *très* cool, Meyers," Robin said, feeding me a spoonful of ice cream.

"About?" I asked, passing the stem back to my left.

"About being here with all these strangers and knowing Glenna invited her ex-boyfriend. Especially a guy like Rick Siner. He's going to be an orthopedic surgeon, tools around on a Harley, and could win a Tony Curtis look-alike contest."

My rush of jealousy wasn't slowed by the opiated hash. I remembered Glenna mentioning Rick; he was the one who had recommended that she buy me Henry James's *Portrait of a Lady*. I felt like Glenna had suckered me. She knew the party was freaking me out, so what was the purpose of inviting him?

"You knew, didn't you?" Robin asked.

I lied and said yeah, when the truth was that I'd avoided asking Glenna about her past because there was no percentage in asking any woman about that stuff, particularly a real looker who was an acrobat in bed. My philosophy was simple: better to enjoy the skills Glenna had learned than to worry about where she had learned them.

Robin said, "Different strokes for different folks, Meyers. But it would bother me." She stood up, then nodded toward the front door. "See, Rick just came in."

I stood and saw a Tony Curtis double in a belted suede jacket, and he had one arm draped over Glenna's shoulders. Before the adrenaline stopped surging through me, Glenna was looking over at the alcove. She said something to Rick and slid out from under his arm as they walked toward us.

I was less philosophical now, and Robin must have noticed, because she said, "Relax, Meyers. I got a secret for you."

I listened to Robin's secret and smiled at Glenna, hoping to hide my anger from her.

It took them a minute to get through the people packed into the living room. Then Glenna said, "Rick, this is Gordon."

Besides the belted suede jacket, Rick had on pear-green bell-bottoms with wide, white stripes and black motorcycle boots. He stuck out his hand with the exaggerated affability of a used-car salesman. I shook it, and he said, "Great to meet ya, man. Glenna says you're a writer. That's far out. Writing's what I always wanted to do."

"What a coincidence," I said. "I always wanted to operate on somebody's knee."

The budding orthopedic surgeon was not as mentally agile as I'd expected. His face was screwed up in confusion, as if he were trying to determine whether I'd insulted him. Glenna, far quicker on the uptake, was frowning at me.

I said to her, "So why'd you invite the sixty-second man?"

Even under the black lights, I could see her face flush.

Rick said, "What's he talking about?"

"Instant oatmeal," I said. "Done in sixty seconds."

That comment didn't clear up Rick's confusion, but it did make Robin giggle.

I said, "Glenna, what you gotta do is tell your guys to think about their jump shot. That way they'll last all night."

Glenna snapped, "Robin, can't you keep your fucking mouth shut?"

Calmly Robin replied, "Hey, it's a party."

Glenna was giving me the full eyeball, not a particularly pretty sight. I should have flipped her the bird, but settled for telling Rick, "It's been real, man. Good luck with the writing."

As I left the living room, Rick said, "Yeah, same here, but what's with the oatmeal? I thought Palmer made Cornish game hen," and Robin let loose with a burst of laughter so loud that I could still hear it after I grabbed my peacoat from one of the sagging Lucite branches of the coat-tree and walked out the front door.

I DROVE into the city and went to see Todd at his studio above Incense & Peppermints. The apartment was also used as storage for the head shop, so Todd shared the space with stacked-up Oriental rugs, bushel baskets of hash pipes and incense burners, and floor-to-ceiling shelves lined with lava lamps. But he didn't have to pay rent, which enabled him to maximize his investment in hallucinogenic futures.

"Where's your lady?" he asked.

"At a party."

"Why aren't you with her?"

"I didn't have an old girlfriend to bring."

Todd seemed puzzled by my reply. "This'll straighten you out," he said, handing me a tab of white lightning. "Comes direct from Owsley's lab in Point Richmond, California."

"Or a Mafia basement in Bensonhurst."

"Whatever. I'm scorin' three bucks a hit for this batch."

I swallowed it, acid being the pluperfect drug for the TV Generation—do a hit and wait for the show to start inside your head. We smoked cigarettes while we waited for our brains to boil, then Todd turned on the lava lamps, and when the colorful segments of wax began dividing like cancer cells in the oily liquid, we went out to the fire escape. Below, junkies were staging a be-in around Tompkins Square Park, the flames of their trash-can fires licking at the inky sky.

Todd said, "I'm splitting for the Coast by the end of the year. What's happening with you and what's her name?"

"Glenna," I said. "She keeps falling over her own feet and landing on my heart."

Todd laughed. "That's too country and western for me."

Just mentioning Glenna's name had been a bummer, let alone imagining her back at the party with Rick. I inhaled and the world moved close, and when I exhaled, it moved away. I inhaled faster, trying to cling to the world, but I became light-headed and gazed up at a thin, icy slice of moon. I envisioned myself as an exploding star, fragments suspended in space, forever.

"Bad trip?" Todd said.

"I've had better."

"Let's go over to the Second Avenue Deli for pastrami."

I nodded. Todd was the only person I ever met who got hungry tripping.

Todd said, "Then we can go down by the Fillmore and you can find some more loonies to write about."

The wind wailed. I hugged myself, and the world was far away. Todd grabbed the sleeve of my coat, and I followed him back through the open window into the apartment.

Chapter 17

Rosy scratches of dawn were nicking the darkness above the Henry Hudson Bridge when I made it back to Spuyten Duyvil. The living room reeked of smoke and beer. Garbage bags heaped on the hearth overflowed hen bones and paper plates, and people I didn't recognize were passed out on the floor.

I tiptoed upstairs, planning to sneak under the quilt beside Glenna. Problem was, Glenna wasn't sleeping. She was sitting on the bed in her crimson-velvet party dress.

"How could you do that?" she said, and a soda can sailed past my head, plinking against the wall.

"Do what?" I asked, flipping the empty can into the wastebasket.

"Walk out on me at my own party?"

"Who told you to invite ortho moron?"

"God, it's not like Rick and I were married. We dated for a year."

"Dated?" I said. "Don't be polite. *Dating's* another word for *fucking*."

"Rick and I are just friends."

This status report, I surmised, meant that it was obligatory for me to pretend I wasn't pissed. Instead, I suppressed an

137

impulse to strangle her. "The section of guys' brains in charge of friendship with chicks is directly connected to their dicks."

"What complete horseshit," she said. "But *chicks* and *dicks*—now there's a real groovy rhyme."

"Bottom line, Glenna: if Rick's your friend, he's only hanging around to freak out some other chick or he's hoping to get laid."

"Rick and I care about each other. That's it. He's happy for me, that I have you."

Her tone was overly patient, as if she were addressing her pet orangutan, and it did not temper my urge to throttle her.

She said, "I invited Rick because I thought you two would get along and you'd be more comfortable."

"Why would we get along? I like to fuck for more than sixty seconds."

"Should I have invited everyone in my class except Rick? Say, 'Gee, Rick, we slept together so don't bother showing up.' You know how embarrassed I would've been? Don't you care about that?"

"That's better, Glenna. Be honest. At least now we know it was all about you."

"You tell me, Gordon. What was I supposed to do?"

"You could've told me about him so I didn't feel like the only jerk there who didn't know you were screwing him."

"If I told you, you would've freaked."

I said, "Maybe you should've given me a chance."

"Maybe I was trying *not* to hurt you by *not* mentioning Rick. And maybe you should trust me."

"Maybe I did till you—"

"And maybe you're a fucking bastard," she said, then ripped her Indian-print quilt off the bed and stormed out.

Without bothering to undress, I stretched out on the mattress. A door opened and closed on the second floor. I hoped Glenna was going into Robin's room, not Biff's, and I would've gone down to check if I hadn't been unconscious.

I AWOKE in the afternoon, my body aching from the strychnine in the acid. I went downstairs to shower, discovering that Glenna had relocated to Robin's. I poked my head into the corner room, the sweep of windows and southern exposure providing the requisite sunlight for Robin to cultivate her marijuana plants. Robin and Glenna, their hair wet from the shower, were wearing terry-cloth robes, sipping Constant Comment tea, and sitting on Robin's queen-size bed with medical texts scattered on the baby-blue satin comforter that Robin's mother had recently shipped to her from Neiman Marcus.

"Studying?" I asked.

"Girl talk," Robin answered.

"You're not speaking to me?" I said to Glenna.

She stared down at an open textbook, and Robin said, "She's not speaking to you."

I said to Robin, "Then please ask Miss Rising if she's coming back to her room."

Robin asked her, and Glenna, without glancing up from her book, said, "Please ask Mr. Meyers if he's double-jointed."

I said, "Glenna, what the hell are you talking about?"

Glenna said, "Robin, if Mr. Meyers *is* double-jointed, please recommend that he go upstairs alone and fuck himself."

Robin was beaming like a kid at the circus. Her envy of Glenna was understandable, but I regretted that it had a habit of poking me in the eye.

I said to Robin, "You like this little drama, hunh?"

"Lighten up, Meyers," Robin said. "Glenna should've told you she dated Rick. And when you flipped out—which you definitely would have—she should've told you that Rick's one of our nation's foremost premature ejaculators. That way you both would've been happy. I only did what needed to be done."

Still eyeing her book, Glenna said, "You did what you always do."

"Bring some reality to the situation," Robin said.

"No," Glenna replied. "Stick your nose in my business."

Robin said, "Everyone needs a hobby."

"Nice poster," I said to Robin.

Tacked to the wall above her bed was a blowup of Huey P. Newton, minister of defense of the Black Panther Party. Huey was as angelically handsome as the late soul crooner Sam Cooke, with the same little-boy-lost eyes that women reputedly find irresistible. In the blowup, Huey was perched on a peacock chair in his beret and leather jacket, holding a spear.

I said, "When my sister was in ninth grade, she hung posters like that over her bed."

With a high-and-mighty sneer, Robin answered, "They didn't have posters of Brother Huey P. when your sister was in ninth grade."

"Right, only Ricky Nelson and Paul Anka."

Glenna started to smile, but she saw me watching her and stopped.

Robin said, "Meyers, you're a prick. You think I'm some teenybopper with a crush?"

"Nah," I said. "You're too old to be a teenybopper."

GLENNA BUNKED with Robin for the next five days. I was still angry at her and thought about going back to Brooklyn, but I would have had to explain to my mother and father why I was home, and I was in no mood for parental explanations. In lieu of leaving, I avoided her, and we skipped the knockdown dragouts, though we did have our share of skirmishes.

One evening, when I entered the kitchen, Glenna was about to stick a Swanson frozen dinner in the oven. She said, "Aren't you sorry for leaving my party?"

"Sorry I went to it."

"Won't happen again," she said, tossing the foil-wrapped tray into the sink and stalking out.

With our different schedules it was easy for me to keep out of range, but I couldn't avoid the bathroom, and so we clashed there often enough in the mornings that I should have nailed one of those historic-battlefield signs to the door.

Standing in the hall in her robe with her hair wrapped in a towel, she said, "When you met Rick, you could've had a little class."

"And I could've been a contender."

"What does that mean?" she asked.

"A line from *On the Waterfront*. It's on the *Late Show* tonight. Check it out."

Glenna was waiting for me the next morning. "I want to tell you something."

"Must we?" I asked.

"It'll take one minute, Gordon."

"Forget it," I said, going past her. "I wanna get fucked for a minute, I'll call Rick."

"You're insane!" she shouted as I closed the door.

The final volley came two mornings later. I was fed up with our skirmishing and fired a preemptive salvo. Before she could utter a word, I said, "Where do you get the nerve to defend inviting him without telling me? Even my father knew he was out of line taking my mother to Zalman's so he could see Tamara, and my folks have been married twenty-eight years. There are boundaries to their craziness. Dad broke the rules, and Mom shot him with seltzer. What are the rules with you, Glenna?"

She glared at me. "I like it better when we're not talking."

"I can understand why."

The following day she came back to her room, but neither of us said much and sex was out. I did press myself against her one night when we were both restless, but she sat up and said, "I can't. I've got a cough. Listen."

She faked a cough that sounded like an advanced case of TB, and I said, "You can't use a phony cough for an excuse until you've been married to a guy for ten years."

"Feels like thirty."

Chapter 18

For the next few weeks, we lived together like shadows.

As a rule, not talking or making love to Glenna for so long would have sent me around the bend and kayoed the concentration I needed to work. However, I was popping black beauties like pistachios to research and write my Madame Restell story. The deadline was tight; it was my longest assignment to date; and I was either at the Brooklyn College library or pounding away through the night on my typewriter in the kitchen, where I had relocated so as not to disturb Glenna's sleep.

Every now and again, despite the vitality and fearlessness that amphetamines supply, whenever I'd stop working long enough to go outside and smoke a cigarette, I had moments of bewildering loneliness that served as a scary preview of what life would be like for me without Glenna. But then I would down another black beauty and get back to the story, and in this manner I persuaded myself that Glenna and I would get it together when the article was done.

Too bad then that on the day I delivered the piece to Garden City and came back to the house to crash, Glenna, Biff, Robin, and their NYMSRAL cronies were on a bus to Albany to attend the Assembly's final debate on the abortion-reform bill.

Assemblyman Cohane had assured the media that he had eighty-two votes in support of reform, six more than needed for passage. What Cohane hadn't counted on, according to the news I listened to that night on the clock radio, was Assemblyman Martin Ginsberg, a Republican from Nassau County, who had contracted polio as a baby. As the five-hour debate dragged on, Ginsberg stood up with the aid of crutches and leg braces and attacked a provision in the bill that would permit doctors to abort a fetus if there was evidence that the child would be grossly malformed. Ginsberg declared that if his colleagues were willing to prevent a person from entering this world malformed, weren't they saying it was proper to remove a person, currently in the world, who became malformed?

Since the bill didn't mention executing the handicapped, Ginsberg's objection wasn't exceedingly logical. But an orderly mind isn't a prerequisite for political office—some would say it's a detriment. For as Ginsberg lowered himself into his seat, he was rewarded with a standing ovation from the legislators, fourteen of whom defected from Cohane's camp, and abortion reform was defeated for the third year in a row.

I fell asleep and dreamed that someone was whispering my name. The dream improved when a tongue darted into my ear. I rolled over, and the lamp on the apple crate snapped on. I opened my eyes, and Glenna was sitting beside me in a pleated, black skirt and white blouse.

"You're not still mad?" I asked.

"I miss you too much to be mad. You mad at me?"

"Always." I smiled. "But mostly I don't get why you invited Rick without mentioning you went out with him. And I'm scared that I don't get it. And I was wondering if it might not have scared you, too—inviting him without thinking it through."

"You reading my mind again?"

I shrugged. "Trying to."

"It did scare me when I thought about it afterward. Why I didn't think about Robin telling you—which she can never resist. Why I spaced out on the whole thing." Glenna took off her black pumps. "This morning, on the bus, somebody was playing the guitar and singing 'In My Life.' I've heard that song a hundred times. But today—today, it's like I finally got it— how pale my past seems when I think about us now. I don't know. Maybe I invited Rick to remind myself that I had a life before my memory's completely filled with you. Maybe it was to push you away, but not too far, because one thing I'm sure about is how much I want you to be mine and how much I want to be yours. Okay?"

"Better than okay."

She kissed me. "Did you hear about the vote?"

"It was on the radio. Tough break."

"There's worse news," she said. "Was the bust in Riverdale on the radio?"

"The raid on the abortion clinic in the apartment?"

"A luxury apartment on Arlington Avenue for God's sake. The doctor doing it was Andy Westrich, a friend from P and S. Andy phoned Palmer from jail. His bail's five thousand dollars, and Palmer's paying it."

"What happened to Andy's dough? The radio said he was operating on two dozen women a day at four hundred dollars apiece."

"Andy's not what you'd call a master criminal. Palmer said he had forty-seven thousand dollars in a savings account, but the cops searched the apartment and impounded his bank book as evidence."

I'd been stroking her calf as we talked, and Glenna exhumed her burlap shoulder bag from under a pile of her clothes.

"I got you a present," she said, removing a three-pack of Trojans from her bag. "Gordo, I'm going to switch to a lower-dosage pill. My tits are sore. I think the estrogen and progesterone are too high. Till I do, you have to wear one of these."

"You know how to put one on?"

"I'm going to be a doctor, aren't I?"

"They teach that in med school?"

"You're expected to learn it along the way," she replied, dipping her hand back into her bag. "And I got you another present. At a shop in Albany."

She took out a Picasso drawing in a silver frame—a nude, just the lovely curve of her right hip and her rounded buttocks. I'd seen the drawing before, but it was still astonishing that such an erotic image could be created with four simple lines. I looked up to thank Glenna, but she was already over at the rubber tree, taking her reflex hammer out of her lab jacket. She came back, handed me the hammer, then held a nail for me to tap into the wall.

"There," she said, straightening the frame on the nail and standing back.

"She looks familiar. Do I know her?"

"Very funny. Now all she needs is a name."

"Picasso called her *Femme*."

"How'd you—" Glenna smiled sheepishly. "Let me guess. You read it in a book?"

"A book."

"You can see *Femme* from the bed when you're writing. She'll keep you company till I get home from the hospital. And there's a surprise for you. On the back."

I took down the drawing and read the inscription written on the cardboard backing in Glenna's neat, efficient hand:

> G: *Never fear. 10 yrs from now, when*
> *you're looking at this picture, I'm going to*
> *be looking at it with you.*
> *I love you,*
> G.

Replacing the picture, I said, "Thank you. This is great."

Then I hugged Glenna, and we stood in each other's arms, with *Femme* standing by on the wall.

Chapter 19

On the Sunday my Madame Restell story appeared, Glenna and I got up early and zipped over to a candy store on Johnson Avenue, where I bought ten copies of the *Long Island Press*. My story had made the cover of the magazine, with a byline right above a four-color artist's rendering of Madame Restell dead in her ornate marble tub, one fleshy arm hanging over the side.

Glenna and I ordered coffee and cinnamon Danish and sat at the counter. I was still admiring my byline on the cover when Glenna finished reading the story.

"This is terrific, Gordo. It's fascinating."

Glenna had a half smile on her face, and her gaze was so warm it felt as if I were sitting under a sunlamp.

She said, "I know there are people who can write well."

"Because they have libraries and such."

Her smile widened. "Because my boyfriend can. And I love it—that you write so well, and your story's on the cover. Want to go home and celebrate?"

What I felt like doing was driving to Brooklyn, slapping the magazine down in front of my father, and saying, *Read this. And dig it—they paid me two hundred and fifty bucks.*

It was a tempting fantasy—tempting enough that it was a good thing my folks had gone to Montreal for a long weekend with Aunt Lil and Uncle Jerr.

"Breakfast's on me," Glenna said, and asked the kid behind the counter how much we owed. He told her, and she began digging into the front and back pockets of her Levi's. She dug through all of her pockets twice and came up with a dime and two pennies.

"Wrong jeans?" I asked, trying not to laugh.

"Wrong jeans. This guy I live with took the right jeans off me last night and tossed them behind a rubber tree."

"Sounds like a smart guy." I put a five on the counter.

"Oh, yes," Glenna said, taking my arm. "He is."

AT HOME, our celebration lasted until late morning. When we went downstairs, talking about where to go for lunch, Biff and Robin were in the living room.

"We certainly can do it," Biff was saying.

"Do what?" Glenna said, as we sat on the couch.

As Robin opened a fresh carton of Breyers, she said, "Palmer had breakfast with Andy Westrich."

"How is he?" Glenna asked.

Biff said, "He's out of jail. But his lawyer says he'll eventually have to do a year. And he's going to lose his medical license."

"What a drag," Glenna said.

"I liked your article," Robin said to me, holding up a copy of the *Long Island Press Sunday Magazine*. I'd left my copies on the coffee table when Glenna and I had come in from the candy store.

"Same here," Biff added. Since I'd threatened to strangle him with his scarf, he had cut out his condescending digs, but his mentioning that he liked the Restell piece should have tipped me off that something was up. "Your article and Andy's arrest gave me the idea."

Robin said, "NYMSRAL is branching out. Taking over for Andy."

"You're gonna help?" Glenna asked Robin.

"She's chicken," Biff replied. "Some revolutionary."

"I'm a practical revolutionary," Robin said. "Marx wrote that nothing can have value without being an object of utility. If I got busted, my MD would be useless; I'd never get a license."

Biff smirked at her. "And your parents would kill you."

"That, too," Robin said, and ate a heaping tablespoon of mint chocolate chip.

Biff looked at Glenna. Robin was also looking at her. "I don't know," Glenna said.

Was this douche bag for real? Just when Glenna and I were in the groove again, and her worst rotations were behind her, she's supposed to hide somewhere with Biff the Brooks Brothers Mouse and do abortions?

Biff said, "NYMSRAL worked within the system and then Ginsberg gives a speech and that's why abortions are illegal? Because of that drivel? That's ludicrous. It's in Gordon's article. Until 1828, abortion was the termination of a pregnancy at roughly eighteen weeks, past the quickening, when the mother could feel the baby move. Before then, abortion didn't violate any laws. The legislature outlawed it because doctors didn't want lay people performing them. Doctors didn't want to lose their monopoly. It wasn't about morality for doctors. All they cared about was money."

"Unlike today," I said.

Biff replied, "I'm a doctor and I don't care about money."

"Lucky you have a trust fund," I said.

Biff shot Glenna a disapproving stare.

"Don't stare at me," Glenna said to Biff, and glanced over at Robin, who, naturally, was the one who had told me about his family dough.

Robin said, "You shouldn't be so modest about it, Palm. It's not like you got rich inheriting railroads. Didn't your great-grandfather invent instant coffee?"

"His own brand of it," Biff said. "Now, can we get back to the topic at hand?"

"Good idea," I said to Biff. "Even if outlawing abortion had to do with money, it also had to do with the fact that women were constantly dying from unskilled abortions. So, to some extent, the law was passed to protect them."

He said, "Madame Restell did her thing before Joseph Lister. Do you know what that means?"

"No Listerine and lots of bad breath?" I said.

Glenna and Robin laughed. Biff ignored them and said, "Before Lister, doctors didn't wash their hands or clean their instruments. Infections were rampant. Lister used phenol to kill bacteria and drastically lowered the rate of postsurgical infection."

Now Biff ignored me and, shifting his gaze between Glenna and Robin, said, "It's the moral thing to do."

"It's dumb," Robin said, and cleaned another mound of ice cream off her spoon.

"Dumb?" Biff replied. "Is it smarter to pretend you're going to start a revolution in the most materialistic society in history? Or stop a war that will not end until Nixon gets good and ready to end it?"

Robin said, "I'll still be a doctor."

Biff said, "There are more important things than being a doctor."

By this point, I thought Glenna would have spoken up, but she just sat there, staring down at the wide-pine floor.

Chapter 20

On JULY 1, Glenna entered her last year of med school. I knew that if I wanted to be with her after she graduated, I'd have to get a real job or feel like a freeloader next summer when she began her internship. My best prospect was to catch on as a staff reporter with the *Long Island Press*. I asked Mack Grunch about it, and he said, "All our new hires got diplomas. Don't mean these pinheads can read and write, but they got a sheepskin. You get one, kid, I'll hire you."

I registered for summer courses at Brooklyn, figuring that I could keep doing freelance pieces and complete the last thirty-seven credits for my degree by the end of next summer. For now, I was no longer worried about the draft. The war was winding down, and on December 1, men between nineteen and twenty-six would have a number assigned to their birthdays by lottery, and this would determine the order in which you were called. Estimates were that in 1970 only the top third of the list would have to report for physicals, and the bonus was that if you weren't summoned during the year, you were done with the draft. All I'd have to do is draw a lucky number, ditch my 2-S, and wait.

Life should have been easier for Glenna—the pressure on fourth-year students is not as intense as on the third-years—

but she had a new distraction. I heard about it on an overcast Sunday afternoon when we were walking on a path along the bank of Spuyten Duyvil Creek.

"Palmer rented the second floor of a town house on Madison," she said. "Between East Ninety-Seventh and Ninety-Eighth."

"Biff's moving out?" I replied with phony good cheer, knowing that she meant he'd selected a site for his clinic.

"It's less than a block from Mount Sinai Hospital," Glenna said. "Palmer says Andy Westrich messed up being in Riverdale. It's too residential. With Mount Sinai nearby our area's loaded with doctors, med students, and nurses. We won't stick out."

"How do the women find you?"

"They don't. They go through people Palmer has helping us. They're the ones who collect the money and make the arrangements. And there are only two people who bring women to the town house. We wear surgical greens, caps, and masks so we can't be identified if we ever have to stand before one of our patients in a police lineup."

A steady drizzle began to fall.

"Who's 'we'?" I asked.

"Palmer, another resident from Presbyterian, and one from Mount Sinai." Glenna pulled up the hood of her bright yellow rain jacket. "I'm the only med student."

"Do you know how to do this?"

"I'll do the endometrial aspirations. They're done when a woman's about a month late with her period. I thread a tube into her uterus. The outside end is attached to an empty syringe, and using suction, I extract the mucous lining the uterine wall. It's simple. Lots of times, the woman's not even pregnant."

"What about the other kind—the dilation and curettage?"

"Palmer and the other residents will do those," she said. "That's for a pregnancy up to twelve weeks. The woman has to be anesthetized, and you insert a curette—a metal loop on a long handle—into her uterus and scrape the lining. You have to be careful or you'll puncture the uterine walls. I know how to do it, but I won't. It feels—"

We stopped walking and watched the raindrops dimpling the water of the creek. Glenna slid her arm under my poncho and around my waist.

I said, "Feels?"

"At twelve weeks, the fetus has eyelids, and you can see fingers and toes, and the external ears. It would feel like—I won't do it. The aspirations are different. That feels like birth control."

We stood in the cozy gloominess of the rain. Glenna said, "You understand why I want to help with this?"

"Your friend Vicky?"

"My friend Vicky. I've been thinking about her lately. I even had a dream about her two nights ago. She was onstage at camp singing 'Moon River,' and I was sitting with you in the audience and waving at her. She wouldn't look at us, and I kept waving, but she still wouldn't look. The more she ignored us, the angrier I got."

I pulled Glenna closer to me.

"I wish Vicky were alive. And even with what I know as a med student, if I'd done her abortion, she probably would be."

It was raining harder now. Fog was wafting over the creek and swirling through the trees.

"You don't see me, do you?" Glenna said.

This sounded like the start of a fight, so gently I asked, "What do you mean?"

"Glenna the looker. Glenna the smart girl, the med student. That's all you see."

Her perceptiveness caught me off guard, and before I could come up with an answer, she said, "You think it's wrong, what I'm doing, don't you?"

"Not if it's done early. First of all, like you said, sometimes with the endometrial aspirations the woman's not pregnant. If she is, it beats having a child no one wants. And since women are going to have abortions whether they're legal or not, it's best that they're done by people who know what they're doing or they'll—"

"They'll what?"

"I meant—"

"Or they'll wind up like Vicky?"

"Like Vicky," I said.

"That's true. So why don't you want me to do it?"

I could have responded with my old story that I wanted her hanging out with me, not Biff, but that wasn't the case, not now. My objection was that for rookie do-gooders like Biff and Glenna, jail and the loss of their medical careers were as hypothetical as death is to teenagers—a fate that befalls the calamitously unlucky and incurably dumb. But since Biff didn't know squat about being an outlaw, I presumed that the cops would bust him as they'd busted Andy Westrich, and my goal was to protect Glenna from going down with him. Yet, I hesitated mentioning it because I felt she'd see my protectiveness as an affront to her independence, and she'd ridicule me for it, for feeling as I believed I should feel.

Which is precisely what she did. I explained that I didn't want her to get into trouble, and she laughed. "You're goofy,

Gordo. If you didn't want me to get into trouble, you should've
stayed away from me."

"I don't want you to get into any trouble I can't get you
out of."

"My hero," she said, and then we stood in the fog, our arms
around each other, and listened to the rain falling through the
trees.

THE WOMEN Glenna worked on were in their late teens and
early twenties. She said that they came in flipped out, chat-
tering about having met a guy at a bar or party, and winding
up at his place, smoking a little weed, drinking a little sangria,
you know how it is, don't you? You're making out, and that's
cool. But before you know where your head's at, he's got your
clothes off. It isn't like you planned it or anything, and I guess
everybody does it. Maybe it's a downer, but you're supposed
to do it, aren't you? It's not like we do it because they want us
to. Women can do what they want—not like our moms. Guys
don't have more rights than we do, and besides, they won't kiss
you if you don't fuck them. All through it, though, I'm trying
to remember when I had my last period. Some big turn-on,
hunh? Then after it's over, and he's asking you to swear to God
that this stupid one-night stand was the best sex ever, I'm saying to myself, I need to get on the pill. Fast. But like that was
then and this is now, and I'm late. I don't wanna know if I'm
pregnant, except if I am I don't wanna be, so please, won't you
please help me?

And help them Glenna did. Usually, she said, the girls
weren't pregnant, only freaked about missing their periods,
and Glenna performed four or five endometrial aspirations
a week. Neither of us anticipated that treating these women,

witnessing their terror and listening to their stories, would touch Glenna in ways she found inexpressibly painful, and at first, there was no sign of her distress. Glenna took me to Pearl's in the city for Peking duck when I had a near miss with a short story at *Esquire*—an encouraging note from the editor who rejected the story but asked me to send him another. We went to Shea with Dad and Uncle Jerr and saw Tom Seaver throw eight and a third perfect innings against the Cubs. A single broke it up in the ninth, but the Mets won, drawing to within three games of the first-place Cubbies. We drove out to Manhattan Beach to swim and went to the Wollman Rink in Central Park to hear Van Morrison. Glenna's room wasn't air-conditioned, and many evenings we opened the windows and fired up a joint as we lay on the quilt and listened to music, our skin on fire, and the faint breeze sighing through the screens carrying the happy scent of honeysuckle.

So the summer flew by without a hint of disaster. That is, not until late one Saturday night in early August.

"Can we do something tomorrow?" Glenna asked, sounding as irritated as a bored child.

"There's a demonstration in the Village I could write up for the paper."

"Like wow." Glenna's sarcasm stung me. Ever since coming to night court, Glenna had said that she wanted to join me on another assignment, but we could never arrange our schedules to do it. Last week, Mack Grunch had asked me to cover the Friday opening of Woodstock. The three-day concert would start on August 15, and Glenna was supposed to come upstate with me for the weekend.

"What else you wanna do?"

"The Village is fine," she said, switching off the lamp on the apple crate.

A minute later, her voice cut through the darkness. "The guys don't come with them. They knock them up and send them to us like they're having their teeth cleaned."

"Do they know their girlfriends might be pregnant?"

"They're so fucking insensitive."

I said, "Could the guys get past your security?"

"That's not the point."

"What's the point?"

"I don't know," Glenna said, and I felt her turn over on the mattress, and shortly, much to my relief, she was asleep.

Chapter 21

T HE NEXT DAY Glenna and I took the train into Grand Central and a subway to Greenwich Village. Coming up from the darkness of the station into the hot afternoon light, we were swept along by a wide, ragged column of demonstrators marching to Washington Square. In front, some of the marchers were holding up banners, which seemed to be powering us forward like the sails of an armada, while all along that rambunctious column demonstrators were chanting, "One, two, three, four, we don't want your fucking war."

The neighborhood was predominately working-class Italians, and the men and women sitting on the stoops and the lawn chairs along the sidewalk were eyeing the demonstrators with the same hatred with which the colonists must have eyed the redcoats. Farther up MacDougal Street, under an OPTIMO CIGAR sign outside a candy store, men with the knotted, muscled arms of laborers were cursing at the column, and as Glenna and I went by, the guy with the loudest mouth spit an oyster of phlegm near my sandals.

"Filthy fuckin' queers!" he shouted. "Go back to Saint Mark's Place where ya belong. Look at dis. Ya can't tell de boys from de girls. Hey, honey," he said to Glenna. "Y'ain't gonna have no fun wid your girlfriend there. And you, wid de faggy hair," he yelled at me. "*Vaffanculo!*"

The laughter of the men was fierce, like concrete being sledgehammered to dust, and a stab of fear twisted through me as Glenna said to Loud Mouth, "Stick it."

"Stick it where, honey?" he said.

Glenna said, "Even a cretin like you could figure that out."

The bane of civilian life is that you almost never have an automatic weapon around when you need one, and if Glenna didn't shut up, I was going to be in need. Loud Mouth was leering at Glenna in her skimpy peach sundress, but he was glaring at me, and evidently Glenna didn't comprehend Loud Mouth's perverse brand of chivalry. He'd mess with her, but when he and his buddies got fed up with her ragging, the ambulance crew would be scraping me off the curb.

I grabbed her hand and accelerated up MacDougal, elated to be away from them, but oppressed by the cloud of humiliation scudding along behind me, and angry at Glenna for her contribution to it.

I said, "Were you trying to get me killed?"

"He was an asshole. I probably cleaned out ten of his girlfriends."

Washington Square Park was rocking and rolling like a psychedelic bar mitzvah. People stood on the walls, shouting, giggling, the lovers kissing, as wineskins and joints proceeded down the line. Beyond the stone arch a platform had been set up, and a band was playing, while hippies, hoods, burnouts, bums, druggies, and students gathered around the high, silvery mist of the fountain.

Still irritated at Glenna, I started to say something, but she was staring into the park at a couple of crispy critters, a girl and a boy, stick figures sketched in skin with the death stares of speed freaks. They were holding hands and gazing at an empty bench. Greasy strands of hair dripped from under the bandannas tied on their heads, and their dungaree bells were ragged, their feet caked with grit. I could identify the girl only because a hint of her breasts drooped under her grimy tank top.

"Gordo," Glenna said, her gaze so cold and flat it scared me, "they wanna be like men. That's why they ball for the hell of it. I feel like telling the girls that come in, 'Keep your legs closed. Those fucking bastards don't give a shit about you.'"

"And that women can't be men?"

Studying the emaciated girl and boy who were standing as steadfast as a monument, Glenna snickered. "But they certainly can look alike."

"Maybe they think if they look alike, they won't hate each other so much."

Her voice sharp as a scalpel, she said, "Don't they seem happy?"

"Glenna—"

"Why don't you interview them?" she said coldly.

I watched anger, confusion, and the bitter remnants of Glenna's past assail her face. The vivid colors of her eyes and hair, and the beautiful lines of her features, faded and blurred. Her face became a charcoal sketch, and to see this happen was as disconcerting as seeing darkness come suddenly to a brilliant morning sky.

I said, "No one's been at your clinic because of me."

Nodding, her gaze still fixed on the boy and girl, she replied, "Sorry. You're right. I'll go over by the music. Catch up with me when you're finished. And Robin says she's making dinner for us tonight."

"Ice cream for dinner?"

"Lasagna first."

THANKS TO Loud Mouth and Glenna I had enough to write about, but I thought it would be interesting to ask a cop if any of the locals had ever beaten up on the freaks coming to the park. However, when I located one of New York's finest, I couldn't tell who looked more bored—him or the horse he was sitting on.

All the cop said was "I don't talk to reporters," to which I replied, "Mind if I ask Trigger?" And the cop said, "Okay, but her name's Cocoa. Make sure you spell it right. She's sensitive."

I took off in the direction of the music, shouldering through the noisy mass of people, walking around the crowd by the fountain, and finally breaking into the open.

Past the arch, the band on the platform had launched into a respectable cover of the Rascals' "How Can I Be Sure"—a song full of doubt and anguish, a brooding song about love in a world spinning out of control. I counted eight couples dancing on the grass to the right of the platform, and then I spotted Glenna farther off to the side. She was dancing alone between two cherry trees, and I'd never seen her move with such languorous grace—at least not with her clothes on. She was moving as though the rhythm of the music had somehow gotten inside her and was now trying to get out, shifting her side to side, as if she were being buffeted by waves of summer air.

Gradually, the other couples became aware of Glenna and stopped dancing to watch. I had thought about joining Glenna, but I was spellbound by the sight of her, this supple enchantress, her bare arms and legs, browned from the beach, and the tops of her breasts, visible in the scoop-necked dress, white as cream. My heart pounded as her hands pushed back her long hair, and she shimmied down, then up and down again. Her eyes were shut and aimed toward the rays of light filtering through the leaves of the trees, and a small smile was on her face, a strange smile, as much sadness in it as happiness, and as her hips rotated under the peach cotton in perfect time to the bittersweet melody, I felt frightened and jealous, as if Glenna had betrayed me by making love to the sun and sky—by dancing alone, encased in the music, on that grassy, sunstruck patch of Washington Square, happy all by herself.

The song ended, and Glenna opened her eyes and saw me and the others watching. She glanced away, as if she'd been caught running naked through the park. A few of the onlookers clapped as she walked over to me.

"Done, Gordo?"

"Done," I said.

ROBIN HAD bought a big bottle of Chianti and made a spinach salad dressed with basil vinaigrette to go along with the lasagna. We ate outside in front of the house, under the oak trees, sitting on Adirondack chairs with the plates set on a big weathered-wood spool that had once held Con Ed cable.

"Can I ask both of you a favor?" Robin said.

I wasn't surprised. Robin seldom cooked, and when Glenna had told me she was making dinner, I'd figured she wanted something. But Glenna didn't respond to her question. She had been remote during the meal, hardly touching her food or wine.

"What's up?" I asked.

Robin said, "Can I come to Woodstock with you?"

I was hurt that Glenna didn't immediately tell Robin to forget it and annoyed that she was leaving it to me by sitting there and gazing out at a kayak knifing across the glassy surface of the creek.

Robin said, "I know three's a crowd, but I won't be any trouble. I bought a ticket and really want to go, except I don't have anybody to go with."

Glenna looked at me. "You should take her. I don't think I can make it."

Anger suddenly swelled up in me, and I felt as abandoned as I had watching Glenna dance. Robin must have seen a change in my expression because, acting out of character, she chose to exercise some tact by saying, "I'll get the dessert."

When she had gone into the house, I said to Glenna, "I thought you wanted to go."

"Palmer has all these procedures scheduled for me to do."

"Can't they wait three days? I want you to come. Like you said you would."

Glenna shrugged. "I've got to do them. I've got to get through this."

"Through what? You hate doing it. All it does is piss you off."

"You noticed?" She laughed, a short, unhappy sound.

"You can stop."

Glenna said, "Not till I'm comfortable with it."

"Why?"

"Because I know what I'm doing is right. And I want it to feel right."

"And me going to Woodstock with Robin feels right?"

"I trust you."

"Not Robin?"

"Not Robin," she said. "You."

The kayak had vanished. With the sun going down, the water had darkened to stone gray.

Glenna said, "Please, don't hassle me about it. Let me do what I have to do."

I nodded, then washed my anger down with another glass of Chianti, and Glenna soothed me with an exquisite smile, her eyes a deep shimmering green, like a memory of the ocean in a childhood summer.

Chapter 22

BY ELEVEN O'CLOCK on Friday morning, Robin and I had made it to the parking lot of the Goose Pond Inn in the town of Monroe. We had taken a Short Line bus upstate from Port Authority. Monroe was about fifty miles from the concert site, but in the city the buses heading closer to the festival—Monticello or Bethel—had been backed up. We'd heard on Robin's transistor radio that 175,000 people were already there, and our plan was to hitch from Monroe, but I refused to stick out my thumb because the town cops kept passing by in their patrol cars, glowering at us and giving me the distinct impression that they would enjoy tossing some hippies in their jail.

Robin and I looked qualified. She was decked out like Lady Fidel Castro in a guayabera—a loose, white Cuban-style shirt—olive-drab pants with constellations of red commie stars sewn on the legs, and, to add a dash of capitalist panache, a ribboned straw kettle hat fancied by lady horse lovers from Churchill Downs to Saratoga. I had an army-surplus knapsack on my back and a Baggie of Robin's pot hidden in my right sweat sock, and I wondered if it was legal for a cop to make you remove your shoes and socks like a mother checking if you'd washed your feet.

"We better get the Monticello bus," I said.

As Robin hoisted her backpack, an old black hearse drove up alongside us. An ankh was smeared in psychedelic paint on the hood, and a girl in her teens poked her head out the passenger-seat window.

"You got any dope?" she drawled, her head bobbing as if her neck, decorated with a choker of shark's teeth, did not take orders from her brain. "Get us high, you get a ride to Woodstock."

The rear seat was stacked with crates of record albums, and Robin was barely able to fit in.

"I'm Marty," the girl said, sliding over to make room for me in front. "Martha for short."

She started giggling at her little joke. Robin introduced us, and the driver, a guy no older than Marty, stepped on the gas. He was lanky with wiry bristles jutting from his pointy chin, and over his bare chest he wore a red-white-and-blue-striped vest that matched his pants.

"This is Sam," said Marty.

"Uncle, no doubt," Robin said, and Sam cracked up as if he were listening to Lenny Bruce.

The rain came as we booked west on Route 17. I lit a joint, then passed it. Marty, who was in a doeskin minidress, lifted her legs, planting her bare feet on the seat and giving me a bird's-eye view of her zebra-striped panties.

Sam glanced in the rearview mirror and said to Robin, "What you two plannin' to do at Woodstock?"

"Listen to music," Robin said. "What're you going to do?"

"Nembutals," Sam replied. Then he looked at Marty with her spread knees. "Tell them what you're gonna do, baby."

"Ball a buncha strangers," Marty said.

"She always does," Sam said, his attention coming unglued from the road.

Robin, her voice wobbly with fright, said, "Sam, could you watch—"

"At least give Gordon a blow job," Sam told Marty. "You gotta be polite."

"Maybe," she answered.

"I said do it!" Sam shouted, grasping her nape and forcing her face toward my lap. Marty swung at him, and Sam's other hand slipped off the steering wheel. He slammed on the brakes, the tires sizzling on the wet highway. The hearse spun, and I heard the high-pitched complaint of glass headlights cracking, the dull thud of crunching metal, and my body was jolted by the impact. The hearse had sideswiped a tree along the shoulder and stalled, facing the wrong direction on 17.

"Turn this fucking thing around!" I yelled at Sam.

"Mellow out, man," he said, restarting the engine, hanging a U, and taking off down 17.

I glanced at Robin. Her usual chip-on-the-shoulder toughness was missing. I reached back to squeeze her hand, and she held on for an extra beat before releasing my fingers.

We drove in silence till the rain stopped. Then Sam said to me, "So, you wanna ball my old lady?"

"Not now," I said.

"She ain't good enough for you?" he asked indignantly.

Robin came to the rescue by saying, "He can't with you watching. It's against his religion."

Perking up with boyish curiosity, Sam said, "What religion?"

"He's a mensch," Robin said.

I was glad Robin thought I was a person of noble character, but apparently Sam was not up on his Yiddish because he
asked, "Is that like Hindu or something?"

"Just like," Robin said. "But you eat greasier food."

"You ruin everything," Marty complained. "Nobody wants
me with you around."

"He's a mensch," Sam said. "What can I do?"

"You can down me out," Marty said. "Give me a Nembutal."

"The aspirin bottle in the glove box," he said.

Pouting, Marty took out a pill and swallowed it, then
rested her head back on the seat and nodded off, remaining in
that condition for what was indisputably her finest hour.

CARS AND vans were stuck on the shoulder of Route 17B, their
tires whining in the mud. Thousands of kids had abandoned
their vehicles and were hiking to the festival. Robin and I had
jumped out of the hearse a mile back and climbed a hill above
the traffic jam.

"People are strange," she said.

I agreed, but I understood Sam's hustle. Marty fucks me,
she's a slut, and he's free to chase other chicks or pop his Nembutals in peace.

Was that what Glenna was doing with Robin and me?

"Do you know where we are?" Robin said.

I consulted my Texaco map and told her that we were near
Route 55, about six miles from the party. Exhausted, Robin
sat on the grass, slipped off her backpack, and exhaled sharply.
Sweat was soaking through her guayabera, the damp cotton
sticking to her breasts.

"We've gotta keep going," I said, averting my eyes from her
shirt and picking up her pack. "Let me carry this for you."

"No guy's ever carried anything for me before."

I gave her a hand up. "Guys *have* helped you up before?"

"Mostly down," she quipped.

"Ha-ha," I said, hoping to discourage any more double entendres.

The sun was radiating an unmerciful iron light, and Robin had trouble keeping up, so I slowed to let her walk ahead.

"I got this hat last summer for Chicago," she said on one of our frequent stops for her to rest. Robin had removed the indigo ribbon with white polka dots from the brim of her straw hat, and she was using it to mop the sweat off her forehead. "For the Democratic Convention."

"Isn't it kind of bourgeois for an SDSer?"

"Not if you don't pay for it, Meyers. All you have to do is dress up, go to the concierge at the Plaza, and say you lost your hat. You give him a generic description, with an accent on *straw*. He dials the front desk, and since rich ladies love to shop, they're always losing their shit so they can reshop for it. Nine times outta ten the concierge has a hat for you."

"Wouldn't it be easier to ask your parents for the money?"

"Asking Esther and Phillie for stuff is a drag. They fork it over, but I have to answer a million questions about when I'm planning to get married."

We detoured onto a trail that ran through a forest. The trail was cooler with the shade and went upward between the trees, steadily upward for a few miles, and finally evened off before dropping to a clearing from where we could see rolling, green meadows and flat, yellow fields.

Robin and I were kneeling at a stream replenishing our canteens when we heard music simmering beyond the woods.

"You missed the opening," Robin said. "That's what you had to write about?"

"Don't worry about it."

"I'm wiped. Go on without me. I'll camp here and catch up with you tomorrow."

I was disappointed at missing the kickoff, but I couldn't abandon her. "Smell the smoke, Robin."

She sniffed. "Somebody's doing a joint."

"There're people all around us who didn't make it. I'll interview them."

I took off with my pen and notebook. The freaks scattered around were upbeat and neighborly. The sole unhappy camper was the curly-haired Miss Phyllis Goddard of Pound Ridge, New York, who was clad in what can best be described as a tie-dyed ball gown, complete with a plunging neckline and a bow at the waist. She said, "I promised to call my mother the second I got here, and I can't find a phone. Do you know where there's a phone?"

Pointing toward Route 55, I said, "Saw one at a general store. But that was six or seven miles ago."

"My mother's gonna kill me." My last sight of her was with tears on her face as she stumbled through the woods, tripping over the ruffled lace hem of her gown, and calling out, "Has anyone seen a phone?"

While I was gone, Robin had shampooed her hair and organized a campsite under a stand of pines. Our sleeping bags were spread a few appropriate feet apart, and a fire was going. Her long raven hair hung wet and straight, and she had exchanged her sweat-soaked guayabera for a gray Barnard T-shirt. We smoked a J as I heated Chef Boyardee spaghetti over the fire, and I was so starved from the hiking and the dope that it tasted like the homemade pasta at Grotta Azzurra.

After dinner, Robin mixed Gatorade and vodka in her canteen. "Instant buzz," she said. "But no damage to your electrolytes and no hangover."

It was a decent drink once it deadened your taste buds, and as Robin and I passed the canteen, she said, "Don't you think I'm ironic?"

"I think you're high."

"And ironic. I want to change the world and I can't even lose three pounds. That's ironic."

"Or crazy."

"Crazy I got from Phillie and Esther. Since grammar school, my father's been showing off my report cards to strangers in restaurants. And all my mother cared about were my clothes and my weight. Mainly my weight. Like she was worried that because I wasn't a size six, I'd be mistaken for an elephant and shot for my tusks. Every summer she used to send me to a camp where the daily caloric intake was lower than Auschwitz."

I finished the Gatorade and vodka in the canteen and lit a Marlboro.

Robin said, "My self-pity getting a little thick for you?"

"I prefer you ironic."

"You should talk." Robin reached into her backpack for a box of Entenmann's chocolate-chip cookies. "All you've been doing is moping around trying to figure out why I'm here and Glenna's not."

Robin opened the box, then put it between us, and we attacked the cookies.

"Meyers, you don't get Glenna, do you?"

"She said something like that to me not long ago."

"Well, she's sick in love with you. That's why she's such a pain in the ass."

I felt vaguely unfaithful talking to Robin about Glenna, and yet it was comforting. "Explain."

"Say you have everything. You're smart, gorgeous, guys chase you. Then you fall in love—not the puppified variety. Now you have a lot to lose that you're not in charge of, and so it stops feeling like you have everything."

I flicked my cigarette into the fire, my feelings about Glenna pinwheeling from anger to an unbearable longing for her.

Robin said, "And the reason Glenna's not here is because we were eating lunch at the hospital with Palm, and when Glenna mentioned going to Woodstock with you, Palm told her he needed her at his clinic. I knew Glenna wouldn't come."

"Which is when you bought your ticket?"

"That's my secret. And here's a secret for you. Our first year of med school, Palm tried to put the moves on her."

"And?"

"Don't get jealous, Meyers. Glenna shut him down, but he doesn't want anyone else to have her, and he still tags after her. See, it's not like she ditched you. She does have a bug up her ass about abortion, but it's also that Palm's her souvenir from the days when she had nothing to lose. And everyone keeps souvenirs."

We finished the cookies, and after I tossed the box in the fire, Robin said, "Chicago was shitty."

"Last summer? What made you think of that?"

"Camping. Remembering how angry I was having to go to chubby camp. You."

"Me?"

"You love secrets," she said. "And you keep them."

"Because I don't have too many of my own."

"That's what Glenna said."

"I was kidding, Robin."

"Glenna wasn't. She meant that you go your own way with your life, and you're not ashamed of much. She's my best friend, but I don't tell Miss Universe my secrets. Secrets are things you're ashamed of."

"Like what?"

Robin laughed. "Like when I was thirteen I read the *Communist Manifesto* and masturbated to the portraits of Karl Marx and Friedrich Engels on the cover."

I laughed. "You'll have to do better than that." God, I liked Robin.

"I was ashamed last summer."

"Didn't you threaten one of Mayor Daley's cops with a hypo of LSD?"

"Not that. I was ashamed afterward." The warm blue air had been washed away by the chillier purple of twilight. Robin draped a Barnard sweatshirt over her shoulders and spoke to the fire. "Afterward, after the Democratic Convention, everybody went camping at this state park outside Chicago. At night, we toasted marshmallows, if you can dig that—forty radicals toasting marshmallows. Then some jerk-off launches into a speech about monogamy letting men exploit women, and there's been a shitload of exploitation in SDS, and what were we gonna do?"

"Did you tell him to get real?"

"No. Everybody was wrecked on Lebanese hash, and the guys wanted it to happen. I remember a radio was on. Aretha was singing 'Chain of Fools,' and we're dancing and then we're fucking. I didn't know the one I started with or ended with. But I felt ashamed. Those schmucks could've been humping ground-hog holes for all they cared."

Robin glanced up from the fire. I didn't feel disgusted, only sorry that she'd been hurt. I smiled at her.

"I'm tired," she said, and I learned another secret about her as she traded her olive-drab pants for white long johns; she didn't wear panties; and the momentary sight of her dense triangular mat turned me on.

It was pitch-black when Robin shook me from sleep. She was sitting beside me, giggling. "Listen," she said, and I heard the rhythmic moaning of sex reverberating above the gurgling stream. Robin explained that she'd awakened me because the noise belonged in my article.

"It woke you?" I asked.

"I had a bad dream—that I had breast cancer. It's a med student's dream. I got up to examine myself."

"No cancer?"

"Nope. Here. Feel." I was too surprised to resist as she guided my right hand under her sweatshirt to one of her high, round, incredibly firm breasts. "'Press your fingers in a circular motion around an imaginary clock,'" she recited. "'Begin at noon, then one, two.' That's it. You're feeling for any abnormal thickening. Rigid tissue in the lower curve is normal. Press there, Meyers, there. Go in, to the nipple. Squeeze it between your thumb and index finger. Is there a discharge? No discharge. Keep squeezing it, will you?"

A thickness rose in my throat. Robin didn't have the confidence to kiss me, but she was confident about her knockers, and like a boxer leading with his best punch, she shoved them in my face. I wasn't sure if she had the slightest feeling of affection for me or if she was intent on paying back Glenna for her effortless allure and for all those Friday and Saturday nights that Robin, unlike Glenna, had spent alone. Yet, as we rolled on top of my sleeping bag and I pressed myself against Robin, and she wrestled off her long johns and my Jockey shorts, I couldn't have cared less about her reasons. Her skin was so warm in the nighttime chill, and I listened as the flattering urgency of her sighs and whispers became part of the rustling of the wind in the leaves overhead. Moving my mouth from her breasts, I raised up and looked off in the darkness, where fireflies lit up the woods with flashing yellow lights. Fear gathered in my chest; and I couldn't catch my breath again until Robin's legs came up around me, and I closed my eyes. The ride began, slow at first, as if we were being carried through the dark by the wind, but soon Robin was digging her fingers into my shoulders and bucking with the lust of the desperately lonely, and I rode along with her, pushing and pushing, shocked at how easy it was for my own anger and unbridled need to masquerade as passion, while Robin moaned, "Thankyouthankyouthankyou," as though it were a declaration of undying devotion.

When it was over, I rolled away from her, hopping into my jeans, jamming my feet into my hiking boots. Robin said, "We shouldn't—"

"It's cool," I lied, furious with myself for allowing Glenna to shove me into this trip. "Be back in a minute."

I grabbed a flashlight and went toward the stream. I hadn't thought about Glenna while we'd been going at it, but now I couldn't stop, and I was nauseous. I took a leak, and as I knelt by the stream to rinse off my face, it began to rain. Not the rain you expect in summer, but cold and hard like the fall, and I turned away from the water and threw up thinking about how secrets can't stay hidden forever.

At the campsite, Robin had fastened my poncho between two pines for a roof against the downpour. I thanked her, stepped out of my boots, got into my sleeping bag, and fell asleep with the rain slanting in on me and the taste of vomit in my mouth.

Chapter 23

IN THE MORNING, Robin and I were talking and laughing about Marty and Uncle Sam and eating Ritz crackers with grape jelly and drinking Tang just like the astronauts.

"You rested?" I asked her.

"I'm not tired, but I'm cold and wet. Can we get back to civilization?"

I was all for returning to Spuyten Duyvil. The rain had quit, but the overcast sky promised more, and I was spooked about spending the next two nights with Robin. The problem was that I didn't know if we could make it to the city. As Robin packed up, I ran around interviewing people who had camped near us. A guy who had staggered in after hiking through the night said that the Thruway was closed, and Routes 17 and 17B were clogged with traffic.

I told Robin, and she replied, "We could find a motel."

I let that suggestion sail by, and Robin said, "I know we're splitting. And don't worry. You're safe. No weepy confessions to Glenna. I'm often miserable—never hysterical."

Beneath her reassurance, I detected a note of hurt, and I figured my best move was to ignore it by consulting my map. Our options were limited to roads through Pennsylvania and

New Jersey, so we hiked to Route 55. We stopped at a gas station to use the restrooms and Coke machine, and for thirty bucks I persuaded a tow-truck driver to drop us at the bus station in Shohola, Pennsylvania, where we continued on to Port Jervis and then caught another bus to the terminal in Irvington, New Jersey. It was three o'clock, and there was a four-fifteen bus to Port Authority. Robin saved us seats on a bench while I got in line to buy lemonade and soft pretzels. Robin's parents lived in South Orange, a half-hour ride from Irvington, and when I joined her, she said that she was going to take a taxi to her folks and visit until Sunday.

I said, "Because Esther and Phillie will dig hearing about you camping with the Now Generation?"

"And doing drugs and sleeping in the rain."

Our joking didn't cover up the awkwardness. Robin picked the salt off her pretzel and said, "I thought it would be easier for you. If you went to the house and I didn't."

"Robin—"

"It's all right."

"It isn't all right."

"But it will be," she said with a melancholy smile.

"Friends?" I said, extending my hand, palm out.

"Friends," she said, slapping me five, and then I went to find her a cab.

I WAS shaved and showered and had ordered Chinese food for two when Glenna came in from the abortion clinic.

"Gordo!" she said, hurrying across the kitchen. "You're home!" I stopped unpacking the spareribs from the aluminum-lined sack, and she hugged me. She tried to stand back, but for an instant I was scared to let her see my face, thinking that she would detect my guilt with a single glance, and so I hid from her by pressing her to me and burying my nose in the sweetly scented flow of her hair.

Over dinner, I explained about Robin's exhaustion and the rain, and choosing to do my piece about the people who had missed the concert. If Glenna had the faintest suspicion about Robin and me, she didn't show it.

I was convinced that Robin would find owning up to our adventure as irresistible as a virgin quart of mint chocolate chip, and I believed it would happen soon, since she and Glenna were doing their neurology rotation together. My one hope that Robin would restrain herself was because Glenna seemed to be her only friend, and Robin wouldn't want to lose her.

For the moment, even though Robin appeared to keep our secret, she developed a brazenness around me that I was sure Glenna couldn't help but notice: she popped into the bathroom when I was showering; she traipsed around naked under her robe with the sash untied; and one Sunday, as Glenna and I ate brunch, she marched into the kitchen in jeans and holding a shirt in her hand, poured herself a glass of grapefruit juice, took a seat, and rested her bare breasts on the table.

Glenna's reaction?

She chuckled, saying to Robin, "Show-off," and cut a wedge from her waffle.

I was so anxious about the situation that on a few occasions I nearly confessed. Yet, because I was almost certain that a confession would mean losing Glenna, I copped out in typical writerly fashion by recording my self-loathing in a story entitled "About the Author":

Let's just call it fate, bad luck. Mother was pregnant. The morning sickness came. A doctor prescribed thalidomide. It worked. I am a thalidomide baby.

I am ugly. My arms extend from my shoulders like the flippers on a seal. I am bowlegged, three feet tall, and weigh one hundred pounds. I waddle when I walk.

Father left home immediately after I was born. He did not believe himself capable of siring such a monster. He blamed Mother and the doctor and me.

I attended Brooklyn College, and sophomore year I had a crush on a biology professor who was interested in birth defects. We made love. I felt used. It ended badly.

After graduation, Mother found a husband, and I found a studio apartment in the East Village and began writing a novel. To support myself I worked as an artist's model. Surrealism was popular. I was a natural.

"Is this supposed to be funny?" Glenna asked, reading over my shoulder as I typed.

I turned around in my chair. Glenna was glaring at me, and for one terrible moment I thought Robin had told her.

"Sort of," I said. "The narrator goes to Atlantic City, meets a runner-up in the Miss America Pageant, and they fall in love. A beauty-and-the-beast thing. But the narrator doesn't feel better. He feels uglier."

"Thalidomide's not funny."

"It's a metaphor and—"

"It's not funny, Gordon."

"Got it. Thalidomide's not funny."

Her glare stayed on me for several seconds. Then she went off to bed.

I WAS taking care of business at school to hang on to my deferment, but every now and again I found myself fantasizing about taking off for Vietnam, usually when I got tired of sweating out Robin and her big mouth or hearing another of Glenna's tirades on abortion.

"The guys," she'd say. "They're irresponsible dickheads. But the girls—they whine about being pregnant like it happened to them without their permission. Like it's a curse. Shit, I met patients on my ob-gyn rotation who'd kill to get pregnant."

My fantasies of running off to war were tempered by bouts of common sense, and other moments with Glenna that were so loving I couldn't conceive of life without her. On weekends, we glided through New York on the burnished drift of autumn, with the car horns and policemen's whistles blending like the music of a calliope. I remember the excited hum of the fans at Shea during the fifth game of the World Series as part of this bright October melody. The Mets had come from behind to win the Eastern Division, then captured the pennant by sweeping the Braves in the play-offs, and now led the Baltimore Orioles in the Series three games to one.

Glenna had finagled a day off from the hospital, and we were with my father and uncle in Danzig's box on the first-base line. Dad sat on the aisle, next to Glenna, opening up her program and pointing out the players. I sat next to her, explaining the sacrifice fly, and Uncle Jerr was seated on the other side of me, as far from his brother as possible, because they hadn't spoken, except when forced to at work, since June.

Their fight, according to my mother, started on a Friday evening. My mother and Aunt Lil had met my father and uncle at Grotta Azzurra. *Life* had recently done a cover story on a week's worth of Americans who had died in Vietnam. The black-and-white photos of the 242 dead were arranged like graduation pictures in a macabre yearbook. My uncle had taken the magazine from his briefcase and was doing his shtick about the war's being a sin when my father said, "*Life* should be publishing shots of the bastards we killed." Uncle Jerr said, "You're a lunatic," and my father retorted, "You were born an ignorant pansy, you're gonna die an ignorant pansy." The brothers sprang from their chairs, cursing each other. *The Godfather* was a bestseller that season, so when Uncle Jerr flung the magazine at my dad, who retaliated by flinging a slice of calamari at him, Grotta Azzurra's better-read patrons thought a Mafia hit was imminent and ducked under their tables, until two waiters escorted my father and uncle out to Broome Street.

Their feud lasted till the eighth inning at Shea. With the game tied 3–3, Oriole pitcher Eddie Watt hung a curve, and Ron Swoboda lined the ball to left, knocking in Cleon Jones. By then, my father and uncle had swilled enough beer to be on a first-name basis with the guy selling it, and as if drawn by the same magnet, the brothers turned toward each other and began to laugh, their laughter drowned out by the roar of the fans as Swoboda scored on an error, making it 5–3 Mets. In the top of the ninth, the brothers cheered every pitch thrown by Jerry Koosman. He walked Frank Robinson, but got the cleanup hitter, Boog Powell, to ground into a force. Then Brooks Robinson flew out to right, and Davey Johnson flew out to left.

"They did it! They did it!" my father whooped, and he kissed Glenna on top of her head, then embraced me, and moved on to enfold his brother in a bear hug, the two of them jumping around as if they were amped up on speed and dancing the hora.

In retrospect, I don't want to get sentimental about it, but my father's witnessing the Mets winning the World Series before he died was a lot like God permitting Moses to enter the Promised Land instead of confining him to the bleachers on Mount Nebo.

Letting go of Uncle Jerr, Dad gazed at the fans kicking up a reddish-brown haze of dust as they swarmed over the infield. An immaculate contentment descended on my father's furrowed, handsome face, and he closed his eyes, savoring the victory as a reaffirmation that discipline and commitment pay off, that the son of poor Jewish immigrants can marry his girl, earn the Silver Star fighting Nazis, own a house free and clear, see his children grow, and direct the PR operation of a publicly traded company.

I remember feeling such joy for my father, for the palpable innocence in his gaze as he opened his eyes and contemplated the scoreboard in right-center field, where the miraculous numbers were agleam for the universe to behold, proving that if chronic patsies like the Mets can be redeemed, then redemption for all was just around the bend.

I was calculating the odds on my own salvation when Glenna said, "Unbelievable, isn't it?"

"A million to one," I replied, staring at the scoreboard and inhaling the fading ballpark fragrances of roasted peanuts and spilled beer.

Chapter 24

SNOW FELL ON Thanksgiving. The floodlights above the train-station platform shone dully through the trees, and I sat upstairs in the bay-window seat watching the silvery flakes spinning through the glow of the lights before settling on the tracks.

Biff was on call at Presbyterian, and Glenna had gone to her parents' for dinner with Robin, who had chosen not to join Phillie and Esther for a cruise to the Caribbean. Having no desire to hear Glenna and her mom snipe at each other, or to get blitzed with Dr. Rising in his fallout shelter—a scene I'd endured twice since the Super Bowl—I begged off with the excuse that I had to be with my family at my aunt and uncle's. I had driven out to Jersey, but I didn't stay long, claiming that I had to finish some schoolwork.

Now, I heard a car chugging through the snow on Edsall Avenue and looked out the window. Robin's Volvo skidded down the lane, plowed through a snowbank, and narrowly missed the GTO. I was sitting in the window seat when Glenna came racing up the stairs.

"Enjoy yourself?" I asked her, as she sat beside me, bringing the cold, clean smell of the outdoors with her.

"As much as you'd enjoy a hand job with brass knuckles. Everything tasted like overdone white-meat turkey."

"It is Thanksgiving."

"My mother served roast beef."

"Very avant-garde," I said.

"She claims turkey takes a day to cook, and she's been swamped redecorating the kitchen at the Ethical Culture house."

"She was doing that months ago."

"Next subject," Glenna said, the iciness in her voice a concoction of frustration and remembered rage that she reliably brought back from dinners in Riverdale like leftovers in a doggie bag.

Happily, the next subject involved Glenna's gluing her mouth to mine, and then we did what we usually did after Glenna visited her folks, only now we did it with her maxi coat on.

Later, Glenna fished a pair of gold peace-symbol earrings from her bag, holding them out in her palm for me to inspect and saying, "I bought a present for us yesterday."

"For us?" I said, appalled, being about as inclined to wear an earring as I was to wear high heels. "What's a matter, I'm not sufficiently pussy-whipped I gotta pierce an earlobe and insert one of those?"

Glenna grinned. "No, silly. I'm going to wear them, but they're for you. For luck. On Monday."

"Monday?"

"The draft lottery. You get your number. Did you forget?"

"Not exactly." Truthfully, I'd been more nervous about Robin's telling Glenna about our campout than I was about getting drafted.

Dropping the earrings behind her on the floor, Glenna snuggled next to me, murmuring, "If you forgot, you're *not* sufficiently pussy-whipped," and I could feel her mouth, against my cheek, curve upward in a wicked grin.

ON MONDAY evening, December 1, we were on the couch, and *Here's Lucy* was on the tube. Glenna was wearing her new earrings, and I'd been watching Lucille Ball in the midst of some screwball misadventure, when the CBS Special Report screen appeared, and the announcer said that *Mayberry R.F.D.* would be back next week at its regularly scheduled time, and then I was looking at newsman Roger Mudd, who was covering the lottery from a front-row seat in an auditorium at Selective Service headquarters in Washington.

General Lewis Hershey, the white-haired director of the draft, summoned a congressman, who plucked a capsule from a glass cylinder and passed it, like a priceless gem, to a graying colonel, who broke it open, withdrew a slip of paper, and announced, "September fourteenth," which meant that males born on that date between 1944 and 1950 now had the honor of being drafted first.

A crew-cut, eighteen-year-old four-eyes from Selective Service's Youth Advisory Committee plucked the next capsule, and the colonel said, "April twenty-fourth."

Only the first four numbers were announced before CBS cut to a commercial for Norelco electric razors. I was drinking a can of Dr. Brown's black cherry when Mudd came back on, and the camera zoomed in on the board, where the draft numbers were posted next to the birthdays.

"There you are," Glenna said, and I heard the trembling in her voice.

"Number five," I said.

There was something shocking about a TV image's possessing such power over your life. Television was the kingdom of make-believe, homeland to the likes of Rocky and Bullwinkle. That colonel playing bingo with boys' lives couldn't possibly be real.

The phone rang in the kitchen, and Glenna got up to answer it.

"Gordo," Glenna called out, "it's your mom."

I went to the kitchen and took the phone. "Hi, Ma."

"Gordon . . ." Her hesitation alarmed me. I thought something had happened to my father. "Gordon, have you signed up for your classes next semester?"

So she had been watching the tube, not rushing my father to the hospital. "I haven't finished my exams for this semester."

"Should Dad write you a check?"

"I'm all set, Mom. I'll register for classes in January."

"Honey, if you need a check from Dad, let me know."

We said good night, and I returned to the couch. Glenna looked up at me. Her eyes were wet.

"It'll be all right," I said.

"Drafted is not all right. The war's not some comic-book adventure. You could get killed over there."

"Could also get run over by a cab."

"There's a higher probability in Vietnam."

"Not likely," I said. "There are more cabs in New York."

"Gordon, number five is no joke."

"I still have my Two-S."

Glenna was studying me and smiling her knockout smile, but her look was something else. There was love in her look, though it wasn't the bubblegum variety they sang about on AM radio. This love was laden with doubt and fear.

Glenna said, "At least there's some good news for you."

"What's that?"

"I'm as worried as your mother," she said, and took off her peace-symbol earrings and tossed them on the coffee table.

Chapter 25

Two weeks after the lottery, I stopped by my folks' at noon to grab some winter clothes. Luckily, my mother wasn't home, because there it was, on the floor under the mail slot, an envelope marked SELECTIVE SERVICE SYSTEM: OFFICIAL BUSINESS.

I tore it open and read the letter: *You are hereby directed to present yourself for Armed Forces Physical Examination by reporting at: armed forces examining and entrance station bldg. no. 116, Ft. Hamilton, Bklyn., N.Y.—on December 22, 1969 at 7:00 a.m.*

The letter was undeniably more real than the TV colonel, and I raced out to the GTO, sped to my draft board in downtown Brooklyn, and presented the letter to the kindest-looking person I saw, an elderly lady who bore an uncanny resemblance to Mrs. Santa Claus.

"I have a student deferment," I said. "Can they draft me?"

"Heavens no," she said, studying the letter through a magnifying glass that dangled from her neck on a chain. "This is a common misunderstanding. Your deferment's safe. But now that you youngsters have numbers, the physicals can be conducted in an orderly fashion. Let me get your file."

She disappeared behind a fortress of olive-drab filing cabinets and reappeared with a cardboard file mottled with stains like port-wine birthmarks.

"Excuse the folder," she said. "The protesters came in and poured pig's blood on our records. Let's see. . . . Oh, my. You're missing Form 109."

"Is that bad?"

Smiling at me as though I were a good boy needlessly afraid of finding coal in his stocking, Mrs. Claus said, "It's the form your school files to let us know you're enrolled. The form is in your file for every other semester. I'm sure the missing one was an oversight. It's easily corrected."

Licking her forefinger, she slid Selective Service Form 109 from a stack of papers in a wire basket. "Here. You bring this to your registrar, and he'll take care of it. Don't forget or you'll lose your Two-S."

"Merry Christmas."

"Why, Merry Christmas to you, young man."

I went to Brooklyn College and took my last final, then headed to Spuyten Duyvil, glad that I was done for the semester and that I couldn't get dragged off to war against my will.

I was calm now, and although I didn't want to worry my folks about the physical, I was anxious to tell Glenna.

I didn't get the opportunity. Not that night. Not ever.

"FUCK YOU, Palmer!" Glenna was yelling. "Fuck you where you breathe! You promised we wouldn't!"

They were standing at the bottom of the staircase and must have gotten in a minute ahead of me. Glenna was still in her coat, Biff in his sports jacket and scarf.

Patiently Biff said, "What're you freaking about? It's a straightforward procedure."

"That's a crock of shit and you know it. That woman's what? Nineteen weeks pregnant? We have to induce labor. In thirty percent of induced abortions, there're complications. She could go into shock from the saline injection. She could die from it."

I hooked my peacoat on the Lucite tree. Glenna and Biff and Robin frequently argued about medicine. Who cared?

"She's divorced," Palmer said. "She can't take care of the children she has."

"You promised we wouldn't do abortions after the first trimester. The fetus—"

Coolly Biff said, "The fetus will have no heartbeat."

"You have no fucking heartbeat!" snapped Glenna. "If you do this, I quit!"

Good, I thought. There'll be more of you for me.

Biff wasn't so cool now. He ran his fingers through his thin straw-colored hair. "You wouldn't be upset if—"

"Palmer!"

"You wouldn't," he said. "You know you wouldn't."

"If what?" I said, catching on, anger rising, fear coming along for the ride.

"If nothing," said Glenna.

"You're pregnant?"

"I'm late."

"Five weeks late," Biff said.

"You keep track of her tampons?" I said to him, and lit a Marlboro, exhaling smoke at him.

He stepped back. Then, with the autocratic inflection that is so characteristic of doctors you figure that med schools must give elocution lessons, Biff said, "Glenna's pregnant and ... I ... will ... take ... care ... of ... it."

"Bet you will," I replied, feeling like I was peering backward into my brainpan, watching Roman candles spit and burn. "Be your big chance to get her pants off."

Glenna said, "Gordon, try not to be a dipstick," and stamped up to her room.

I can't describe how intensely I hated Biff just then. Had he proffered one haughty piece of doctorly advice, I would have stubbed out my cigarette between his eyes. I opened the front door and shot the butt into the yard, then closed the door and felt like a nitwit because while I was hating Biff, I knew that it wasn't his fault.

Upstairs, the overhead Japanese lantern was on, the muted colors of the light sparking in the specks of mirror that dappled Glenna's plum-red, embroidered tunic. She was sitting on the bed, her back propped up against the pillows.

I sat across from her. "You tell Biff and not me?"

"I was upset. Palmer asked me what was wrong. He's my friend, and I told him. You make it sound like I was unfaithful to you."

She stared at me, and for one terrifying blink of an eye, I thought Robin must have given her chapter and verse on our trip to Woodstock when they had gone to the Risings for Thanksgiving.

I said, "How could you be pregnant? You were supposed to be taking the pill."

"You think I want to be pregnant?"

"Do you?" I asked, vaguely hoping her answer would be yes. It wasn't.

"Are you high?" she said.

"No, but you musta been. How do you get pregnant if you take the pill?"

"Remember when I told you I was switching my prescription to a lower dosage? Well, I finally did. Two months ago."

"So?" I asked.

"So something went wrong. You need more, Palmer can give you a lecture on ovulation."

"When—"

"How do I know when? You fuck me every day like I'm some broodmare."

This wasn't going as well as I'd hoped. She seemed to be suggesting that I'd knocked her unconscious with a Louisville Slugger and ravished her.

"I'll marry you," I said. Technically, I'd never considered marrying her, and the proposal had seemingly come without my consent. Yet, I had considered losing Glenna, and I couldn't envision going through it.

"Marry me? Where will we live? Who will take care of the ..."

"The baby?"

"Just because you can say the word doesn't mean—"

"I'm serious," I said, reaching for her hand.

"You're serious?" she echoed, pushing my hand away. "You go to school, you don't go to school. You're a reporter, you're not a reporter. You write fiction, you don't write fiction. You're real serious. You're real prepared to be a husband and father."

She was right. I wasn't ready. Which was why I was terrified that she was pregnant. But hearing her honest opinion of me hurt.

"Glenna, don't you love me?"

"Yes, but what's that got to do with this?"

"I don't feel like you do."

"Gordon, I can't help what you can't feel."

We were silent. Then Glenna said, "You know what my mother would think?"

"Since when do you care what she thinks?"

"What I think. What I was raised to think. This could be my child."

"Our child," I corrected her.

She shook her head, unwilling to concede that this was about me, too. I could have the blame for knocking her up, not the credit.

"I take care of those girls at Palmer's clinic. This is different. This is me. This child is mine."

"You mean you'll keep it?" If she did, it might also mean that I'd never lose her, that finally she'd be mine.

"I didn't say that."

"Don't I get a say?" I asked.

"You got your say. That's why I'm—"

"Why you're . . . ?"

"Look, I can't do this now. I have to fly to Palm Beach tomorrow to be with my parents. I'll be back New Year's Day. Can we talk then?"

"Maybe you could skip Florida?"

"I would—believe me. But my father's making a surprise fiftieth birthday party for my mother on New Year's Eve. I have to be there. Can't we talk about it later?"

I wanted to tell her that I loved her, that everything would work out, that I could deal with a baby if I could only have her. "Glenna, I want to talk about it now."

"You want and you want and you want. Maybe it's not your fault. That's what men do. They want. And my tit's run dry. I need to think about this. Leave me alone."

Not bothering to undress, she lay down, turning away from me on her side, and I waited until her breathing had the subdued rhythm of slumber before I stretched out beside her in my clothes and clasped my hands under my head, careful not to bump her, not to rile her again.

Perhaps Glenna would get her period while she was sleeping, and I could have her without changing my life, without the complications. Like survivors of any battle, we could laugh about the scare later, when we were safe, when we had our children. Sure, we could go on and on, I thought, and that's when Glenna sat up, took her plastic packet of birth-control pills from the apple crate, and flung it at the rubber tree across the room.

Then she curled up in a ball and slept, and I spent the night gazing at the ceiling.

Chapter 26

At dawn, with only three shopping days left till Christmas, I got in line with hundreds of other young men and filed through the sleet to take my physical at Fort Hamilton. Soldiers with flashlights herded us through the darkness into a cold, cavernous building, where a bald, baggy-eyed sergeant was sitting at a metal folding table and drinking coffee from a styrofoam cup. In a weary voice, he told us to pick up our questionnaires and pencils, then directed us to the rows of benches.

"I'm burning my draft card!" shouted a tall, skinny kid in a coonskin cap and a bright red nightshirt that hung past his knees like a dress. He was standing in front of the sergeant, right arm extended, pinching a flaming scrap between his thumb and index finger.

A desultory round of applause came from some of the guys on the benches. Destroying a draft card was a federal offense: it could cost you ten grand in fines and five years in prison. But the sergeant just belched and shambled from behind the table with a Tiparillo clamped in his teeth. Seizing the kid's wrist and ducking his head toward the flames, he lit his cigar with the burning card and said, "Numbnuts, that's your driver's license."

Letting go of the charred scrap, the kid bent down to inspect it, then announced with disbelief, "I burnt my license; I can't believe it; I burnt my fucking license."

The sergeant gave the kid his paperwork and shuffled back behind the table.

After finishing my questionnaire, I spent the next few hours waiting in various lines, taking off my clothes and putting them back on, and answering questions, all the while wondering whether Glenna was pregnant with our son or daughter.

Since I had neither a terminal illness, drug habit, nor an unnatural fondness for men or beasts, I passed my physical with flying colors. Brooklyn College was closed until Monday, January 5, so I couldn't submit Form 109 for my deferment to the registrar until then. Still, I wrote my name on the form, signed it, and tucked it into the glove compartment of the GTO.

With Glenna in Palm Beach, Palmer visiting his old college roommate in San Francisco, and Robin at a dude-ranch spa in Arizona with her parents, the house was quiet, and I occupied myself by hunkering down at the typewriter and trying to write about the kid and his driver's license. When Todd called to say that he'd copped us fourth-row seats for Hendrix's late show at the Fillmore, I told him that I was working.

"You're certifiable, Meyers. This is Hendrix."

"Next time."

"Not in this city, man. In two weeks I'm off to Hollywood. Let me know if you wanna come."

I hung up the phone and typed away, but the sentences wouldn't behave. Early on New Year's Eve, I tore another false start out of the Smith-Corona and rode the trains down to the Village.

The Eighth Street Bookshop was closed, but the holly and tinsel and lights were up in the stores. People hurried home from work, kicking up the slush on the sidewalks, eager for the party to begin. Behind plate-glass windows, waiters in black bow ties and starched white aprons were already seating couples at candlelit tables, and whenever anyone tramped in or out of a bar, snatches of conversation, music, and laughter filtered into the street.

Easy Rider was at the Waverly. I was hungry and bought a ticket and a bucket of buttered popcorn. Afterward, on the subway uptown, the movie stayed with me, the images of Fonda and Hopper on their bikes, racing down the open road under an endless sky, and suddenly I felt that I couldn't take any more limbo with Glenna. I should split and it didn't matter where.

There was Vietnam, but I had less drastic choices. Drive to California with Todd or go visit my sister, Elaine, who had relocated from Europe to Boston, where she had a job as a social worker.

My resolve to beat it weakened considerably when I walked into the house and spotted Glenna's leatherette valise under the Lucite coat-tree. Assuming that she'd cut her vacation short to spend New Year's with me, I grabbed her luggage and bounded up the stairs, calling her name.

She was standing by the desk in her terry-cloth robe, depositing a soiled sanitary napkin in the wastebasket. Far out; her period was here. I dropped her bags and noticed that she was bent at the waist, as if she had cramps, and holding on to the desk chair for support as she hobbled around it and lowered herself onto the bay-window seat.

Then I saw the long-stemmed rose lying on top of a stack of books on the desk. The petals were wilted. Cheap rose, sad rose, the consolatory rose that each woman was given after her abortion at the clinic.

"Are you all right?" I said.

"Yes."

"Can I get you something?"

"The ginger ale on the nightstand."

I gave her the bottle of Canada Dry. She drank from it. I sat on the chair, anger saturating my arms and legs like molten lead.

"Biff came home early, too?" I asked.

"He did."

"Where is he?"

She said, "I told him to crash with friends."

"Too bad. I could have used the exercise."

"That's what I thought."

"How'd you get out of your mom's birthday party?"

"My mother found out about it. She hates surprises and got in a big fight with my father. The party was canceled."

Glenna set the bottle by her bare feet and looked at me, her face pale as first frost. "I want to talk to you," she said, a sentence that has probably, in various languages, preceded most every heartbreak since the Stone Age. "I did some thinking in Florida."

"That's a lousy idea," I replied, telling myself that if I cracked wise for another hour and fifty minutes, 1969 would be 1970, and a whole new decade might furnish her with a rationale to reconsider.

"I'm not—" Glenna said, and then she stopped.

I could live with that. Silence. Everything the same. It was the dim light in her eyes that scared me. Like that first day, generally right after Thanksgiving, when you know that the autumn has gone and winter is going to be around for a while.

Glenna said, "I'm not very good at relationships."

"As good as I am."

"Gordo, don't debate with me. Listen to me, okay?"

"Okay."

"It's not only that I'm not good at relationships. It's that I've lost interest in them."

"I don't get it, you 'lost interest.'"

"I don't get it, either," Glenna said. "And maybe *lost interest* is the wrong word."

"Or the wrong two words."

"Don't talk horseshit, Gordon. I get an ear infection from it."

"So explain what you mean."

"I can't connect anymore," she said. "I have no interest in it. Not with anyone."

"Why?"

"I don't know."

"Is there something you're not telling me?" I asked, wondering if Robin had finally told her about our trip.

She shook her head, and I wasn't sure if that made it better or worse. At least if she was dumping me for cheating on her, I'd understand it.

Glenna said, "Don't look at me like that."

"Like what?"

"Like I'm some SHPOS," she said, using an acronym for SubHuman Piece Of Shit, a term that was used to refer to the bums who stumbled into the ER.

"Goddamnit, Glenna, tell me why you're breaking up with me." My anger was no longer leaden; it had sprouted wings and hovered in my chest like a predatory bird.

"I can't. I'm not a writer. I can't use words like you do."

"You make it sound unfair."

"It is. I'm being as honest as I can."

"Honest?" I said, and the bird broke out of my chest. "You wanna be honest? Stop talking about saving Vicky, and tell me how your abortion got you even for your brother, Richard."

"What?"

"Call Richard's mother—what's her name, Felice? And tell her you just did what she should've done."

"Fuck! You!" she screamed.

"Tell her. Tell Richard. Tell your father. Go on. Be honest."

"You believe that, Gordon? You're sick."

"Then tell me why you want me to leave."

"I can't do this anymore. I want it to be over."

"Tell me why. I'll try'n fix it."

"I don't want you to fix it. It's me, Gordon. You can't fix me."

I was aware of what was happening, but it seemed like I was observing a conversation between two people I'd never met.

I said, "Don't you feel anything about the abortion?"

"About what? A cellular mass?"

"Now that it's gone, it's a cellular mass. Before it was *your* child. You said it, Glenna, not me. *Your* child."

There was a sudden intake of breath, as though I'd slapped her.

I said, "You think if you get rid of me, then you'll get rid of this, too? That if I'm not here, you won't have to think about it?"

Glenna was screaming again. "You asshole! Get out! And when you're driving away, tell yourself how nice it is that *you* have nothing to do with how screwed up your life is."

I unplugged my typewriter, snapped the case shut, then began stuffing my clothes, papers, and books into the shopping bags that Glenna kept wadded up in the closet.

As I filled the bags, things stood out in bold relief: the *Re-*

volver album cover on top of the stereo with the pen-and-inks of John, Paul, George, and Ringo; the Indian-print quilt on the bed; the rose on the desk; and the framed Picasso drawing on the wall.

Gazing at the curves of *Femme*, I recalled the inscription Glenna had written on the cardboard backing—her loving assurance that I had nothing to fear because ten years on we would be looking at this picture together.

"Take it," Glenna said, her voice hoarse from screaming.

"I can't."

"Just take it."

I shook my head, and when I put the calfskin case with her house key on the desk, my throat got so tight with sadness I thought I'd choke.

Going up and down the staircase and out the front door to load my belongings in the GTO, I realized that I was done walking across these warped pine boards—done sitting in the living room, done seeing the posters on the white plaster walls, done building fires in the fieldstone fireplace.

Yet, somehow, as I reentered the bedroom again and again, I was convinced that Glenna was going to say, *Don't be goofy, Gordo, don't leave. I love you.*

Instead, she sat staring at me, the muscles twitching around her eyes. She didn't speak until I picked up the last bag.

"I used to think . . ."

Softly I replied, "Think what, Glenna?"

Her voice barely above a whisper, she said, "I used to think the happiest day of my life would be having a baby with you."

She began to cry, a spate of sharp sobs that shook her from head to toe. I felt myself sag, drained from our fighting. I put down the bag and went to her, kneeling in front of the window seat and wrapping my arms around her. She held on to me, sobbing on my shoulder. "I'm sorry," I said, and I could feel Glenna nodding against me, still crying, and I felt as though I could kneel there forever—as long as Glenna let me hold her, as long as I didn't have to lose her. Slowly, her sobbing and quivering subsided. I knew this meant that we were approaching our end, and I held her even tighter, closing my eyes, wishing myself a future with Glenna that I knew we wouldn't have. She pulled back from me, whispering, "Go now," and I got up, and she tilted her head toward me, and a sob caught in my throat when I said, "I don't want to," and she said, "Please, Gordon, please go," and I picked up my bag again, and before leaving I paused in the doorway, watching Glenna wipe the tears from her face with the sleeve of her terry-cloth robe while the moonlight shone through the window behind her.

OUTSIDE, I took several deep breaths of the frosty air and tried to wrap my mind around the fact that I would never return to this place.

Turning around for a last look at the house, I remembered the first evening I'd come to pick up Glenna, a warm September evening so full of promise, and the sense that I'd had as I rapped on the door with the brass knocker that once I went inside, I'd never want to leave.

I didn't want to leave now, though there didn't appear to be any choice. Moving out from under the bare branches of the gnarled oaks, I glanced up at Glenna's window. Her Japanese lantern was still on, and I saw her standing and staring down at me, a silhouette sealed behind glass and backlit by a pastel glow. I started to wave, but before I could get my arm all the way up, the lantern went off and the window was dark.

I stood there, shivering, and it seemed as though all the hours of love and comfort and pleasure that I'd discovered in that room with Glenna were compressed into a single moment, and in the next moment, quick as lightning, I lost them all, and the feeling of loss that raged through me was so excruciating it doubled me over.

It was a minute before the pain receded and I could stand up straight, and then, careful not to slip on the ice, I went down the steep set of stairs, opened the rusty iron gate, and got into my car.

I RANG in 1970 and mapped out my future speeding past the Bridgeport exit on I-95. I made it to my sister's apartment, on the decaying cusp of Roxbury, at 3:00 a.m. I explained what had happened and said that I couldn't deal with Mom and Dad.

Elaine treated me to a charitable dose of sisterly compassion. I hung out with her for three weeks, taking in the sights around Boston and talking nonstop about Glenna.

What I decided *not* to do during those twenty-one days was submit Selective Service Form 109 to the Brooklyn College registrar or enroll for the spring semester.

By the time I said good-bye to Elaine, I'd been drafted.

Part V

Present: New York

Chapter 27

"Bliss," GLENNA SAID.

"It was only a club sandwich," I replied.

"Not the sandwich. You and me."

"What'd you mean?"

Looking down at the Rémy Martin in her snifter as if she expected the cognac to start boiling, Glenna said, "After you left New Year's Eve, I began to ache. Every bone in my body hurt. Even my elbows. I was scared about developing an infection. I took my temperature every fifteen minutes. I thought something had gone wrong with—"

Glenna put the snifter on the plate with the remains of our sandwich.

"My temp didn't spike," she said. "But the aching went on. It lasted for weeks, and I went to see a doc at the student health service. An older woman. She's peering at me over her bifocals and asking me about myself. I tell her I'm a fourth-year, I recently broke up with my boyfriend, blah-blah-blah. She examines me, and I'm starring in the usual med-student horror show, convinced that I'm about to be diagnosed with Hodgkin's, leukemia, or cancer—either osteosarcoma or multiple myeloma—I know I've got one of them. Then the doc says I'm fine, and I burst into tears. She pats my hand, and I ask her when the aching will stop. She says, 'Why, dear girl, you'll have to wait till you fall in love again.'"

The pair of twentysomethings who had been drinking at the bar went out the front door, letting in a wintry gust of air. In their stocking caps and overcoats, I couldn't tell which one had reminded me of Alex.

Glenna said, "I fell in love again and the aching disappeared. But there was no bliss. Not like with us. And I don't know why."

I was overwhelmed by Glenna's confession, yet indignant with her for making it. Why tell me now? What purpose did it serve? I wanted to scream at her, and I wanted to lean through the muted gold light and kiss every inch of her face.

I said, "I never trusted enough to feel that way about anyone else."

Glenna winced, as if I'd pinched her. "It's my fault—"

"I'm not blaming you. It's the feeling I didn't trust—that deep sudden connection, that—"

"Chemistry?" she said, tossing her silver-threaded brown hair back from her shoulders.

"Chemistry makes it sound like it's only sexual attraction."

"You weren't—"

"Of course I was. But if that's all it was, it would've burned out in a month. My connection to you came out of nowhere. As if you stepped out of one of my dreams. It was magic for me the moment we met at Presbyterian, and a lot of the magic was that I felt so safe with you—so sure that the closeness would go on and on. When it ended, I figured I was crazy to believe it had ever existed in the first place. I was like a priest losing his faith."

Glenna grinned. "So you're a priest now?"

"You get my drift."

"Trying to." She gave me a piercing look—her doctor's look, contemplating symptoms and treatments. "How would we have worked, Gordon?"

"Can't say."

"We wouldn't have."

I shrugged.

"I broke up with you, and I was miserable. That doesn't mean I made the wrong decision. Neither one of us was— what, mature enough?—to really be in love. The right decision doesn't always feel good."

"Glenna," I said, then drank the rest of my martini. It was my third, and on top of the vodka I'd downed at the hotel, it transformed Lally's Tavern into a revolving restaurant. "Glenna, it hurt so much for me to lose you—guess what? I never did. Somewhere inside me, I just held on."

I longed to hear the same thing from her. I didn't. She nodded sympathetically. "Is that what you came to tell me?"

I looked over at the gas flames in the fireplace, and a familiar panic crept over me, with a fury hiding beneath it, like a snake coiled under a rock.

Glenna said, "Every once in a while it crossed my mind to get in touch with you. Eight months ago, I got your address and phone number on AnyWho dot-com."

"Why didn't you get in touch?"

"Because most normal people wouldn't."

"That must be one of those left-handed compliments."

"I'm not upset you did. But it is kind of nuts—maybe more than kind of. You can't go backward. I'm sure you know that. So why did you show up at my office?"

"I'm nuttier than you?"

"Obviously," Glenna said, laughing, and I marveled at her ability to mix so much gaiety and poignance in a single sound. "If you tell me, Gordon, I'll let you see where I live. Where are you staying?"

"The Hyatt."

"I catch my train at Grand Central. It's a twenty-minute train ride to my place. You can catch a train back. They run late, and you'll be right next to your hotel."

"You don't live in the city?"

"I did. On the Upper West Side with my husband. The apartment was sold a year ago. David was living there when I met him. I had lifetime tenantship, but David willed the proceeds from the sale to his sons, and I knew his boys could use the money. So I moved. Do we have a deal?"

"I have to go to the men's room," I said, and stood, holding on to the lip of the table until I was confident that the martinis hadn't rubberized my legs.

I stood at the urinal, wondering why I didn't lay out the facts for Glenna and wait for her response. I told myself that it was because I couldn't predict how she would respond.

What's the real reason, Dad? I imagined Alex saying.

I smiled, imagining the sound of my son's voice, so full of impatience for any shade of gray.

Maybe there's more than one, kiddo.

You're in Dorkville again. She'll understand.

How could she? I wondered, since I could barely understand it myself.

I want you to, Dad. I want you to tell her. Please. It's not your fault. Tell her what happened.

I could do that, just blurt out the facts. But once I was done with the story I would have to return Glenna to her future, and I dreaded saying good-bye to her again.

Since Alex didn't offer any solutions to that little problem, I washed and dried my hands, checked my voice mail even though the icon reported no messages, and went back to the table.

Glenna was gone, and I panicked until I saw her coat draped over a chair. She came out of the ladies' room and put on her coat before I could come around to help her with it. She slung her leather briefcase over her shoulder and followed me through the arched doorway. No one was at the horseshoe bar. The bartender stopped watching the flat-screen, tore our check off a pad, and gave it to me.

"Split it?" Glenna said.

"I've got it," I said, giving the bartender a $100 bill. "You paid the last time, remember? At the Fickle Fox."

Glenna frowned. "You said you were done."

"I had a relapse."

Her frown curved upward until it was almost a grin.

As the bartender got my change from the register, Glenna and I glanced up at the TV. MSNBC was running the footage of the marine convoy that had been hit in Afghanistan. The talking head announced that three marines had died in the attack and ten had been wounded.

Glenna said, "The news was awful when we were young, and it's no better now."

"My opinion, it's worse."

"How come?"

"There's a lot more of it," I said.

*   *   *

THE SNOW had let up, but the streets were deserted as we walked toward the rainbow blaze of lights in Times Square. The wind had blown the snow across the sidewalks, and we had to high-step through the drifting powder.

As we crossed Broadway and headed to Grand Central, Glenna said, "Be easier if we had snowshoes."

I was too winded to answer and watched the huffs and puffs of my breath smoke in the cold. I wished Glenna would take my arm, but she kept walking ahead of me and climbing over the hard mounds of snow the plows had packed in along the curb.

"Glenna, if I keel over, you'll know what to do?"

"Call 911."

"Nice," I said.

"Hey, I'm a pediatrician, not a cardiologist."

"I guess 911 would be better than you telling me to take two aspirin and call you in the morning."

"Aspirin would be good," she said. "Prevents blood clots."

"I knew that."

"And think of the money you saved not going to med school."

At the corner of Forty-Fourth and Fifth, Glenna was walking over a snowbank when she suddenly sank to her thighs. She tried to climb out by herself, but it was like being stuck in quicksand.

"Need some help?" I asked, my grin stretching ear to ear.

"Don't you dare make fun of me, Gordon. Be a gentleman and help me out of here."

"I have a medical question."

She arched her eyebrows, and I recalled that look, equal parts annoyance and amusement. I wanted to laugh; I wanted to jump into the snow with her.

"What's your question, Gordon?"

"Well, ever since I turned fifty, whenever I see a doctor, he wants to stick his hand up my ass."

"Terrible, isn't it? Now help me up."

"Seriously," I said, taking her gloved hands in both of mine. "I tell the guy I've got a backache; he says, 'Oh, let me check your prostate.' I tell him my knees hurt; he says, 'Gee, bend over.' Why is that?"

"We like a patient to get his money's worth."

I tugged her up out of the snowbank. After Glenna brushed off her coat and dug the snow out from the top of her boots, I offered her my arm.

Glenna said, "You'll tell me why you're here, right?"

I brought up a vague imitation of a smile, and she hesitated, studying me, then threaded her arm through mine.

Part VI

Past

Chapter 28

BY JUNE, I had completed basic and advanced infantry training and flew to New York from Fort Jackson, South Carolina. My most vivid memories of those ten days in Brooklyn before leaving for Vietnam were my father's interminable advice on how to stay alive, my mother's ferocious silence, and my struggling against my impulse to call Glenna. I had written her a letter from South Carolina, explaining where I was, and I had received a postcard in return. It said:

> *Please take care of yourself.*
> *Glenna*

I spent ten months in I Corps, the northernmost military region in South Vietnam. I was assigned to the provisional recon element of the Red Devil Brigade, and we were tasked with peeking around the uglier corners of Quang Tri Province, 2,000 square miles of jungles, mountains, and deep-serious trouble. My first week in-country I wrote Glenna another letter, but I never received a reply.

I rotated back to the World with plenty of stories to tell. Those first couple of years I was back, you may have heard some of them if you met me in an airport bar. You might have heard what it was like lying along a spur of the Ho Chi Minh Trail, setting ambushes, calling in artillery fire or air strikes on convoys, and running search-and-rescue missions to recover downed pilots.

What you would not have heard about was my wrestling with the greatest irony of all: I went off to war and it was my father who died—died right in our backyard, sitting at the redwood table with Uncle Jerr, Aunt Lil, and my mother, who held his hand until the ambulance came, too late as it turned out, to do anything for his overworked heart.

I was granted an emergency leave to attend the funeral, and my commanding officer, a lifer who had done three tours of the Nam, used his contacts to arrange an early-out discharge for me at Fort Hamilton. I had kept a journal over there, and I was considering turning it into a book when my former CO phoned. He was retiring and planned to set up a consulting firm in DC. He had been a fan of my after-action reports and asked if I'd like to work with him.

Truthfully, I had no desire to relive my war in prose, so I moved to Washington. Over the next two years, I often thought about Glenna, but couldn't see any reason to get in touch with her. Washington is a lonely town because it is loaded with transients, which also makes it perfect for the hit-and-run relationship, and I had as many of those as possible between cab rides to and from the airport.

Our business took off. I bought a town house in George-town and made a hobby of trying to quit smoking. My aunt and uncle sold their place in Jersey and rented an apartment in Manhattan, and my mother followed suit, taking a two-bedroom on East Thirty-Fifth Street. My sister, Elaine, came from Boston to lend a hand with the move, and I took the train up the next week to help my mother settle in. We spent the day unpacking boxes, and it was after five when we went to sit on her small terrace. I was drinking Michelob out of the bottle and wishing I had a cigarette, while my mother kept glancing nervously at her watch.

"Mom, you got an appointment?"

"I may have made a mistake."

"What happened?" I asked.

"The day before I left Brooklyn, the phone—"

"The phone what, Ma?"

"The phone rings."

"The phone rings and?"

"And it was Glenna."

I was excited at first and then incensed at Glenna for calling. "What did she want?"

My mother shrugged. "Who knows? We only talked a little. I told her you'd be here today and gave her my address and my number. She said she'd call around five."

"Ma, you didn't even like her."

"I never said I didn't like Glenna. I said she—forget what I said. You've been—I don't know, you've been so sad."

The phone started ringing inside the apartment.

"Go on," my mother said. "You'll never know if you don't answer it."

I went in and picked up.

"Gordon? How are you?"

I hadn't heard Glenna's voice in more than three years, but the soothing familiarity of it made it seem as if we had spoken yesterday. I wanted to hang up while simultaneously wanting to slip through the wires and wrap her in my arms.

I said hello, and she said, "Sorry about your dad. He was so nice to me."

"Like his son, Glenna, he was a sucker for a pretty face."

I heard her breathing into the phone, a fragile, windy sound, like her breathing on the nights after we'd made love. That memory made me feel as if I were choking.

I said, "How come you're calling? You okay?"

"More or less. Can we get together?"

I kidded myself that I'd say no, even pursed the word on my lips. I couldn't say it, though, and I was exasperated at myself for my weakness. "Where are you?"

"I'm in a deli a couple blocks from your mom's."

"I'll meet you in the lobby in fifteen minutes."

I got out my toilet kit, brushed my teeth, shaved, and splashed on some Old Spice. I don't know precisely what I'd been searching for since returning to the World, but when I glanced in the mirror, my face had the tense expression of someone who was growing weary of the search.

My mother was waiting for me when I left the bathroom. I put on my olive-drab field jacket and said, "You going to warn me about Glenna again?"

"Sometimes people will surprise you," she replied.

"Pleasantly or unpleasantly?"

"That's the surprise. Have fun."

Chapter 29

As I STEPPED off the elevator, Glenna said, "You're home."

My heart was racing, and I was scared to touch her, but she was in my arms before I knew it.

"You're taller," I said, releasing her.

Her flowing lilac skirt was printed with pink dogwood blossoms, and she raised the hem, performing an impish tap dance in her cork-heeled platform clogs. Then she said, "You hungry?"

"Weren't you in a deli?"

"I couldn't decide what to order."

"Nothing changes," I said, gratified by her consistency.

"Not true. I used to be able to order by myself."

Looking at Glenna, I felt happy and confused, and I had so many questions for her I didn't know where to begin. "What's going on with you?"

"Long story," she said. "Can we go?"

On Lexington Avenue, people were gliding through the warm, windy evening, rushing to go home or out for a night on the town.

Glenna said, "Let's eat at the Fickle Fox, East. It's on Twenty-Third. A friend owns it. Roland."

"Roland?" I echoed, wishing she'd said Suzy or Jane.

As I hailed a cab, Glenna unbuttoned her pink cardigan. She was wearing a lilac tube top underneath, and her midriff was still as sleek as a stripper's.

"The taxi," she said, grinning. "You can look later." Mercifully she added, "Roland's not what you think."

In the cab, Glenna told me that the Fickle Fox, East, was named after a popular hangout in San Francisco, which meant nothing to me until we entered the restaurant with its baroque wine-and-gold floral carpet and drapes, gilt-edged mirrors, and a mural of a bedroom-eyed Oscar Wilde standing in a fur-collared overcoat and holding out a pearl-handled walking stick as if he were about to part the Red Sea. At the tables, nattily dressed older men were sampling food from each other's plate and toasting friends as though they were at the nightly feeding of a fraternity.

"Glenna, what's this?"

"A wrinkle restaurant."

"A wrinkle restaurant?"

"An eating establishment for aging homosexuals," she said just as a slim young man, with a frothy copper shag and an armful of menu boards, hurried toward us.

"Glenna! Oh, Glenna!" he called. "You're here!"

"Roland!" Glenna said. "The restaurant is incredible!"

He bussed her like a Frenchman. "Everyone loves the Wilde," he said, leading us between the tables. "I was in the gallery to see Hildegard about another mural, but she's such a queen bitch about money. Glenna, you must speak with her."

The booth was in a secluded corner, and I guessed that this was where Roland hid the heterosexuals. He handed us menus. "All right, children, what would we like to drink?"

"To Hell with Swords and Garter," said Glenna.

"What's that?" I asked, irritated that she hadn't requested her standard gin and tonic.

Roland replied, "It's her usual: scotch, vermouth, and pineapple juice. Care to try one?"

"I'll pass," I said, reluctant to sample a drink that sounded like a line from the Prince Valiant comic strip. I was also put out that Roland knew something of Glenna I didn't and annoyed at myself for being so childish. I asked for a Jack Daniel's on the rocks, and as Roland took off, he said, "Don't forget, Glenna. You speak to Hildegard."

"Hildegard?" I said.

"Hildi's my roommate and owns the gallery where I work. She's from Switzerland."

"You work in an art gallery?" I asked, stunned, recalling how driven Glenna had been in med school. "You're not a doctor?"

"Technically, I am," she said, poring over her menu as if attempting to decipher Sanskrit. "I graduated P and S in May while you were at that fort."

Roland brought the drinks. "Decided yet, children?"

I smiled. There was one thing he didn't know about Glenna: he hadn't given her an hour to make up her mind. Flustered, she thrust the menu at Roland. "You choose."

"The chicken-and-cashew quiche. It's to die for."

I ordered scallops, and when Roland had gone, Glenna said, "After graduation, Robin and I drove cross-country with Palmer. We crashed with Elliot Mintz, Palmer's pal from Columbia undergrad. Elliot has this rambling Victorian in the Haight and owns a big chain of health-food stores. That's when I met Roland. Before buying this place, he managed the Fickle Fox in San Francisco."

"Why didn't you do your internship and residency?"

"One afternoon, Robin and I took the ferry to Sausalito. The town knocked me out. The hilly, crooked streets. The fog rolling off the bay. And we went into an art gallery and met the owner, Hildegard. There was a HELP WANTED sign in the window. As a goof, I spent some of my vacation working at the shop. I felt so good, so relaxed—*not* being at the hospital, *not* listening to the girls at Palmer's clinic. The morning before we were supposed to go home, I told Robin and Palmer I was staying in Sausalito. They freaked. You would've thought they'd paid my med-school tuition."

Roland served our meal. I was starved and forked the plump sea scallops from the pewter plate, mopping up the lemon juice and melted butter with a hot sourdough roll.

"I called my folks," Glenna said, sampling her quiche. "They freaked, too. But they *had* paid some of my tuition, and I had all these loans, so I got on a plane and started my internship at Presbyterian. The legislature had legalized abortion in the spring, so I was happy to be done with the clinic, but I couldn't stand being at the hospital and didn't make it through July. I was in the cafeteria, facing a shelf of rice pudding, and I walked out. I couldn't even remember why I wanted to be a doctor. I moved to Sausalito and worked with Hildi till this January, when she decided to open a gallery in SoHo. I came back to work with her. Robin and Palmer said I was crazy. You wouldn't believe Robin. She looks great. She kicked her ice cream habit, made it to a size six, burned her overalls, and won't wear anything she doesn't see in *Vogue*."

I was astonished that the subject of Robin still made me nervous and studied Glenna over the rim of my glass, trying to determine if she knew about Robin and me. I finished my drink and concluded that, against the longest of odds, Robin had kept our secret.

"How'd that happen?" I asked.

"She fell in love with Palmer's friend Elliot Mintz. He'd been in SDS back in New York, but he's now the organic-food king of the West Coast. He turned Robin onto a macrobiotic diet and got her into hiking and kayaking. They got married when Robin finished her internship at Columbia. She's doing a dermatology residency at UC in San Francisco. You should've seen the wedding Esther and Phillie threw them at the Plaza. I was the maid of honor. After the ceremony, Robin said to me, 'You're always a bridesmaid, never a bride.'"

"She showed you."

"Maybe she did," Glenna said.

"Where's Biff?"

"Palmer joined a practice on Seventieth and Park."

"So he's doing classy abortions."

Glenna sliced her quiche with deliberate strokes, as if she were limbering up to sever my vocal cords. "You didn't want a child. All you wanted was to tie me up and tie me down."

There was more than a little truth in her claim, and I was glad that she changed the subject and asked me about my life. I told her about the war, nothing heavy, describing it as a bad movie with no plot.

"You going to write about it?" she asked.

"Not now. A guy I served with, we've got this company in Washington, and we have a contract with the Defense Department. We're going to Germany, France, Italy, and Spain next month to observe some military exercises."

"Are you in love?"

I shook my head. "You?"

"No."

"Is that good for me or bad?"

She laughed that dusky laugh I'd have been better off not remembering, and a rush of excitement and fear shot through me.

Roland dropped off the check. Glenna and I reached for it. She got there first.

"My treat," Glenna said.

Given her history of offering to pay and then not having any money, I was surprised when Glenna came up with the cash.

"The new and improved me," she said, and I can still remember how desperately I wanted that to be true.

Chapter 30

GLENNA AND I strolled arm in arm past the Flatiron Building as an April breeze rustled in the trees of Madison Square Park. Her hair was grazing my shoulder, and a whiff of her perfume, keen as ripe berries, went riding off into the starless night. Under the glittering lights, we strolled in unison, a lover's stroll, our private rhythm.

"You'll come up and see my place?" she asked as we turned onto Seventh Avenue and passed under the globe lamps outside a police station.

"Sure."

Her place was in a row of five-story brownstones. In the vestibule, a brass chandelier cast a musty light on the gray-veined marble floor, and I trailed Glenna up a staircase, captivated by the bouncy ellipses of flesh under her skirt.

"Race ya," Glenna shouted gleefully, breaking for the fourth landing, a rerun of our old game.

She got to the door first, with me right behind her, and she unlocked it, and we stumbled into her living room, laughing. The apartment was so stylishly spick-and-span, so unlike her house in Spuyten Duyvil, I couldn't believe that she lived here. Bulbs in polished brass sconces burned on both sides of a window. The freshly painted white walls were decorated with posters in chrome frames, and a tawny shag rug was centered perfectly on the dark hardwood floor. In front of a sofa covered in tweedy earth tones was a low table of varnished driftwood and a semicircle of vanilla-and-chocolate beanbag chairs.

"Hildi's a neat freak," Glenna said, and shrugged awkwardly, as though apologizing for no longer residing in a labyrinth of withered plants, dirty laundry, and junkyard furniture.

Stepping from her clogs, she tossed her cardigan on the sofa. The soft, rounded contours of her breasts were outlined against the snug lilac tube top. To my right, I noticed a hallway that presumably led to the bedrooms.

"Do I get the grand tour?" I asked.

"Drink?" she said, going into the kitchen, which was separated from the living room by a butcher-block counter and stools.

"Any kind of bourbon," I said, tailing her. Skillets, cooking utensils, a spice rack, and a wok were fastened to the brick wall. Weird. Glenna had considered cooking an art practiced at McDonald's.

On tiptoes, she searched the skyline of liquor bottles on the refrigerator. Her leg muscles stretched, sinews straining, like in that breathless instant before she came. I retreated to the living room, and Glenna walked out of the kitchen, empty-handed. "No bourbon. I have wine, sherry, scotch, vodka, or gin."

Her face tilted toward me, and I knew she would have let me kiss her. I took a breath and wished I had a cigarette.

"No, that's all right," I said.

"There's a liquor store on Eighth. I'll go in a minute. You'll stay for a while, won't you?"

I unzipped my field jacket, and she sat on the sofa, her hair breaking over her green eyes in a shimmering wave. Like Veronica Lake, my father had said. A knockout.

"Glenna, do you ever wonder—"

"Wondering makes me sad," she said, looking up, and the wave receded over her shoulders.

"In Vietnam, I did a lot of sitting on LPs—"

"LPs?"

"Listening posts. Where you hide and watch. That was my main job. Hiding in the jungle, watching trails. We did it in five-man teams. I was bored and terrified, and I made up this family. You, me, a little boy and girl. Like a TV show. I called it *The Adventures of Us*. I felt better, imagining a family. Then the team would have to make it to an extraction point to get on a helicopter. We were maybe three kilometers from North Vietnam. Ambushes. Mines. You had to be heads-up or you were all done, so I had to stop imagining the family. I hated that. It was like losing you and—"

Massaging the cushion next to her, Glenna said, "Sit with me."

I sat just as footsteps pounded up to the fourth landing. Glenna stiffened; a key jangled in the lock; and in stormed a woman immaculately turned out in a skimpy rawhide jacket, glossy black Qiana shirt, crushed-denim elephant bells, and platform clogs. Her blond hair, as short and tidy as a British schoolboy's, was woven with gray, and her face was an enchanting collection of smooth planes and angles. In more tranquil moments the face would have been pretty, but not now—not with anger sharpening the features like a whetstone.

Glenna stood, and the woman glowered at her, saying, "What is it you are doing?"

Glenna said, "Hildi, you told me you were going to West-port for the weekend."

"I am, but I was late at the gallery and I go to the Fickle Fox and Roland said you were in for dinner with—with him."

It didn't immediately dawn on me what I was witnessing, even when Hildegard began glowering in my direction. Something about her stare was familiar, but I couldn't place it.

"And now, Glenna," Hildegard said, "I feel you take me for the idiot."

"Hildi, I told you this morning; I don't want to do this anymore."

"You tell me? Now I tell you: if you take me for the idiot, you are barking at the wrong tree."

Hildegard drew a pack of Marlboros from her jacket, put a cigarette in her mouth, and lit it with a black Bic lighter. I thought about bumming a smoke from her. Christ, it was even my brand.

"I'm Gordon," I said, standing.

Judging from her scowl, I could forget about the cigarette. But I figured out why her stare was so familiar. It reminded me of Glenna's mother. Her eyes contained the same disappointment and sullenness, the same barely concealed outrage.

"I know who you are very well," exhaled Hildegard. "The question I hope to know is, does my Glenna know *who* she is?"

"Can't we discuss it later?" Glenna said.

"Ach!" Hildegard exclaimed through the tobacco haze. "First, my Glenna is swinging one direction, and next she is swinging another, and she will not discuss her swinging."

I began to feel sick.

"Hildi!" Glenna said.

"I must know what is it you want. Me or this man."

"I'll go by Monday," Glenna said coldly. "You go now."

"I will leave, but you will leave, too. You will not only leave *my* apartment, you will leave *my* gallery and *my* life."

Hildegard left without closing the door. Glenna slammed it for her.

Part of me couldn't believe what I'd witnessed. I needed to see their bedroom, needed to know if I had been so love blind that I hadn't even conceived of the possibility that it was men—and not just me—that Glenna had lost interest in. I moved down the hall and heard her trailing behind me. There was a queen-size brass bed with a burnt-umber coverlet, a brass lamp, and an oak wardrobe, vanity, and stereo cabinet.

"Was Hildegard the first?" I asked, despising myself for caring about her answer.

"That's none of your business."

"Was she?"

"Why do you—"

"Goddamnit! Was she?"

Quietly Glenna said, "First. And only."

"Why didn't you tell me?"

"I did. At dinner. You asked me if I was in love. I said no. And I'm not."

Glenna's eyes were narrowed in concentration, as if she was trying to reach a decision.

I said, "You could've been honest with me."

"Don't you dare mention honesty to me!" she snapped. "Don't you dare!"

"What are you talk—"

"I'm talking about you—you garbage dick—and Robin."

I had always thought that if my screwing Robin had come up, I would be contrite. I wasn't; I was enraged. "Isn't that what you wanted, Glenna? Isn't that why you sent me to Woodstock with her? So I'd fuck her and you could dump me?"

"Is that what you think now?"

I was vibrating with rage and bewildered by my ability to hold on to anger and pain. "You bet."

"And what were you thinking back then? That Robin wouldn't tell me *my* boyfriend made it with her? And that what? I'd stay with you anyway?"

"I didn't think you cared enough for it to bother you."

"That was your problem, wasn't it? And guess when Robin filled me in? At her wedding. Right after the ceremony. Made me buy a ridiculous lime-chiffon, fairy-godmother, maid-of-honor dress and then took me over by an ice statue of David pissing whiskey sours into a punch bowl."

"I'm sorry."

"Sorry about what? That Robin waited so long to tell me?"

"I—"

"You know what she said, Gordon? That she was just bringing some reality to the situation. That I didn't really want to be with you. That it was better if we found out sooner rather than later."

"Was Robin wrong?" I asked.

"I was having a hard time. With our relationship, with Palmer's clinic, with myself. And so you and my friend decide to help me out by—"

"Glenna, I'm—"

"Can we stop talking about it now? Can't it be over with now?"

"We can stop talking about it," I said.

Kneeling down, Glenna took an album from the cubby below the turntable—the Beatles' *Revolver*. Old album. Long-ago album. "Gordo, go get your bourbon. I'll put some music on."

I was a block past the liquor store when I spotted Hildegard at the curb. She was outlined in the aura of a streetlamp and scanning Eighth Avenue for a cab. She must have seen me out of the corner of her eye, for as I approached, she spun around and stepped boldly in front of me, saying, "You must explain why does my Glenna hurt people like this? It is not something I can very much understand."

"Me either. But I don't think she means to."

I had to steady the Bic in her hand for her to fire up a Marlboro. She offered me a cigarette. I could almost feel the soothing blast of the smoke in my lungs, but my willpower held, and I told her that I'd quit.

"This is very smart." She took a deep drag off the Marlboro and exhaled a stream of smoke. "You being so smart. What shall we do about our Glenna?"

"We could have a duel."

"A silliness for men only." Hildegard smiled at me, a pained smile, both hopeful and resigned.

Earlier that evening, as I rode the elevator down to meet Glenna, I'd thought of nothing but holding her again. Now, with her waiting for me in her apartment, ready to climb into bed, all I could think about was how much I wanted her to love me, not for a night but forever. That wasn't going to happen. Not now. Not ever.

I said, "Go home, Hildi. Maybe things'll work out."

"Maybe," she said, but she didn't sound convinced, and I couldn't blame her.

Hildegard walked away, then she turned and waved, calling out good-bye, and I waved to her and wished her luck and listened to the wooden clip-clop of her clogs receding in the night until all I heard was the hum of the traffic around me.

Part VII

———————

Present: New York

Chapter 31

I HAD THOUGHT GLENNA was kidding right up until the Metro-North train stopped in Spuyten Duyvil.

"You live here?" I asked, after we had stepped out into the glow of the gooseneck lamps on the station platform.

"I do."

We went into the skyway above the tracks, then down the steps and outside, where the snow had started up again and moonlight fell across the black water of the creek like bars of silver.

Glenna said, "Right before I finished med school, the house came on the market, and my dad bought it as an investment. He rented it out and held on to it until he died. I was never wild about the city, and as I got ready to sell the apartment for David's boys, I bought the house from my mother, renovated it, and moved in."

The road had been plowed, and as we went past the parked cars buried in the snow, I said, "Is it weird?"

"Not at all. It's comforting."

"Didn't you just tell me you can't go backward?"

"With people. Not real estate."

The road curved up through the woods. Glenna was

a step ahead of me, and as we passed between patches of moonlight and darkness, it seemed as though we were literally treading through time—from what lay ahead of us to what was gone.

I said, "You never told me how it ended with you and Hildi."

"I suppose I realized that whatever my problems were, I wouldn't fix them by crossing the street. After Hildi came back to the apartment, we talked, and she went to Westport, and I packed up and left. I was at my parents' for a month, which was enough to convince me to find an apartment and start my internship."

Glenna opened the iron gate, but before going up the steps, she said, "There's something I've wanted to say all night."

New pole lights topped with beveled glass had been installed on either side of the gate, and they were bright enough for me to spot the angry tightness in her jaw.

"When I got your letter from Vietnam, I was relieved we'd broken up. I didn't want to live every day being afraid you might die. I didn't want to carry that heaviness in my heart." Glenna paused. "But I—I still loved you. And every Monday, when I was in California, I'd open up the *San Francisco Examiner* and read the names of the boys who were killed that week. I'd get nauseous reading the list, and I'd feel such joy when your name wasn't there. I did that every week for a year."

"Why'd you wait to mention it?"

"Because I thought I'd stop being mad at you for going. But all these years later, I'm still mad about it. I used to think you were paying me back for—for the abortion and for ending our relationship, and then I'd feel guilty, that it was my fault you went."

"There are lots of reasons boys go to war. I was considering it before I met you. You're not responsible."

She nodded.

"Feel better?"

"Not really," she said.

Our breath rose in small, white clouds that evaporated in the snow-swept air. It seemed that one of us should speak, though I hadn't the foggiest notion of what to say. Snowflakes had formed a lacy mantilla on Glenna's hair, and she was as hauntingly beautiful as I remembered, standing there framed by the white light and falling snow. I leaned closer, planning to kiss her, but she abruptly turned away, saying, "Let's go in."

SINCE NEW Year's Eve of 1969, I had revisited this house so often in my dreams that watching Glenna tap her alarm code into the numeric pad behind the door and take off her boots, I had to remind myself that I wasn't sleeping. A sense of unreality came over me, a soporific murkiness that even turned Glenna's hanging our coats in the closet into a barely comprehensible act. Yet, as I put my boots next to hers on the carpet mat, I worried that one wrong move would wake me from my slumber and the dream would slip from my grasp.

"What'd you think?" she asked, going over to a wall switch in the living room and bringing up the lights recessed into the ceiling.

"Terrific."

The fieldstone fireplace had been repointed, and the refinished pine floors gleamed. The shabby furniture had been replaced by two easy chairs with ottomans, a love seat, and a sofa covered in a richly textured, ruddy-brown fabric and complemented by an assortment of needlepoint scatter pillows.

"No black light or posters," I said, glancing at the oil paintings on the walls, an impressionistic seascape with a young woman strolling alone on a beach, and a meadow of wildflowers with a towheaded little girl and boy dashing through it.

Glenna said, "Robin took them when she moved out."

Just her mentioning Robin's name made me uncomfortable, and while she gave me a tour of the renovated dining area and ultramodern kitchen, I avoided her eyes.

On the second floor, Robin's room was now the master suite, and Biff's was a guest room. The third story had been converted into a study and gym with its own bath. The overhead Japanese lantern had been replaced with two rows of track lights, which Glenna switched on with a remote control. To the left of the bay window was a caramel-colored leather couch surrounded by lopsided stacks of books and journals. To the right of the window was a U-shaped desk with a notebook computer and laser printer, which was all I could see of the desktop because it was piled up with mail, magazines, and half-filled bottles of Dasani water. On the far side of the room was a treadmill and Universal gym, both with towels draped over them, and a glass entertainment center with CDs, videos, and DVDs wedged haphazardly into every cubbyhole.

Glenna said, "This is the only spot I don't let my maid service clean."

"You might want to rethink that."

She laughed.

"Is that—" I stepped over to the wall behind the treadmill, too startled to finish my question.

Glenna didn't answer, but she walked over with me and stood in front of *Femme*, the Picasso print she'd bought for me in Albany.

Glenna said, "You wouldn't take it when you left, and I wanted to throw it out. But I'd written that promise on the back, that you, me, and *Femme* would still be together in ten years. And it felt—I don't know—wrong to get rid of it. I stuck it in a box and put it in the basement, and when I came back here, I hung it up because I felt like this was where she belonged."

Sadness welled up in me, and I was afraid if I looked at Glenna, I'd start to cry. I wandered over to the bay window. Snowflakes sparkled as they fell through the icy glitter of the moon.

Gently Glenna said, "Was coming here too hard?"

I shook my head.

"What's bothering you, Gordon?"

"Dylan went electric."

"Like forty years ago," she said.

"It's taking me a while to get over it." I was dizzy and sat on the couch. I said, "I'm glad you kept *Femme*."

"I'm glad I kept her, too."

When the room stopped spinning, I handed my iPhone to Glenna. "That's my son, Alex. I took the picture when we were at a baseball game in August."

"What a good-looking young man." I felt her sit on the other end of the couch. "I see you."

Glenna returned my phone. I placed it on a stack of journals.

"Did I tell you how funny Alex is?"

"You didn't."

"Even as a little boy, he was funny. Once, when Alex was five or six, we were at the Washington Zoo and a deer bolts out of Rock Creek Park and into the lions' area. The cats go after the deer, and Alex says, 'I didn't know the lions get room service.'"

Glenna said, "Sounds like he inherited his father's sense of humor."

"And my curiosity. Right after he came to live with me—he was what, fourteen?—I find him in the basement going through my army trunk, and he pulls out my medals."

"You won medals?"

"The Purple Heart because a sniper nicked my arm. And the Bronze Star."

"What'd you have to do for that?"

"I had to be ignorant. My sergeant was up ahead of me in a field of scrub bamboo, and he starts shouting that he got bit by a snake. So I run out into the field and carry him back so the medic can check him out. It was a dry bite—"

"No venom?"

"No venom. And when our lieutenant catches up with us, he says that another recon team had marked the field as mined, and he writes me up for the medal. Truth is, and I told Alex, I doubt I'd have run out there if I thought my ass would get blown off. But I'm Alex's dad and he figures I'm a hero—especially since he knows a little about the work I was doing. Alex is real smart, and he begins reading about Vietnam and has a million questions. I try to answer them, but I'm nervous, because my dad's Silver Star got me interested in war. Which is why I pushed Alex to go to Berkeley, since from what I heard nearly all the profs and students there hate capitalistic American warmongers, and I'm hoping my boy becomes a commie peace freak."

I went over to the desk, took the Dasani bottle with the most water in it, and sat down again. I still couldn't look at

Glenna. After taking a drink, I said, "Alex graduated with a double major—in computer science and Middle Eastern studies. As a kid, he was into computers, and the summer he was in ninth grade, I took him to Israel, Jordan, and Egypt, and he loved it. Junior year of college he studied in Jerusalem and Cairo, and he graduated Berkeley fluent in Hebrew and Arabic. And he comes out after 9/11, patriotism's in the air, we're in Afghanistan and Iraq, and Alex informs me he's enlisting in the army. Wants to be a Ranger. Scared me shitless."

"God, what'd you do?"

"Convinced him with his degree and language skills he'd make a bigger contribution as an intelligence analyst. I had some contacts, and I promised Alex—if he let me help him get a job—to buy him a Mazda RX-8."

"Did the bribe do the trick?"

"Bribery is the parental ace in the hole. Alex got a sports car, his own apartment, a girlfriend, and a job he liked at the National Security Agency."

I put the bottle of water on the floor. "Ten days ago, my phone rings, and it's my ex. Beth says that Alex and his girlfriend—her name's Julie—were supposed to come for dinner, but Julie just called—in tears—saying that Alex had gone off to Baghdad. Beth starts shouting at me, asking how I could be fucking stupid enough to let Alex go to Iraq. It's the first I knew of it. I knew Alex and Julie had been fighting, but not that he was going anywhere. So I calm Beth down, and I check with a friend over at the NSA. He asks around and gets back to me. He can't give me the details, but he says Alex is safe, and he'll be flying back to the States on Christmas. I call my ex, tell her Alex is fine, and he'll be home in a week."

I was silent. I wasn't sure how long my silence lasted, but it must have been awhile because when Glenna said, "Gordon?" her tone was laced with fear.

My voice was weak and far away when I said, "The morning after Christmas my NSA friend shows up at my house."

I turned toward Glenna. It was as though I were peering down at her underwater; her image wouldn't hold still.

I could hardly hear myself when I said, "My friend says Alex was with a convoy out along the Saudi-Iraqi border when it was attacked. Every soldier was killed, and Alex and some NSA operative are missing."

Tears hung at the edges of Glenna's eyes. I glanced away and said, "My friend says the guy with Alex is former Special Forces, a good man in a pinch, and maybe they're on the move—escape and evasion it's called. No videos of captured Americans have shown up, and our people are out in force searching for them. But after two days—nothing."

Glenna slid over close to me.

I said, "I drive over to Potomac and tell my ex. Beth starts screaming, 'How could you let this happen? Why did I ever let Alex live with you?' Her husband tries to calm her down—he's a decent, levelheaded guy—but Beth won't stop. And while she's carrying on, I'm thinking she's right: it's my fault. I go home, and I'm sitting around trying to figure out what I did— maybe letting Alex see the medals—I don't know. I was losing it. I get in the car, and on my way to New York I stop at the cemetery in Jersey. I'm standing in the snow, asking my mom and dad and Aunt Lil and Uncle Jerr to find Alex, and I'm thinking that if someone hears me, they'll call the cops and I'll get locked up in a rubber room."

Glenna said, "You can't blame . . . ," but that was all I heard before a familiar tightness in my chest squeezed the air from my lungs, and I sat back, trying to catch my breath and staring up at the track lighting, imagining that moments ago Glenna and I had returned from Little Italy, and I was about to kiss her for the first time.

"Gordon, are you all right?"

"Glenna," I said, and then I said nothing, because I couldn't figure out how to explain myself without coming off like a twenty-four-karat head case.

I was still trying to figure it out when Glenna placed her hand on my forearm and said, "This is me, Gordon. You can tell me. You can tell me anything."

I shifted my gaze from the ceiling to Glenna, and it struck me, as it had so many times before, that I never tired of looking at her, never stopped being overwhelmed by the contours of her face, the high cheekbones, the obvious intelligence in her expression, and how her eyes, when she studied you, appeared to brighten from jade to emerald.

"The reason—the reason I came to New York was that if I could get back into the past with you, I could . . ."

"Could?" she said.

"Could pretend none of this had happened. That everything was in front of me. In front of us. It sounds crazy, but I wanted—for just one night—to believe I was going to have a different future. A future with you. A future where my son wasn't missing in the middle of a goddamn war."

"Not so crazy."

Outside, a train whistle wailed in the distance, and suddenly I was crying. The worst of it wasn't the rapid, deep-lung sobbing that shook me like a seizure, nor the feverish terror that had been searing me from head to toe since Alex went missing, nor the photo album I kept behind my eyes—Alex building a sand castle; Alex learning to ride a bike; Alex in a tux the night of his senior prom. No, as agonizing as these images were, the worst torment was the conviction that I'd failed to do the one thing, above all others, that I was supposed to do—protect my child. And the punishment for this abject failure was to pass most of each day and night suffocated by my guilt.

I was gasping now; my throat burned from crying; and gradually I became aware of inhaling the crisp autumnal smell of apples and that the soothing fragrance was coming from Glenna's hair. She was hugging me, and her hair, still damp from the snow, was rubbing against my face, and her breath was warm in my ear. As desperate to breathe as a drowning animal, I pressed myself against the dips and swells of her body, determined to take whatever air Glenna would relinquish into my constricted lungs, and I kissed her, deeply, greedily, and she kissed me in return, generous Glenna, sharing her cognac-sweetened breath with me.

Yet, for an instant, I wasn't sure if I was kissing Glenna or a recent acquaintance from an airport bar. It was strange and exciting and painfully disappointing, because I desperately wanted it to be Glenna, and I drew back from her and opened my eyes.

"Are you okay?" she asked, and I combed my fingers through her hair and kissed her again, but now it was all achingly familiar—the slow, exploratory softness of her lips, the stirring insistence of her tongue, and the way she scissored her arms around me, holding on as if she might tumble off the couch and go plunging through space.

We fell back on the leather cushions, my hands caressing her as though the memory of her body's tantalizing geography had been stored in my fingertips, and I felt the years fall away. Glenna held up her arms, and after helping her pull off her shirt, I nibbled at her ears, and she tilted her head back, and I kissed the graceful line of her neck and the rise of her collarbone. Her bra fastened in front and I unhooked it, and her breasts were fuller and softer but with no less power to comfort, and my mouth went from one to the other. As her breathing quickened, her hand came down to unbutton her slacks, and she rose up, shimmying out of dove-gray wool and then lacy ecru cotton. She was watching me, and from the look on her face, a rousing blend of hunger and uncertainty, you'd have thought we'd never made love before, and she only closed her eyes when my hand moved lower to touch her. Tenderly, she stroked my head, my shoulders, my chest, and let out a long, shuddering sigh, murmuring my name, her hips rising and falling in time to my touch. I knelt on the floor, thrilled by that downy fragrant shadow, lingering at the center of her until her sighs became a more urgent music, and I stood, peeling off my clothes, and then I was on the couch again, above Glenna, looking at her lovely tear-streaked face and wistful smile.

"I love you," she said, reaching up to guide me, and I assured her that I loved her, too—always had, always will—and when I entered her, a shiver ran the length of our bodies.

"Don't move," she said, pressing up hard against me.

I held on, tumbling backward through my history with Glenna, released from the bleak gravity of now, momentarily weightless and free, riding a wave of pure exhilaration, because joined to Glenna it was so easy to fool the present with the past, to trade my terror for delight.

"Remember?" she whispered as her knees came up, but before I could reply, she began to move with a fierce and deliberate rhythm that was as recognizable to me as the beating of my own heart, and she crooked an arm over my neck and pulled my head down and said breathlessly, "Remember I remember," and so, as we had, long ago, in this room, we comforted each other with the erotic wisdom of our flesh.

Chapter 32

"D**AD!**" **ALEX CALLED** out, waving at me as he hurried through the crowded concourse at Dulles. "Over here, Dad!"

Glenna and I were on the moving sidewalk, but it was too slow, so I got off and dashed toward my son, weaving between the arriving and departing passengers as if I were running back a kickoff. People were staring at me and stepped aside to let me pass, but I almost collided with a young man who walked out of Brooks Brothers. He reminded me of Biff with his candy-striped, button-down shirt and striped tie, and I passed the duty-free shop, a newsstand, and a Starbucks, the line backed up onto the concourse and the air suffused with the aroma of brewing coffee.

I held out my arms, and Alex was a step away from me when I woke up alone on the couch, feeling the joy of the dream draining out of me and the sadness flooding in. Glenna must have covered me with the fleece blanket, and I lay there in the dark, drifting in and out of sleep. I dreamed about summer mornings when I'd awake in this room with the breeze coming through the windows as refreshing as cool silk on my skin, while I listened to the symphony of crickets outside, their steady, peaceful chirping like a metronome keeping time for the world.

The chirping grew louder and louder in my dream, unnerving me enough that I woke up, blinking against the light shining through the bay window and realizing that the chirping was coming from my iPhone.

I snatched the phone off the stack of journals on the floor and read the screen. It was my NSA friend. Sitting up as if I'd mainlined a double espresso, I tapped the ANSWER button and said, "What'd they find?"

"A blood trail."

I felt sick. "Where?"

"Leading out of a cave."

"Were they both hit in the ambush?"

"How the hell—"

"Goddamnit, you—"

"We don't know," he said.

"No bodies?"

"No bodies. There was a bloody pressure bandage in the cave."

"They have a first-aid kit?"

"We're hoping," he said.

"Water?"

"Hoping about water."

"But no water?" I asked.

"You do understand that you're not on the need-to-know list?"

"If—"

"I hear something, I'll get back," he said.

"If it was your boy, I'd—"

"That's why I'm doing it. Gotta go."

I ended the call, threw on my clothes, and cleaned up in the bathroom. It was eight thirty; I needed to catch a train to the city; but I was reluctant to leave and sat in the bay-window seat, watching the band of lead-gray water flow through the cold, white world until I heard Glenna's voice and her footsteps on the stairs. She walked in talking on her cell and wearing a tartan flannel nightgown and sheepskin-lined slides.

"If Rachel's fever's gone already, it wasn't the flu. If her fever comes back, you call me. . . . You're welcome. Bye-bye." Glenna put her phone on the desk. "Hi," she said.

"Good morning."

She sat next to me in the window seat. I wanted to kiss her, but suddenly felt shy about it.

Glenna said, "I tried to get you up to sleep downstairs, but you wouldn't budge."

"Tired."

"Last night . . ." Glenna said, and glanced out the window.

"Yes, it was."

We were quiet.

Glenna looked at me. "I feel terrible about Alex."

"I know you do," I said, deciding that I'd skip updating her. One of her hands was holding mine. I squeezed it and let it go.

"Glenna, I should've told you sooner. I didn't want to burden—"

"It's not a burden, Gordon."

We gazed out at the snow. It was sparkling in the sunlight like ground glass.

Glenna said, "I have orange juice, coffee, bagels, muffins. You hungry?"

"No thanks. I have to check out of the Hyatt and get my car."

"I've been thinking about that."

"Thinking what?"

"I want to meet your sister."

"You do?"

"I do. Take me with you to Boston."

Her request caught me off guard, and before I could answer, she asked, "Elaine won't mind, will she?"

"I think she'd like it."

"How about you?"

The possibility of going off with Glenna seemed more fantasy than reality. But the idea of waiting for word about Alex without her was far too real, and I didn't know if I could stand the emptiness.

I said, "I think I'd like it, too."

"Think?" She punched me lightly on the arm.

"Can you get away?"

"I'm in a network of pediatricians, and we cover for each other. I can take a few days."

"Elaine's husband, Charlie, is a golf junkie, and there's a dinner dance at their country club. Do you have a nice dress?"

"I have a gorgeous dress."

The sun had disappeared, and the sky darkened to a dull steel-blue.

Touching my cheek, Glenna turned my face toward her. "They're going to find Alex."

"Promise?" I laughed at asking such an absurd question.

Glenna didn't laugh or even smile, but put her arms around me, and I held on to her, running my hands over the flannel of her nightgown and burying my face in her hair. We stayed that way, holding each other, until Glenna said, "I've got to get ready. Keep me company."

"Be there in a sec."

She kissed me, scooped up her cell, and went downstairs.

Last evening, when I walked into this house, I had expected to feel haunted, but Glenna was right: it was comforting. I didn't see any ghosts, just the long, jagged arc of my life. I tried to draw strength from that vision, that I had forged ahead following that arc as best I could.

Yet as I sat in the window seat, recalling the hours I'd spent admiring the view, listening for trains, and waiting for Glenna, and now trying to persuade myself that I was simply waiting for Alex, I couldn't muster any strength from my past, because in some dreary recess of my soul I believed that despite our night of passion, I was no closer to holding on to Glenna than I'd been on that afternoon when I'd interviewed her in the cafeteria at Columbia Presbyterian.

I took one last look at the view. Snow was falling, and the flakes vanished into the dark water of Spuyten Duyvil Creek.

Chapter 33

Eᴸᴀɪɴᴇ ᴀɴᴅ ᴄʜᴀʀʟɪᴇ lived in a redbrick, Federal-style house with rolling lawns, a hilly circular drive, and an ornately leaded fanlight over the front door. My brother-in-law, who owned a string of Subway restaurants and Dunkin' Donuts between Boston and the Cape, was at work, but Elaine, after hugging and kissing me and welcoming Glenna as if she were her long-lost college roommate, served us oolong tea and banana bread warm from the oven. Like Glenna, Elaine offered hope for women nearing the outer ring of middle age. Her short, stylishly cut hair was now completely silver, though she was as willowy as she'd been in high school, with legs that would have been at home on a fashion runway, and her voice had the same throaty timbre that used to make my friends blush when Elaine, so benevolent to anyone in her younger brother's orbit, would treat us to ice cream sundaes at Jahn's—our reward, she said, for being the cutest, coolest boys in Brooklyn.

When I'd called my sister to tell her that Glenna was coming, I'd told her that there was no word on Alex, so as we sat in the kitchen I was spared that conversation. Even so, after Elaine suggested that we take a walk to Belmont Center and Glenna went to the guest room to retrieve her sweater, my sister sent a chill down my spine by saying, "My family's your family, Gordie, and we're always here for you." Elaine was a social worker with a busy private practice; like our mother, she rarely spoke to hear herself talk; and her comment, I suspect, was not only meant to be reassuring, but to encourage me to prepare myself for bad news about Alex.

The temperature was in the high thirties and the walk was pleasant, with Elaine and Glenna striding ahead of me, discussing the virtues of spinning classes versus Pilates and the challenges of collecting reimbursements from insurance companies—a task, they agreed, better left to bone-breakers from the Mob. The Christmas lights were still up, and as my sister and Glenna window-shopped, I sat on a bench, fiddling with my iPhone until I got rid of the chirping ringtone that set my teeth on edge.

Elaine and Charlie had two married daughters, who lived nearby, one in Newton, the other in Brookline; and my nieces, their husbands, and their children met us in Boston for seafood at McCormick & Schmick's. My sister's family was a raucous bunch, and the dinner would've been quite a party except that Charlie's light blue eyes were so full of pain. My brother-in-law, a former Boston College point guard, who had retained some of his boyish handsomeness and all of his curly, silver-blond hair, was close to Alex. In one of my son's nascent acts of rebellion, he'd spurned my favorite team, the Knicks, in favor of the Celtics, and because Charlie had season tickets to the Celts and his daughters weren't interested in basketball, I'd send Alex up to Belmont four or five times a year to go to the games with his uncle, a tradition that had been rekindled once Alex had come back East from Berkeley. Charlie didn't mention Alex, but as soon as the maître d' seated us, he draped his arm over me and said, "Elaine's driving home," and then he ordered us the first of too many vodka martinis.

OVER THE next three days, Elaine led us on a forced march through the cultural and historical delights of Boston, with side excursions to fortify ourselves at pubs and chowder houses, and to take advantage of the postholiday sales in stores whose opulence would have shamed the Puritan founders of the city. While shopping on the second afternoon, Glenna and I caught a break. Elaine went into Ralph Lauren with Charlie to look at suits, which gave us a chance to enjoy Newbury Street at a more humane pace.

Glenna said, "I like your sister and her family."

"They're a lot of fun."

Glenna took my arm. "I like this, too. Just being with you. It feels almost normal."

"Normal?"

"Like we're—a couple?"

I smiled at her. She had a point, though I was unclear how I felt about it. I was constantly worried about Alex, but pondering what might lie ahead for Glenna and me was no comfort. Why would it be different this time? Because I had enough money? Because Glenna was a doctor? Because most of the decisions about how to live our lives had already been made? For so long, I was sure that the reason our relationship had ended was a matter of faulty timing—a collision of reality and dreams. I was less sure now and seemed incapable of conjuring up a picture of our future together. All I knew was that even if I didn't lose Alex, I couldn't bear to lose Glenna again.

"Gordie! Glenna!"

We turned around. Elaine was standing outside of Ralph Lauren with Charlie, waving for us to head back down the street.

I said, "My sister's very energetic."

"She's trying to distract you."

"She did the same thing when I came to see her after we broke up. Only now she has more money and refuses to let me pay for dinner."

Our dinners, during these three days, were as arduous as Elaine's version of the Boston Marathon. That evening, we went to L'Espalier, a high-toned French place with authoritative waiters, and a menu and wine list that would have dazzled a finicky dauphin. I ate lemon risotto, sautéed broccoli rabe, roasted duck with orange marmalade, and shared two bottles of pinot noir and a toasted-almond crème brûlée with Glenna. I was drowsy by the end of the meal, wide-awake after Charlie drove us back to Belmont and I climbed into bed.

I was lying on my side, flipping through the pages of a dog-eared copy of *People*, when Glenna came out of the bathroom in a short, white satin nightie.

"Done reading?"

"Yes," I said, admiring how the satin clung to her, dropping the magazine on the floor, and switching off the wall lamp.

She got into the brass four-poster, backing up against me under the covers, and I spooned myself around her, wondering if she was in the mood. The nightie was a positive sign; however, that she was lying perfectly still was not. As I was weighing a variety of approaches, Glenna said, "I've been remembering our first night together."

"What about it?"

"That I had to fight with you to fuck me."

"You had to call me up. That's not a fight."

"Beg you then."

"Beg? Are you nuts?"

Giggling, she began rotating against me. "And now it's this."

"I was scared of you," I said, cupping my palms over her breasts.

"Just because I was pretty. Remember, I told you: you don't see me."

"I saw you. That's why I was scared."

"Are you scared now?" she asked, reaching back to hold my hip as her movements picked up steam.

"This second?"

"This second."

"Not as scared as I used to be."

She giggled some more. "Hooray for progress."

Her hand was on me, and then I was inside her, with Glenna saying, "Hold me tighter, as tight as you can," and I did as we moved together in the dark, round and round, slow and steady, and when it was over, I stayed wrapped around her, happy and at peace.

"Are you awake?" Glenna asked, nudging me with her elbow.

"No, but if you whack me again I will be."

"I've been thinking about hiring an associate."

"Tonight?"

"Not tonight, funnyman. Or maybe I'll take in a partner."

"You have someone in mind?"

"Not yet. But if I had help with my practice, I could go on longer vacations."

"Unh-hunh," I replied.

"I want to travel more. I've been to London for conferences, twice to Geneva, once to Paris. And to the Caribbean. That's about it. Your work took you everywhere."

"Most of those places didn't have clean towels."

"Tell me about one that does."

"The Slovak Republic."

"C'mon, Gordon. Did you have a favorite place?"

"Let me think about it," I said, and recognized, too late, that the subject of this conversation was far different from what it appeared, and that I'd given Glenna the wrong answer.

Sliding away from me without a word, she lay on her stomach and went to sleep.

AT MIDNIGHT, on New Year's Eve, the ballroom of the country club seemed as loud and crowded as Times Square. Balloons dropped from the ceiling; couples with cheeks puffed out like Louis Armstrong in mid-solo were blowing noisemakers; and the band played "Auld Lang Syne" before segueing into a souped-up, earsplitting rendition of "Let's Twist Again." Glenna, recovered from last night's pique, gave me a long, sweet kiss; Charlie, enfolding me in a bear hug, shouted, "This is gonna be a great year. Alex's coming home, and we're gonna make you a Celtics fan"; and Elaine, after kissing her husband, patted my cheek and pulled Glenna onto the dance floor, where both of them, slender and lithesome in their long, shimmery dresses, kicked off their heels and started twisting with the exuberance of two kids on *American Bandstand*.

I watched them dance until the other gyrating couples blocked my view, and then I wandered out to the lounge to escape the noise. I'd been jittery all night, checking my iPhone screen for any signs of voice mails or text messages even though I'd been keeping the phone in my shirt pocket so I could feel it vibrate if anyone tried to contact me. The lounge had three glass walls overlooking the snowy fairways and greens of the golf course, and I stood looking at the snow falling heavy and fast through the wide, bright arc of the outdoor lights, while fear and anger, those birds of a feather, fluttered in my chest.

The band had finished running through a Motown medley when I saw Elaine exit the ballroom. I walked over to her.

Elaine said, "You want to get going?"

"Soon."

"You should bring Glenna to visit again."

"We'll see."

"Listen to your big sister. People change, Gordie."

"You taking bets on that?"

"My work makes me an optimist," she said.

"Mine didn't."

Elaine was eyeing me with the professional gaze I assumed she ordinarily reserved for her clients—curious, compassionate, and all-fucking-knowing.

"I gotta tell ya, Elaine. You and Mom both had a lot of advice for me about Glenna."

"How'd Mom do?"

"A bull's-eye."

"I'm as good a shot as Mom was," Elaine said, planting a kiss on my cheek and heading for the ladies' room.

Glenna was at our table, talking to Charlie. The band broke into "Since I Fell for You," and I asked Glenna to dance.

Charlie said, "Don't forget to bring her back," and I chuckled, promising that I wouldn't forget and thinking that my big sister never missed an angle.

Wedging into an open spot on the floor, I drew Glenna to me, and she rested her head on my shoulder. We were swaying to the mournful notes of the song when I said, "How'd my parents stand it? I was in that jungle for ten months. It must've killed my father."

Glenna moved her head back to look at me. "High blood pressure, heart disease, and cigarettes killed your dad."

"And you're a doctor."

"I'm a doctor. And the doctor says please dance with me."

And so we danced.

With the snow, the fifteen-minute ride to Elaine and Charlie's took over an hour, and after we got home and I was drifting off to sleep, I wished that I could ask my parents to forgive me.

Chapter 34

BY NINE O'CLOCK on New Year's Day, I was driving Glenna to Spuyten Duyvil. Across New England a foot of new snow had fallen overnight, but the roads were clear and the sun was out, enameling the sky to a pale, lustrous blue.

"This is a nice car," Glenna said. "I haven't ridden in an Audi before."

"Alex helped me pick it out. He claimed it would impress girls."

She smiled slyly. "How'd it do?"

"Aren't you impressed?"

"I would be if I didn't miss your GTO."

"Me, too."

For nearly three hours we rode along in a euphoric bubble, as if we had slipped backward through time, a perception heightened by Glenna's tuning in The '60s on satellite radio. Not even the most suspicious, pessimistic observer eavesdropping from the backseat of the Audi would have guessed that my son was missing in Iraq or that Glenna and I had anything before us but a blissful, unbounded future. We talked; we laughed; we stopped at a rest area for cocoa; and Glenna suggested that we take the scenic route through Connecticut, adding twenty or thirty minutes to the trip, and giving us a chance to see the art deco bridges and the slant of the sun on fields of untouched snow.

As we crossed into Westchester, Glenna asked, "Why'd you decide to write again?"

"I'd promised myself to write a novel, and I suppose the promise had no expiration date."

The bubble went pop when Glenna said, "You're welcome to stay with me until Alex comes home. Do some of that writing if you want."

"That's a nice offer."

She said, "And now you've got the end of the story."

"Right."

"Or I could visit you in Washington."

"You said you could only go backward with real estate. Not people."

"Not backward," Glenna replied. "A new beginning."

In my rearview mirror I spotted a New York State trooper, with his lights flashing, gaining on us. I slowed down, and he flew by in the left lane.

"Gordon?"

"Actually, I started writing the book, and I e-mailed the Brooklyn chapters to Todd."

"Todd Elhoff? Your friend who went to Hollywood?"

"He's a producer now, and he loved the chapters. Said he might buy the movie rights from me. And that would help sell the book to a publisher."

"That's promising. Is he serious?"

"Todd's won Emmys and Golden Globes. And he's a big part of those chapters. I'm sure he loves that."

"Knew you could do it."

"You did," I said, recalling the burgundy-leather-topped writing board she'd bought me with the matching leather-bound dictionary and thesaurus. I wondered if she was thinking about those gifts and the encouragement she had given me.

"Gordon, may I ask you a question?"

On the radio, the DJ announced that following the next commercial break, he would play every song on the *Sgt. Pepper's* album without interruption.

"Ask away," I said, looking over at Glenna. She was staring out the passenger-side window, and I regretted that my reply had sounded so flippant.

"Will you—will you ever forgive me?"

I shifted my eyes to the road. "Yes."

"When?"

"I already forgave you."

"Then what is it?"

"I just haven't forgotten how much it hurt to lose you."

I racked up two more miles on the odometer before Glenna said, "I can't change what happened."

She was stating a fact; no reason to debate it.

Her voice cracking along the edges, Glenna said, "Why'd you take me to Boston?"

I shrugged.

"Gordon, please. Tell me. Why did you come back to me? What do you want?"

I knew from her voice that if I looked at her, I'd see her eyes misted up with tears, so I shrugged again and stared at the highway.

Sgt. Pepper's was playing on the radio, and for the rest of the ride neither of us spoke.

*   *   *

EDSALL AVENUE was as narrow as a mountain pass with the snow plowed up on either side, and I was taking the long way around to Glenna's house, through the train-station parking lot, when my iPhone began warbling like a choir of demented songbirds. I parked and took the phone from the cup holder. On the screen I saw a restricted number and felt as if my blood had stopped circulating. I wasn't numb, exactly; more like embalmed.

"Hello."

"Dad? Dad, can you hear me?"

"There's a lag, but I can hear you."

"Dad, I'm all right. Really, Dad. I'm in the hospital—Ibn Sina in Baghdad."

As I was envisioning Alex lying in bed without his legs, he said, "I had some shrapnel in my thigh. A surgeon removed it, and I'm on IV antibiotics. The wound was infected, but I'm fine."

Alex was alive and in one piece. I floated off somewhere. Thank you, God. Wherever You are.

"Dad? Dad, are you there?"

"I'm here, Alex."

"You heard about the ambush?"

"Not the details."

"I don't know how I got out," Alex said, his tone flat, like a hammer tapping tin. "I grabbed some water. The guy I was with grabbed a first-aid kit. We cave-hopped in the hills. Some bedouins came through. I talked to them, and they took us to their camp. A team of army medics was there vaccinating children."

My blood hadn't started moving yet, but I could feel pressure building behind my eyes.

"The ambush, Dad. They hit us with mortars, rocket-propelled grenades, and small arms. I can't stop hearing it. And seeing the bodies. I had to crawl over the bodies to get out of the Humvee."

His tone wasn't as flat now, and I could hear how frightened he'd been, and the hangover of fear.

"Alex, it'll stop."

"Dad, I can't stop seeing—"

His voice broke, and I heard him sob.

"It gets better, Alex. Trust me. You come home, we'll talk."

After a few seconds he regained control of himself. "It'll be at least three days before I get out of here. The infection has to clear up."

"Whatever it takes. I'll be home when you get back. Did you call your mother?"

"Julie did. To tell her I was in the hospital. I'll call her now."

"You and Julie?"

"We're good—I think. And, Dad?"

"Yeah?"

"Dad, I couldn't tell you about my flying over here."

"Don't worry about that, Alex. I love you."

"I love you, too, Dad. I'll call you tomorrow."

After I dropped the phone in the cup holder, Glenna said, "Alex is okay?"

I nodded.

"Elaine asked me to remind you to be in touch when you heard."

I nodded again. While Alex had been missing, I thought that if he turned up safe, I'd feel like popping a cork on a magnum of champagne, but my relief was matched by a gla-

cial fury at my son for scaring me senseless. All the hours of
waiting to learn whether he was dead or alive, all of the rage,
sadness, guilt, and the remembered fragments of his childhood—teaching him to hit a baseball and shoot a basketball,
carrying him to bed and reading him *Goodnight Moon* so often
I could recite it by heart, and stumbling sleepily into his room
in the middle of the night to pour him a spoon of cough syrup
or comfort him after a nightmare—swept over me like a river
breaching a levee, and to say that I began to cry would be to
sugarcoat the experience.

One minute I was staring out the windshield to the southern shore of the creek, where birch trees, white and spidery,
erupted in explosions of light against the wall of evergreens,
and the next minute I was weeping uncontrollably. In my mind
my car was transformed into a cage, and I rocked back and
forth, hurling myself against the bars. The shoulder harness
of my seat belt scratched my neck when my forehead hit the
steering wheel, and I was vaguely conscious of Glenna's hands
on my shoulders, trying to hold me. All I saw as I wept was
the watery outline of her face and that her lips were moving. I
couldn't decipher what she was saying because the one sound I
heard was a horrific, guttural cry, like somebody dying in great
pain, and not until Glenna unbuckled her seat belt and leaned
across me to press the buttons that opened every window in
the car, and a frigid blast of air lashed across my face, did I
understand the hellish cry had been coming from me.

After a while, I started shivering and grew quiet. My overcoat was in the backseat, and I buttoned my corduroy sports
jacket. Then it dawned on me that if I wanted to warm up, the
wiser choice was to raise the windows.

I said, "Sorry for—"

"Nothing to be sorry for," Glenna replied, rubbing the back of my neck.

I drove over to a spot by her gate, popped the trunk, and took my iPhone so I could shoot Elaine and Charlie a text.

"Need help?" Glenna asked.

I shook my head and flopped her dress bag over my shoulder, grasped the handle of her suitcase, and used my elbow to shut the trunk.

When we walked into the house, Glenna tapped in her alarm code, and I put my iPhone on the pedestal table to the side of the staircase and carried her things up to her bedroom. On my way down I started thinking about the New Year's Eve that I'd returned her calfskin key case and, with my throat so constricted by sorrow that I thought I'd choke, hauled my belongings out to the GTO in the shopping bags that Glenna had piled up on the bottom of her closet, all the while hoping that she would ask me to stay, and now that sorrow and that hope and those ghostly footfalls reverberated in my memory.

Glenna said, "Can I give you lunch or a cup of coffee?"

"Thanks," I said, noticing that her mascara had run, leaving squiggly black trails on her face. "But I don't wanna get caught in traffic on 95. I'll stop somewhere."

Glenna slipped her hand inside my jacket and stuck a piece of paper in my shirt pocket. "My numbers and e-mail. If you want to be in touch."

"I'll be in touch. Let me get Alex settled and—"

"It was great seeing you, Gordon."

"Same here."

"And I'll send Elaine a thank-you note. I'm so happy I met her and her family."

I put the palm of my hand against her face. "Your mascara," I said, remembering that night, so many years ago, when Glenna had wiped her tears away with the sleeve of her terry-cloth robe as the moonlight shone through the bay window behind her.

"I know," she said.

I had to get out of there and gave Glenna a quick hug and quicker kiss. We said good-bye and I walked out the door, closing it gently behind me.

I inhaled the wintry air and started down the slippery steps, and again I recalled that New Year's Eve—my conviction that I'd never come back to this place and how I'd mourned the love and comfort and pleasure that I'd discovered here with Glenna even before I made it to my car, and that feeling of loss had been so excruciating it doubled me over.

Yet I had come back. Not every conviction is impervious to the lessons and corrosion of time, and I could feel the past and present gathering together to become, if I was lucky, the future I desired. Out across the gray, whitecapped water of the creek the trees were bent under the weight of the snow, as though heavy with the weight of accumulated memories, and despite the crackling-cold wind of January, as I stood in the radiant sunshine, underneath a cloudless blue sky, it was possible to believe in spring.

I was halfway down when I realized that I'd left my iPhone in the house. Carefully, I went back up the steps and, facing the brass door knocker, remembered another evening, a summery September evening, when I'd first arrived in this exalted, arcadian corner of the city to take Glenna to Little Italy, and I knew that I'd want to stay forever. I ran my fingers over the cold brass and knocked, but Glenna didn't answer. I tried the door and it opened. My phone was on the pedestal table. After sticking it in a jacket pocket, I called out, "Glenna!"

"Upstairs," she called back, and I hiked up to the third floor.

Glenna was sitting in the bay-window seat. Her eyes were red, and she had a wadded-up ball of Kleenex in her hand.

"I forgot to tell you something," I said.

"What'd you forget?"

"I forgot to tell you the truth."

"Which is?"

"I couldn't take losing you. Not again. Ever."

Softly Glenna said, "We won't lose each other."

I sat with her and wondered how old I would have to be before I stopped thinking she was the most beautiful woman I'd ever seen.

"We won't," she said. "You have to believ—"

"I do."

Glenna was holding my hand when she said, "I want to travel more."

"With me?"

"If you insist," she said, and grinned. "But you didn't tell me if you had a favorite place."

A tugboat was heading up Spuyten Duyvil Creek, and I watched it move through the water, feeling the sun on my face and looking into the bright winter light.

"Here," I said, putting my arms around her. "Right here."

Epilogue
Summer: Two Years On

THE SIREN. THAT'S all I could perceive through the pain, the noise swelling in my ears until I felt like the hippopotamus squatting on my chest had started kicking me in the head.

"Let me straighten that," the paramedic said, leaning over to adjust the straps of the oxygen mask covering my nose and mouth. He was a beefy kid in his twenties with a four-leaf-clover tattoo on his forearm. I wanted to ask him if the tattoo helped my chances, but I couldn't talk, so I pointed at it.

"Tattoo's mad lucky. Don't worry 'bout nothin.'"

I wasn't worried. I was too busy wishing the pain would stop.

At the hospital, they rushed me into the ER as if I had a malpractice attorney on retainer. A nurse, a perky redhead in a baby-blue smock, stood to my left and asked, "Mr. Meyers, is this the worst pain you ever felt?"

Before I could reply, a balding guy with the cheery demeanor of a mortician appeared on my right. "Sir, I'm Dr. Silt. Do you have a history?"

I lay on the gurney and peered up at their faces. The worst pain ever? Like most lives, mine had included its share of pain. A history? Hell yes. Who didn't?

"Mr. Meyers?" the nurse said.

"I'm thinking." I laughed, but neither the nurse nor Dr. Silt appeared to get the joke.

MY EKG and blood tests were normal, and the hippopotamus went somewhere else to sit, but Dr. Silt wanted to monitor me for signs of a heart attack, so he admitted me to the telemetry unit overnight. I was given a double room without a roommate and connected to a telemeter, a small box with four wires, which ran to pads on my shoulders and rib cage and hung around my neck like a high-tech ribbon from a country fair. I was sitting in bed inspecting the dinner menu when Glenna walked in, and all at once I felt frightened and relieved. Frightened because if I was dying, I'd have to leave her. Relieved because loving her, I felt as though I'd live forever.

She sat on the bed and kissed me. "I spoke to Dr. Silt. He thinks you had an esophageal spasm."

"That's serious?"

She shook her head and glanced down at the menu.

"Then how come you're—"

"Scared?" Glenna said, staring at me. "For God's sake, you scared me." In late July, for our first wedding anniversary, we had vacationed for a few weeks in Florence, Rome, Venice, and the fishing village of Portofino, and her face was tanned a dark gold.

I said, "What causes the spasms?"

"No one knows. Possibly anxiety."

"Maybe it's that I finished the novel this morning, and Todd called. He's almost got the option contract done, and he gave me the name of a literary agent who wants to talk to me. The pain started when I got off the phone."

"Ah."

I'd written a family saga about three generations of men who go off to war. Half of it was made-up. It was the other half that troubled me, picturing strangers taking a peek at my life. Glenna had read every word, usually responding with a kind comment or two, except for those times when she had said nothing and a shadow of sadness passed across her face.

I said, "If you have to go back to the office—"

"I don't. That's why I have Jennifer." Jennifer Austerlitz was a young pediatrician that Glenna had hired as an associate.

I said, "We still on for tomorrow night?"

"You're fine. No reason to cancel. You'll be out of here before noon."

"I'm fine? You and Dr. Silt—you're sure?"

"You're fine, Gordon. There's only one thing to worry about."

"What's that?"

She gave me the menu. "Whether to order grape or raspberry Jell-O."

BY SIX o'clock the next evening, the pork ribs glistening with my molasses-and-vinegar barbecue sauce were in the oven approaching perfection; my corn bread was cooling in a glass dish on the stove; and I was spreading Mrs. Richardson's butterscotch sauce over a graham-cracker pie crust with a spatula. When that was done, I nuked a pint of Ben & Jerry's vanilla in the microwave, then spread the softened ice cream and topped it off with another layer of butterscotch.

As I put the pie in the freezer, Glenna, who was at the island slicing tomatoes, said, "If an investigator from the Office of Professional Medical Conduct saw this dinner, I'd lose my license."

"You're making salad. That gives you plausible deniability."

The doorbell rang, and Glenna and I went to answer it.

Julie, her long auburn hair pinned up in a chignon, came in holding Danny, my six-month-old grandson. Danny wasn't too happy even though he was outfitted in the red-and-white Washington Nationals romper I'd sent him. He was howling and yanking on the front of Julie's gauzy camp shirt.

Julie, who appeared almost as frazzled as her son, said, "Danny's hungry, he's wet, he has that rash again, and I'm the worst mother in the world—I forgot to pack the Desitin. Can you look at him, Glenna?"

With her arm around Julie, Glenna led her into the living room, then knelt down, took Danny, put him on the couch, and undid his romper and diaper. Julie's mother had died from pancreatic cancer during Julie's pregnancy, and in those last terrible months of her illness, and since Danny had been born, Julie and Glenna had spoken on the phone nearly every day.

My grandson was quieter now, and Glenna said, "Danny's fine. I picked up some Desitin and Pampers at the supermarket. They're in your room. Let me help you."

"That'd be great," Julie said.

As they marched by me, with Glenna carrying Danny and cooing at him, I got a chance to kiss the carroty fuzz on my grandson's head, and Julie pecked my cheek, saying, "Hi, Dad. How are you? I promise—in five minutes I'll hardly be psychotic."

They went upstairs, and I went out the front door. A heat haze shimmered over the creek, and Alex, in a seersucker suit and loosened tie, was trudging across the grass with two duffel bags hanging off his shoulders and carrying a Pack 'n Play in one hand and a bulging knapsack in the other. You can always tell a new father in transit with his family: he looks like the lone bellhop working a convention.

"Hey, Alex," I called out, and he dropped the bags. I crossed through the shade of the oak trees and hugged him. Ever since he'd returned from Iraq, I tended to hug Alex longer than he liked, but he didn't protest.

"Happy birthday," I said, letting Alex go and taking the knapsack and Pack 'n Play. "Work's good?"

"Busy."

"No traveling?"

"No, Dad. No traveling."

DANNY WASN'T ready for ribs or corn bread—the birthday dinner I'd been preparing for Alex since he was seven—but after Alex blew out the candles on the pie, I liberated my grandson from his high chair, sat him on my knee, and introduced him to a spoonful. As his big hazel eyes filled with wonder, Danny cleaned off the spoon and let out a peal of delight, flinging his arms toward heaven as if praising God for creating butterscotch and ice cream. He tasted one more spoonful before his eyes began to close. I held him against me and, for a glorious instant, believed that I was holding Alex again—one benefit of reaching the age where nearly everything reminds you of something else.

"Bedtime for the future Nationals' captain," Julie said. She had the delicate, elegant look of a ballerina; her movements possessed the same lithe grace; and as she took Danny from me and left the kitchen, I watched Alex follow her with his eyes.

Alex said, "Dad, what're you grinning about?"

"Nothing."

"Nothing? No way. What is it?"

Behind me I heard Glenna walk over from the sink. Then she was standing next to Alex's chair and resting a hand on his shoulder.

She said, "He means it's everything."

"Everything?" Alex asked.

"Everything," I said.

Alex chuckled. "You're talking code again. I don't get it."

I stood and kissed the top of his head. "You will."

WHEN I woke up, the clock on my nightstand read 5:59. I thought I'd heard Danny crying, but Julie must have gotten up to nurse him because the house was quiet. Glenna murmured in her sleep, and I slipped out of bed, pulled on a sweatshirt and shorts, stepped into my moccasins, took my reading glasses and my laptop off my dresser, and went downstairs.

Fifteen minutes later I was sitting outside at the wrought-iron table we'd set up under the oaks. The birds were singing, and the rose light of dawn had lightened the sky to lavender and streaked the shoestring clouds with crimson. I sipped coffee from a travel mug and, after the computer booted up, began rereading my novel from the beginning. In the warm weather, I occasionally wrote out here, but I'd done most of the work up on the third floor. We had the entertainment center moved to the living room and the treadmill and Universal to the basement, and Glenna had bought me a mahogany, U-shaped desk to match her own. I offered to pay, but she said no, and when I told her that she was being overly generous, she laughed, saying, "Not really. I expect you to keep my stuff organized," which I would have done anyway, since the books, journals, and mail heaped up on her desk, the couch, and the floor edged me toward insanity. Writing the novel had been a struggle, but working in a room so laden with my past, I frequently had the giddy, improbable sense that the man I'd become was watching the boy I'd been pass through his days and nights.

I heard the front door open, and Glenna came out in a yellow polo shirt, denim cutoffs, and a beat-up pair of buffalo sandals. Whenever I saw her dressed as I remembered from so long ago, I had this wonderful feeling that our time together had been unbroken.

"Do I get to read the ending?" she asked, sitting at the table and running her hand over my arm.

"I'll print out the last chapter for you," I said, and offered her my mug.

She took a sip. "I'm going to make Jennifer a partner."

Glenna had been mulling over that decision for the last year, and I asked her what made her finally decide to do it.

"Thursday, when I had to rush off to Montefiore, I had a waiting room full of children and their parents, and I needed someone to deal with them. Jen was terrific, and I don't want her to leave. So we talked yesterday and we're going to work out a buy-in plan she can handle. And now that I'm going to have a partner, I can travel even more."

"Didn't Italy count?"

She smiled. "That's only one country."

I noticed that Glenna was wearing a gold necklace with a turquoise, leaf-shaped pendant. "That's pretty. I haven't seen it before."

"Julie gave it to me last night after you went to bed. It belonged to her mom."

"Alex told me how much Julie appreciates all you do for her. He said that no matter how lousy a day she's having, when she's done talking to you, everything's fine."

"I adore Julie, and I'm glad to get a chance to treat her the way I wished my mother had treated me."

A warm wind blew through the treetops, and the air was rich with the fragrance of grass and flowers.

Glenna said, "Last night, it took me an hour to fall asleep, and as I was closing my eyes, I remembered that when I was a little girl, I believed that I'd never grow up to be happy. At least not in any lasting way. And that feeling's been with me most of my life."

"And now?"

She half rose out of her chair to kiss me. "Now I don't believe that anymore."

"See, that wasn't so hard."

"A lot harder than I wanted it to be."

A Metro-North train en route to the city pulled into the station. Several passengers were milling around on the platform. They boarded and the train rolled on along the blue water of the creek.

Glenna said, "We should go in and get breakfast started."

"What should I make?"

"After that dinner? Kelp, wheat germ, and Lipitor."

I looked over at Glenna, and we laughed, lingering for a moment, just listening to the vanishing clack of the train and watching the morning come.

Acknowledgments

To be published with great care requires a corps of dedicated professionals, and in this regard I've been extremely fortunate.

I'm grateful to my agent, Susan Golomb, for her wise counsel and her persistence on my behalf; and to my editor, Greer Hendricks, for her keen eye and her talent for making even a criticism sound like a compliment.

Much thanks to Susan's assistant, Eliza Rothstein, who is as efficient as she is pleasant, and to Greer's assistant, Sarah Cantin, whose good cheer is only matched by her patience with my many questions.

At Atria Books, I'd like to thank executive publisher Judith Curr; deputy publisher Chris Lloreda; marketing manager Hillary Tisman; senior production editor Carole Schwindeller; copy editor Steven Boldt; and Jeanne Lee and Laywan Kwan, who are responsible for the beautiful cover.

In a somewhat different form, *Comeback Love* was originally published by Staff Picks Press, a small publishing company founded by Susan Novotny. Susan is a longtime owner of independent bookstores, and she did a marvelous job spreading the word about my novel. One person who heard about it was John Muse, a national accounts manager for Simon & Schuster, and John soon became a tireless advocate on behalf of *Comeback Love*. I owe much to Susan and John.

At Staff Picks Press, Susan Taylor, Melissa Mykal Batalin, Susan Petrie, and Carolyn Wavrin were of enormous help. And the comments of one early reader of the manuscript, Marlene Adelstein, were invaluable.

My family and friends have also been of immeasurable assistance: my sister and brother-in-law, Frann and Eric Francis; my niece, Meredith Francis; and my sister-in-law, Mary Beth Grover. For many years, my friends Tracy Richard and Bruce Davis, Carol and Joe Siracusa, Ellen and Jeff Lewis, Howard Dickson, Howard Sperber, and James Howard Kunstler have provided much kindness and laughter. And I'd like to send a heartfelt thanks to those of you who generously contributed your share to this book—Charles Oransky, Richard Kinley, Darron Leddick, Janet Heinle, Jeanne-Marie Crockett, Jenny Milchman, Meta Weinkrantz Berk, Mark Cudworth, Mary Ellen O'Neil Davis, Dr. Jennifer Shaw, and Dr. Sharon Samuels.

I appreciate all of you who have been in touch on the web. For those of you who haven't found me yet—on Facebook, I can be reached via Author Peter Golden; on Twitter, it's pagolden32; and my website is petergolden.com.

Finally, I'd like to thank the two people who sit at the center of my life and work: my son, Ben, and my wife, Annis.

COMEBACK LOVE

Peter Golden

A Readers Club Guide

1. What do you think *Comeback Love* is saying about first loves, and about long-term commitments? Is love all about timing?

2. Glenna is actively and successfully pursuing a respected career, while Gordon is somewhat fumbling his way through his education and pursuing his own professional dream. How much does this influence their dynamic?

3. What did you make of Gordon's relationship with his father? How do you think their bond affected Gordon's relationship with his own son, Alex?

4. Gordon's mother says, "*I don't dislike Glenna, but I love you, and she's a girl like your sister, and they . . . they hurt men.*" (p. 65) Do you think that, ultimately, Glenna hurts Gordon—or do they mutually hurt each other?

5. What precisely does Gordon's mother mean when she says that Glenna is a girl like Elaine? How would you describe Gordon's relationship with his sister? Does he ever come to see the similarities that his mother sees?

6. Describing his relationships since Glenna, Gordon admits, "*I never trusted enough to feel that way about anyone else.*" (p. 218) Do you feel that this is something that always happens after first love, or was their relationship uniquely transformative?

7. How would you describe the marriage between Glenna's parents? How does it compare to the one Gordon's parents share? Do you think their respective models of relationships impact how Glenna and Gordon's own romance evolves?

8. "[It] would be some time before I understood that this was precisely the problem, the beginning of our end, that Glenna loved me. So much." (p. 109) Do you agree with Gordon's assessment that this moment signified an unraveling? And why is Glenna's love for Gordon the problem?

9. Consider the circumstances (psychological and logistical) that lead Gordon and Robin to sleep together. Do you think Glenna knew this might happen when she suggested that the two of them go to Woodstock without her? Were you surprised by this outcome?

10. What do you think prompted Gordon's father to bring the family and Glenna to Zalman's restaurant? How were these motives different from those that drive Gordon to return to New York to see Glenna?

11. Consider the ways in which *Comeback Love* is simultaneously a timeless story of first love, while also being very much a story of its time. How do current events (in both the past and present sections) inform the action of the narrative and the development of the plot?

12. "'This could be my child.' 'Our child,' I corrected her. She shook her head, unwilling to concede that this was about

me, too. I could have the blame for knocking her up, not the credit." (p. 202) Who did you empathize with here—Glenna or Gordon?

13. Discuss why Gordon failed to submit his Selective Service form. Do you think he wanted to go to Vietnam, or did he want to escape New York? How are these two desires different?

14. Imagine you are the casting director for the film version of *Comeback Love*. Who would you cast as young Gordon and young Glenna? Who would play them in the present-day scenes?